FALLING FOR MY BODYGUARD

He's trying to save her. She's trying to kill him. One indecent outfit at a time.

SEXTON SISTERS SERIES

LYNDSEY GALLAGHER

Copyright © Lyndsey Gallagher 2023

All Rights Reserved

No part of this book may be reproduced in any form or by any electronic means, including information storage and retrieval systems, without written permission from the author, except for the brief use of quotations in a book review.

This is a work of fiction and any characters that bear a resemblance to anyone living or dead is a coincidence. The events are imagined by the author and bear no similarities to actual events.

FOREWORD

Dear Reader,

If you like sizzling fiery passion and irresistible chemistry, you've come to the right place! Have a fire extinguisher at the ready for the lingerie store scene, don't say I didn't warn you!

If you like the sound of that... come hang out with me at my Facebook reader group, Lyndsey's Book Lushes, where you'll find loads of behind the scenes info and inappropriate memes!

https://www.facebook.com/groups/530398645913222

I hope you enjoy Archie & Victoria's story.

Lyndsey xxx

This book is dedicated to the fabulous members of my Facebook reader group, Lyndsey's Book Lushes. Thank you for all the laughter, friendship, and support. I appreciate every single one of you.

PROLOGUE

Victoria

'You know you don't have to do this, right?' My sister, Sasha, flutters her pristinely manicured fingers over the small of my back.

'I know,' I lie.

I *do* have to do this. Deep down, I've always known I have to do this.

The very same night my seven-year-old body was pulled from a car wreck, I vowed to become a doctor. To save lives. I owe my life to the doctors and nurses at Dublin Hospital. I'll never be able to repay them, but I can pay it forward.

It sounds noble, but don't be fooled. Undoubtedly, it's an honourable vocation, but the temptation of six years living the college high life is equally alluring. A fresh start in a new country...

College is supposed to be wild. It's half the appeal. If I don't get trashed on cheap shots and cider at Freshers' Week, am I even a real student? Waking up stark bollock naked in bed with a new classmate and a banging headache is practically a rite of passage, isn't it?

The opportunity to find myself away from the rules and restraints of my well-meaning, but over-protective, famous family, and the castle I grew up in, shines like a beacon of light across stormy seas.

The need for normality gnaws at my soul. Sheer ordinariness and the freedom my peers take for granted. Residing in student digs, embarking on messy nights with new friends where the shots are free-flowing and my body has no choice but to surrender to the rhythmic beat of the music.

The only problem is, now I'm here in Edinburgh, in my brand new three-storey Georgian house, days from starting my six-year degree at the university, I can appreciate that a normal student experience was never going to be a remote possibility.

Not for me.

Not for any Sexton.

I might have moved to another country, but it looks as if I'll never be at liberty to escape my family.

Or my life.

Or who I am.

It sounds terrible. I adore my sisters more than any goosebump-evoking words can ever express. But every family has their woes, and ours is that we can't take a step out the door without risking being mobbed.

It's a first world problem. Believe me, I know.

Chloe, my middle sister, is a ball-breaking businesswoman currently storming the world with her events management business. And my eldest sister, Sasha, is about to marry the hottest rock star this world has ever seen.

Sasha raised me while single-handedly running our parents' luxury castle estate. She's a sister, a mother, and the best friend I could ever ask for all rolled into one sassy, spirited, glamorous package.

I'm even super fond of my effusive, almost-brother-in-law, Ryan. Half the female population is in love with him. But to me, he'll always be my big sister's goofy boyfriend.

Their wedding is two months away. They've been offered billions for exclusive access to their big day. The media's snorting up their whirlwind romance, inhaling it like it's the purest form of crack cocaine, and they're hopelessly addicted.

Hollywood's leading film producer is currently writing the script for a movie telling the love story that has captured the hearts of the entire world. There isn't a person on God's green earth who doesn't want a slice of them.

Which unfortunately means they want a slice of the rest of us by default.

My heels click across the sanded, varnished original mahogany flooring of the master bedroom, towards one of many immaculately restored sash windows. The view from my new townhouse boasts a rich history that my curious feet itch to explore.

My heart skips a beat as my gaze roams the Scottish skyline. The setting sun renders it a warm shade of coral above the unfamiliar but iconic horizon. The famous medieval Edinburgh Castle towers proudly over Princes Street Gardens in the distance.

Tourists and locals swarm like ants across the manicured lawns, revelling in the last of the August sun. Princes Street is thronged with attendees of this year's Fringe Festival. Buses and trams crawl by, starting and stopping with accompanying hisses and chugs. Distant wailing sirens erupt from a fire engine somewhere close by.

Will I ever get used to the noise?

'What do you think?' Sasha crosses the room to stand

beside me, the silky fabric of her shirt brushing against my bare shoulder.

Pastel pink painted fingernails gesture around the spacious master bedroom. 'Paint it any colour you like. Decorate it however you like. It's yours to do with whatever you want.'

Whatever I want? Even sell?

I exhale a slow, deep breath, attempting to rid myself of the ungrateful teenage hormones surging through my blood. This house, a gift from my rock star brother-in-law, is beyond generous. It's ludicrous. But it's not what I want.

I want freedom. Like Mel Gibson in Braveheart. I want to make my own choices. To live my life the way *I* choose to live it.

It could be the most opulent, extravagant house in the country, but all it will ever be to me is another prison. Especially given the pinched-faced warden I'm forced to share it with - my new personal bodyguard, Vince, who lingers in the doorway behind us, eyes darting suspiciously like Chucky himself might just leap out from under the bed with an axe.

Sasha's warm hand rests on my forearm and I turn to meet huge jade eyes which glint with excitement.

I can't mimic even a smidgeon of Sasha's enthusiasm.

'Is this really necessary?' My hands rest defiantly on my hips as I eyeball the mountain-sized man assigned to guard my back for the foreseeable future.

Thoughts of Archie infiltrate my mind, reoccurring repeatedly, no matter how many times I mentally swat them away. Tall, broad, with dirty blond hair and an even dirtier laugh, Archie is like a younger Daniel Craig starring as James Bond, only way hotter.

He also happens to be my first crush.

Why did he decline the position as my bodyguard? After accompanying me to several events as my security, I wrongly assumed he'd jump at the chance. If I have to be tailed twenty-four-seven for the supposed best days of my life, having a six-foot-four blond Adonis doing the tailing might have taken the edge off.

Regret clouds Sasha's previously bright eyes. 'You know it is, sweetheart.' Slim, warm fingers squeeze my arm. 'With the wedding, we can't take the chance. The paps are frantically pursuing all of us. I'm sorry.'

The familiar nausea-inducing guilt threatens inside. The last thing I want for my selfless, stunning sister is for her to feel bad. She already gave up most of her twenties to raise me. I refuse to kick up a stink and rob her of her thirties, too.

'Maybe things will die down, you know, after the wedding...' I glance hopefully at Vince, who's adopted his usual rigid, but ready for danger stance, five feet away from us.

Sasha swallows hard, her dainty neck bobbing as she bites her lower lip apologetically before reminding me about the movie.

A huge sigh whooshes from my chest, but I nod like the good girl I've always tried to be. But being good is getting harder with each passing day. I'm torn between screaming at the injustice of barely being allowed to pee on my own and trying not to rock the boat.

A feisty, independent new adult stirs inside, determined to burst like a piñata, in a glorious hormone-infused display of rebellion.

And I'm not sure how much longer I can hold her back.

Chapter One

VICTORIA

Five years later...

Is it a full moon? Because this shift has seen one lunatic after another arrive relentlessly through doors of accident and emergency.

My scrubs cling to my sweat-sheened skin, along with the thick crimson blood of the patient occupying the hospital trolley before me. It trickles across my forearm, inching closer towards my hand as I attempt to restrain the patient's flailing arms. 'Sit still please, Mr ...' I glance at his chart again, '...Assman.' How appropriate.

He clutches his nose with one hand while the other continues violently lashing out in my direction.

'You crazy bitch!' he shouts, clutching his bleeding nose. Alcohol fumes from his rancid breath sting my eyes.

Unlike most patients arriving through these doors, this one didn't come in bleeding.

No, I 'accidentally' elbowed him in the face. I'm a great doctor, but even I have my limits. When his grubby, persistent hand reached for my breast for the fourth time, I snapped. He'd already repeatedly requested mouth-to-mouth, insisting, as a woman, it's all I'm good for.

If only he knew what this woman is truly good for is a hot shower and several large glasses of wine after fifteen hours of firefighting one catastrophe after another.

My best friends are waiting for me in a fancy bar on George Street and I'm itching to get there before the damn place closes for the night. Work hard, play harder, and all that. Drinking and dancing my ass off is my favourite hobby.

It's tempting to leave the ungrateful fool here unattended, but I didn't put in five hard years at med school to get myself struck off the register mere months before I graduate.

'I can't help you if you won't sit still.'

Jen, a middle-aged, maternal-looking nurse assisting me, tosses me a look that says, *'What the fuck are we going to do with this one?'*

Mr Assman bucks back in the trolley like a wild horse, yelling up to the blinding hospital skylights, 'She's fucking crazy.' Presumably he's hoping someone behind the thin paper curtain might give a shit.

Maybe they do because it's suddenly yanked back with a force more suited to a boxing ring than a hospital ward. The senior house officer on duty frowns sternly at my patient before turning his appraising stare to me.

Doctor David Dickson is my personal mentor, born and bred in this very hospital, by all accounts. He has a sharp tongue and, if you believe the rumours, an even sharper eye for the students under his charge. His buzz cropped hair is greying slightly at both temples. An ever-present pinstripe tie peeks from beneath the collar of his starched white doctor's coat, a perpetual reminder of his importance, to himself, at least.

'Is everything okay in here, Doctor Sexton?' He doesn't look at Jen but clicks his fingers in her direction, motioning for the patient notes, an incomplete form pinned between the metal grip of a weathered looking clipboard.

'She,' accusation weighs heavily in Mr Assman's tone, 'assaulted me in the face.'

'It was an accident,' Jen and I say simultaneously.

'He's clearly agitated,' I explain. Doctor code for "high on something."

I remove a tiny torch from my scrub pocket to examine Mr Assman's pupils. As I raise my hand, Doctor Dickson shakes his head gently and nudges me aside.

'I'll take over,' he offers, nodding at the blood drying on my sallow skin.

I glance at the platinum pocket watch hanging from my breast pocket. 'Are you sure?'

'Go home.' He says it like he's doing me a favour, even though my shift should have ended over three hours ago.

When his palm grazes the small of my back, I have to wonder if he's going to want something in return for this small mercy, but the prospect of the aforementioned shower and wine renders me careless.

A&E is one of the toughest placements I've endured during my five years at medical school, primarily because neither the lowly students or the most qualified senior house officers can prepare for what the fuck comes through the front door on any given day or night.

The sheer magnitude of weird and wonderful injuries and traumas should be enough to put me off applying for a position here when I graduate, but privately, I think I might have just found my spiritual home.

There's something utterly enthralling about not knowing what to expect from one day to the next. Even if it does leave me perpetually bleary-eyed. Amongst the buzz of the beeping monitors, the blinding overhead lights, and the race from patient to patient, I've never felt so alive.

I nod at Doctor Dickson, accepting his offer.

Brushing past Jen, I step towards the clinical waste bin to

remove my personal protective equipment. She winks at me, and I nod a silent thanks for her support today.

'I want to make an official complaint,' Mr Assman rages on. '*SHE* deliberately elbowed me in the —'

'We'll get to that in a minute.' Doctor Dickson cuts him off in a definitive self-assured voice.

Just as I'm ripping the clammy gloves from my hands, my mentor materialises beside me again, a little too close for comfort. The sickly sweet smell of his cinnamon scented cologne is strong enough to penetrate my mask.

'One more thing.' Doctor Dickson's deft hand catches me by the wrist. 'If you need some assistance working on your bedside manner, I'll be in my office tomorrow.' His gunmetal grey eyes hold mine for a second longer than is comfortable.

'Thank you.' I nod to acknowledge his creepy offer. Not to accept it.

I dump the nitrile gloves into the bin and leave before I find myself in any more awkward situations.

Scuttling towards the exit, practically salivating at the prospect of a cold crisp glass of Sancerre, I keep my head down in case anyone else requests my assistance. I'm inches away from the thick, grey double doors when a familiar deep voice booms behind me.

'Victoria.'

I sigh, swivelling on my clogs, plastering a smile on my face in the process.

Harrison Hughes closes the gap between us in three strides with his ridiculously long tree-trunk legs. The guy could have been a professional rugby player. Instead, he chose to follow in his father, mother, and grandparents' footsteps and pursue a career in medicine.

We've known each other for over five years and while he's been openly shagging his way through the women on our campus, I've had to be a little more discreet about my endeavours, unfortunately. Nothing kills spontaneous, passionate hook-ups like the menacing glare of an eternally present ten-tonne-truck of a bodyguard.

Not to say there *hasn't* been any nocturnal activity, it's just I have to plan my activities a bit better than most.

'You finished?' His thick stilted English accent screams 'privately educated,' probably at Eton along with Prince William and Harry and God only knows who else.

'Yeah. Hours ago, actually.' My gaze darts to the patient he's left unattended. 'Can I help you with something?'

In one swift cocky motion, Harrison flicks his dark floppy hair back, revealing eyes so brown they're almost black. 'Go out with me.'

It's not so much a question as a demand. Harrison Hughes is clearly used to getting whatever he wants, or should I say, whomever he wants. Arrogance radiates from his every pore. Confidence. Entitlement. Wealth. Power. Some women may find that attractive. Not me. Being raised by a single female and having attended an all-girl school for most of my life, I find the inflated masculinity he projects borderline aggressive.

My clogs scoot the final foot to the door as I muster an apologetic smile. 'Thanks, but I don't think so. Have a good night, though.'

It *has* to be a full moon.

The female changing room is empty. I peel off the blue scrubs and drop them into the central laundry basket, safe in the knowledge the hospital's wonderful washing fairies will have stacked three fresh pairs in my cubicle before my next shift.

Removing my favourite shampoo and conditioner from my locker, I tiptoe across the freezing cold tiles to one of four communal showers and let the soothing hot water run gloriously over my head.

Twenty minutes later, dressed in an off-the-shoulder cream silk dress and suede ankle boots, I stroll down the hospital corridor towards the family waiting area where my bodyguard, Jared, awaits.

Jared conforms to the stereotype. Tall, broad, stocky and serious. As usual, he's chewing gum hard enough to break his teeth.

He shoves his phone into his trouser pocket and leaps to his feet at the sight of me. 'Doctor Sexton. I was beginning to get worried.'

'Busy day,' I shrug as he steps in line beside me.

He's the thirteenth bodyguard I've had in five years. Vince, my original assignment, barely lasted a month. Apparently, he signed up to save lives, not offer a babysitting service while I tried to get drunk with my classmates. Or laid. Unsuccessfully, I might add. I stuck out like a porn star's prick with a meaty-looking mountain man permanently stationed within five feet of me, twenty-four-seven. No fresher was willing to take that on. Would you blame them?

Around midway through my second year, I discovered it was easier to host house parties than to try to keep up with the student pub scene. At least I could lock myself in my room with whomever I chose, for a short while at least.

The year Ryan and Sasha's movie was released was the only time I took my security seriously, willingly shutting myself away for three months until the press coverage ceased. But when it finally did, boy, did I make up for it! In the six months after that, I managed to rack up six different bodyguards. I was wild.

Now, at the age of twenty-three, I like to think I've gained a little wisdom. Jared's been with me for four months. We struck a deal as soon as he arrived. He accompanies me to and from my hospital shift but doesn't remain in the building for the entire twelve hours, confident in the hospital's own security measures and that my mask and scrubs provide me with a degree of anonymity.

If I go to a nightclub, he waits outside in the car, insisting I call him to meet me at the exit before I step out onto the street.

He lives on the ground floor of my house, and wouldn't dream of climbing the stairs to my private area unless I screamed for him to come up. As far as having a permanent security detail goes, he's the best I've had. Though I'm not sure my sisters would agree if they discovered our arrangement.

We walk side by side out of the Royal Infirmary and, sure as God, a full moon looms ominously in the sky overhead. I fucking knew it!

My black SUV is double-parked at the back doors. Having a super famous family does offer some benefits. Jared unlocks the vehicle, politely opening the passenger door for me, before strolling round to the driver's side.

Eying my outfit, Jared says, 'I take it we're not going home?'

'No. George Street, please. I'm meeting Libby and Melanie for a glass of wine. A girl's got to get her kicks somewhere.'

Fifteen minutes later, we pull up outside the gilded high entrance of one of the most prestigious bars in Edinburgh. A queue a mile long lines the street.

'I'll be right here,' Jared promises, removing his phone from his pocket, presumably to watch Sky News. The man is addicted to scrutinising and dissecting every depressing headline.

That, or he's about to play Tetris, something which reveals more about his age than he'd care to admit.

'Thanks Jared. I appreciate your discretion.' I pat his arm before slipping out of the car and straight to the front of the queue. I know the doormen. More importantly, they know me. Another perk, I'll reluctantly admit.

Inside, it's pandemonium. Sweaty, gyrating bodies jostle against mine as I force my way through the overcrowded dance floor to the VIP area where I'm certain my friends are waiting with a chilled bottle of wine and a comfortable seat.

'There she is!' Mel screeches like a market trader flogging knock-off handbags. Dainty fingers shove her huge thick glasses back up onto the bridge of her tiny button nose. No wonder they're perpetually slipping. She doesn't exactly have a lot to hold them there. Her short pixie hair is spiked up into its usual style, freshly dyed a unique shade of scarlet. Chartreuse eyes glint with devilment.

Libby, my other best friend, leaps up to greet me in a much more graceful manner, kissing each of my cheeks. 'Darling! We thought you'd never get here.' Her long blonde hair cascades loosely to her tiny waist, half-masking the sequinned midi dress that clings to her womanly curves. Bright blue eyes glitter.

Libby's like an adult-sized Barbie doll with an IQ on par with Einstein himself. Her sunny personality and unwavering solidarity at clinic makes it impossible to begrudge either her beauty or her brain.

I glance down at my own dress. I'd been aiming for sophisticated, but next to these two stunners, I feel a tad dowdy. Nothing that a glass of wine won't fix. Or three.

'How was A&E?' Libby asks.

Though the three of us are studying medicine together, we got split up for placements, worse luck.

'Eventful, as usual.' I take a deep breath, readying myself to elaborate even with the ear-splitting bass pumping in the background, while Mel fills a glass for me.

Just as the first crisp cold mouthful seeps deliciously down my throat, a thunderous bang pierces the air.

The music cuts out, blinding overhead lights blink on and someone shouts, 'Everybody get the fuck down!'

All hell breaks loose.

Chapter Two

ARCHIE

Technically, my job title is 'bodyguard', but somewhere along the way it's evolved into 'babysitter' for two tiny twin dictators.

The weak January sun illuminates the manicured lawns of Huxley Castle. It's unseasonably mild and therefore the perfect morning for a little ball practice with my two favourite four-year-olds.

'Hit it hard this time!' I yell at Blake, swinging an imaginary bat through the air. His own bat, a gift from his Uncle Jayden, is almost as big as him.

Nodding at Bella, Blake's twin sister, I signal for her to throw the ball again. Her pursed lips and cute snub nose are a picture of determination. Her arm launches back before propelling the ball impressively high into the air. Bella has more zest than many grown men. Though given who her parents are, it's no surprise.

Blake's little arm swings ten seconds too late. Clearly, I needn't have worried about him breaking a window.

Bella whoops, pink unicorn-embellished trainers hop on the spot in a victorious jig.

'Ah! I'm shite!' Blake cries, throwing the wooden bat to the ground, pouting like only a four-year-old can get away with.

'Shite's a bad word, Blake.' Bella stops dancing, placing one hand on her tiny, legging-clad hip. 'You owe the swear jar five euro.'

'I'm not paying.' Blake's arms cross tightly across his tiny torso.

I march over to stand between them, ruffling Blake's dark cropped hair. Both children are the image of their father, my employer, and treasured friend, Ryan Cooper.

I've worked as private security for Ryan and his brother, Jayden, for years. The position fell into my lap while I was drowning my sorrows in a bar in LA. I'd just been discharged from the British Army. I wasn't in a good place mentally. I boarded a plane hoping to pick up some private security work with a guy I'd been stationed with in the Middle East but got side-tracked by my first taste of freedom and excessive amounts of Macallan whisky.

When a fight broke out in a bar, I apprehended a guy with a knife in less than ten seconds. Jayden offered me a job, and thank God he did, otherwise I might still be in that same bar drowning those same sorrows and battling my PTSD alone.

I don't need to work. Not anymore, anyway. I don't need a lot. I have no interest in materialistic things. Between the military pension and some well-invested bonuses over the years, I could comfortably retire.

But then what would I do?

I was born to protect and serve. Working for the Cooper brothers gave me a purpose. Indirectly, they saved me. I owe them everything.

And I can't help feeling that if I save as many lives as I've taken over the years, perhaps I might somehow balance the invisible scales that hover over me.

Huxley Castle is a far cry from the modest farmhouse in the Cotswolds where I started life. But it's the first place I've felt truly at home in years. Maybe ever. Ryan and Sasha treat me like a member of their family. Which is the main reason I bought one of the luxury cabins situated on the castle grounds. For the first time in my life, I've found somewhere I feel I belong.

My cabin is my private sanctuary, with unlimited access to all the castle facilities, the twenty-five metre glass domed pool, the in-house cinema, and Michelin-starred restaurant.

My favourite facility, though, is the winding gravel trails that blaze through the castle's surrounding woodlands. Sprinting ten kilometres, inhaling the smell of the thick fresh foliage each morning helps eradicate the harrowing memories of the past.

My father always told me I didn't have what it took to be a soldier. It turns out he was right. Still, it's hard to dwell on what's behind me when I'm gauging every gruelling step ahead.

I've lived here for five years, providing security for Ryan, his wife Sasha, and their family, both here and on various tours and trips. Glancing between the twins, my heart swells in my chest. The day they were born seems like only yesterday. I watched them take their first steps. Bella first, of course, paving the way ahead as usual. On their first day of school, I was almost as emotional as Ryan.

It's an honour to live here with them and serve them. It's not how I envisioned my life.

Given the chance, would I change it?

No.

'Besides, Archie should pay up! He says shite all the time.' Blake's high-pitched voice drags me back to the present. His tiny neck arches backwards as he cranes to look at me. Small but savvy, is this fellow.

I drop to my knees, balancing on the grass beside him, producing two fivers from my pocket and tucking one tightly into each of their hands. 'I'm a grown up, so I'm sort of allowed. Don't tell your parents, though.'

As if they've heard me talking about them, Ryan and Sasha appear from the castle together, her hand pressed tightly in his as they descend the taupe stone steps.

Wearing dark jeans, a white t-shirt and aviator sunglasses, Ryan looks every bit the retired rock star he is. Sasha's wearing an oversized jumper dress, stylish and understated. No wonder she's been featured on the front page of every fashion magazine. Pink painted lips are pinched into a tight line, her expression drawn. Something's up. I've been here long enough to know the signs.

As her gaze roams over the lawn and she spots the twins, her mouth curves into a smile which doesn't quite reach those wary jade eyes.

'Mammy,' Blake screeches. Bella might be a daddy's girl, but there's no mistaking who their little boy favours. No matter what goes on outside the castle gates, Sasha and Ryan make it their business to put the kids first. Always.

'I hope you're not hounding poor Archie,' Sasha mock scolds, sweeping Blake up into her arms, even if he is getting on the heavy side.

'He was teaching us how to play baseball but I'm shi...' Thankfully, he replaces the word he was about to use. '...rubbish.'

Ryan snorts. His strong shoulder bumps against mine in a playful gesture. 'The Brits don't know how to play baseball! Ask your uncle Jayden to teach you next time he's home from LA.'

'Don't believe him, kids. Jayden couldn't bat his way out of a brown paper bag!'

Ryan pretends to chase Bella before lifting her high into

the sky and tickling her. A pang of envy flares in my sternum. The Coopers are a walking, talking commercial for the perfect family. Even with whatever new drama is eating Sasha.

'Everything okay?' I glance quizzically between the world's most famous couple as they gently set the kids upright on the lawn.

Sasha turns to Ryan, who clears his throat and pushes his sunglasses on top of his head. Espresso-coloured eyes gaze back at me, blooming with something like commiseration.

'What is it?' Images of the mad bastard I call 'father' assault my mind. I haven't set eyes on him in years.

Could he finally be dead? No. My sister would have called me, not my employers.

Though perhaps not, given that I nearly always reject her calls. If it's not Dad she wants to discuss, it's the hundred acres of family farmland we inherited. I want nothing to do with any of it, but I can't shirk my responsibilities forever.

'It's Victoria,' Sasha blurts. I don't know whether to be relieved or horrified.

Victoria might be the youngest of the three Sexton sisters, but over the past five years she's evolved from shy teenager to **ALL** woman. Even thinking about her makes my dick longer and harder than the baseball bat discarded at my size twelve feet. It's why I tend to avoid her.

'Is she okay?' Stupid question. Obviously, she's in some sort of trouble. Again.

Victoria has a reputation for working harder than anyone belonging to a family as wealthy as hers, powering through long, arduous shifts on an Edinburgh hospital ward in the name of a vocation.

Unfortunately, she also has a reputation for partying harder than anyone too.

She's had more bodyguards than the rest of this family combined.

'What's she done now?' I raise an arm to shield my eyes from the brilliant sunlight.

Ryan steps forward, his arm dropping over Sasha's shoulder, as her face falls again.

'She was involved in a nightclub shooting last night.' His gravelly voice is grim. 'It's all over the news.'

'What?' Adrenaline jacks inside, coursing through my arteries, furiously pumping to every cell.

'She wasn't hurt, luckily.' Ryan's tone is sombre. 'The opposite, in fact. She was trying to help the person who got shot. Typical Vic.'

Sasha pinches the bridge of her nose. 'It's still way too close for comfort.'

'What happened? Where was she? And where was Jared, more to the point?' My chest tightens.

Jared's new to the family and his approach is what some might describe as a little lacking. Personally, I'd call it lazy. When your only job is to protect a person, you do it with everything you've got.

Ryan removes his phone from his pocket, unlocks the screen and hands it to me.

An image of Victoria Sexton smattered with more blood than anyone could survive losing, glares back in technicoloured glory. Crimson stains the front of the ivory-coloured dress which has slipped down off her shoulder, revealing inch upon inch of creamy skin. She's on her knees in a busy nightclub. A man with hair the colour of blazing fire sprawls lifelessly on his back on the floor beside her. Sheer horror is etched into every minute crease of her face.

It doesn't take a doctor to work out he's dead.

'What the fuck?' My stomach jolts like it's been thumped.

'Bad word!' Bella shouts from across the lawn. Little legs power across the grass, the palm of her hand upturned in a silent demand.

'Is she okay?' My fingers locate another crisp note in my back pocket. I hand it over without taking my eyes from the photo.

'She's insisting she's fine, but how can she be?' Sasha pats Bella's head and asks her to pick some daisies to make a chain. Anything to get her out of earshot.

Ryan coughs. 'The thing is, Archie, I had to fire Jared. He's supposed to be within five feet of her at all times. Instead, it turns out he was outside playing fucking Tetris on his phone.'

My blood boils and my facial muscles fight to keep their composure.

'Anything could have happened to her.' Sasha's voice cracks as she clutches her chest. 'I wish she'd just come home.'

She won't. Not until she's a fully qualified doctor. Maybe not even then.

Three things I've learnt about Victoria Sexton during her fleeting visits home over the years is that:

1. She's hell bent on pursuing a career saving people.

2. She's stubborn as fuck.

3. She's never forgiven me for not taking the position as her bodyguard all those years ago.

Point three causes the proverbial penny to drop.

Victoria needs a new bodyguard. Again.

Ryan gauges my reaction tentatively.

I take a step back, sucking in a mouthful of air. I can't do it. I couldn't before, and nothing has changed. In fact, if anything, my attraction to Victoria has only heightened over the years. How can I watch her back when I can't stop imagining her lying on it?

'We need to know she's safe.' Ryan's earnest eyes gaze into mine. 'We need someone we can trust. She only has another six months until graduation. Hopefully, then she'll come home. And so can you.' He points at my cabin. My home. My sanctuary.

Would Ryan and Sasha want me anywhere near the place if they had any inkling I'm borderline obsessed with their little sister? To the point I haven't even tried to date anyone else in over two years.

Then again, will they want me here if something happens to her because I refused to do my job and protect her? My grip on the phone tightens as I search the picturesque horizon I've come to love for some sort of inspiration that might justify my eschewal. 'Ryan, I...'

'Please, Archie,' Sasha begs, a pleading hand palming my shirt. 'You and Victoria used to get on so well. I don't know what happened, but maybe you could put your differences aside for a few months? You might be the only person she'll listen to.'

Doubtful. Very doubtful.

My gaze falls to the bloodbath in the picture again, and a weary sigh slips from my lips.

For fuck's sake.

'Please?' Sasha asks again.

How can I say no when they've been so good to me? When they've become the family I never had. I was at the lowest point in my life when Jayden and Ryan gave me not only a ridiculously well-paid job, but a reason for living when all I wanted to do was curl up and die.

I owe them everything.

One swift nod seals my fate, for the next six months at least.

'When do I need to go?'

'Now.' Sasha throws her arms around me, offering a grateful hug.

Mad how one Sexton woman can touch me and evoke no reaction, and the other only has to appear in the same room and my cock springs like an obedient soldier jumping to attention.

Fuck my life.

All I have to do is keep Victoria safe and out of trouble. It's my job, after all. It's a glorified babysitting position. I've had plenty of practice. Though by all accounts, the twins may be easier to control.

Half of me is horrified.

But what's really horrifying is that the other half of me is secretly thrilled at being forced into her proximity again.

Chapter Three

VICTORIA

Coffee surges from the Nespresso machine into my favourite white cup, nowhere near as quickly as I need it. There's something therapeutic about watching the light china fill with something so dark and delicious.

Why is everyone making such a fuss? Last night wasn't the first time I'd treated a gunshot victim. It won't be the last either. My profession is not one that affords the luxury of being squeamish.

I understand Sasha and Ryan's initial concern, given the photos splashed all over the internet, but when I said I was fine, I meant it.

More than fine. There isn't a scratch on me.

It's Jared I feel sorry for.

He skulks through the kitchen towards the hallway with the last of his belongings, two more suit bags, and a large holdall, his head hanging low in shame as he dumps them at the stairs.

'Coffee?' I nod towards the machine.

'No. Thank you.' His crow's feet have doubled in depth

overnight. 'I truly am sorry, Doctor Sexton. I should have been inside that club with you.' Tired eyes rise to meet mine.

My hand reaches instinctively to take his. 'Jared, it wasn't your fault. It could have happened to anyone.'

His hard jawline lifts rhythmically as he predictably gnaws on chewing gum. 'I'm not paid to protect *anyone*. I'm paid to protect *you*. And I failed.'

A sigh of frustration rushes from my chest. 'Either I'm standing here as a fucking ghost, or you didn't fail! I'm fine. The arrangement was *my* idea. I needed space. The whole time I've been here, I've been made to feel like an overgrown child unnecessarily saddled with a babysitter. You were the first person to respect my desire for privacy. I hated every other bodyguard I had.'

Well, apart from... Never mind. My thoughts pointlessly wander to Archie again.

Archie, who opted to stay at the castle rather than come on an adventure with me.

Archie, who can hardly bear to be in the same room with me these days.

What did I do that was so wrong?

For a while, I thought we were friends. Maybe even with the potential for more. Or maybe that was just my teenage hormones wishfully thinking my crush was reciprocated.

'I should have had more respect for what I was being paid to do. It's been a pleasure knowing you these past few months, though. You're going to go far in this life, Doctor Sexton.' His weathered lips lift into a half smile.

Jared and I hover by the front door in silence, waiting for the car that will take him to the airport, back to his family in Ireland, and drop off the next dictator I'm forced to share my home and my life with.

Some days, I'm seriously tempted to stuff a few precious belongings into a backpack and run away. Dye my hair.

Change my name. Maybe take a job as a cocktail waitress. Jet across the world and bum around a beach on my own.

It's futile though.

My family would tear down heaven and earth to find me.

And how can I save lives if I can't even finish my degree?

I stare into my coffee, contemplating my fate. It suddenly seems less therapeutic and increasingly murky.

I blow my hair from my face with a huff. 'Any idea who they're sending to replace you?'

Jared shakes his head. An engine slows to a stop outside the thick pastel pink front door (Sasha did say I could paint it any colour I like).

We eye each other with wary trepidation. Jared extends his leathery hand for a formal shake, but I wrap my arms around him in an awkward embrace.

Guilt eats at me. It's my fault he's been sacked. 'I'm sorry I got you into trouble.'

He coughs to mask his embarrassment. 'It's fine. I'm getting too old for this line of work, to be honest.'

'What will you do?' I'd hate to see him stuck for a job, even though I know Ryan will have given him a generous pay-off.

'I'm going to take some extended leave with my wife. We might go to Spain for a couple of months.' A small, crooked smile sprouts as he reaches for the front door. 'Try to stay out of trouble, Doctor Sexton.'

'From the look of it,' I pull a face of distaste in the direction of the car outside and the figure clambering out, 'I'll have no choice.'

Jared takes a deep breath and yanks the front door open, finding himself face to face with his replacement.

A broad silhouette towers over him, sneering with an air of disgust.

I'm not sure which of us is more shocked. Time stops and

the rest of the world disappears as I drink in the sight of my new bodyguard.

A crisp white shirt compliments flawless, lightly tanned skin, but it's the trademark black Armani suit that sets my underwear on fire. All Ryan's security wear them, but Archie wears it better than any of them. The way it sculpts those enormous shoulders, showcasing that familiar bulky, powerful physique.

A physique that's born to protect.

Or serve.

Or, in an ideal world... both.

Familiar luscious lips command my attention. Full, plump perfection simply made for sin. Or maybe I've simply been reading too many romance novels.

The hair that was once dirty blond is now darker, a consequence of swapping sunny LA for dreary Dublin, but it's him.

Archie Mason's startling blue eyes finally land on me, boring through my flimsy cami pyjama top, deep enough to sear my soul. Sparks dance across my skin, and my nerves crackle with need.

'You're a magnet for trouble, Victoria.' Archie lifts the suitcase next to him like it's weightless and shoves roughly past Jared, charging straight into my home.

Jared adjusts his jacket, eyeing Archie's disappearing back. 'He looks like a whole heap of fun. Good luck. Goodbye, Doctor Sexton.'

Loitering against the solid wooden doorframe, I raise a hand at the car Jared climbs into. My tongue's so busy hanging out of my mouth, I can barely muster a final farewell.

Not because I'm feeling sentimental.

No.

Because I'm avoiding confronting my new, overtly masculine bodyguard.

The same perfection-personified bodyguard who repeatedly turned down this job before.

The very man who leaves every room I walk into each time I return to Huxley Castle.

What happened to the sunny, funny man I met with Ryan all those years ago? What did I do to deserve the cold shoulder? Other than offer him the opportunity to come here with me?

What changed?

Slamming the heavy oak door shut with a clunk, I pivot on my toes and march upstairs to the middle floor. If the thunderous banging is anything to go by, that's where my new housemate is.

His beguiling aftershave lingers in his wake, a concoction of sage and bergamot blended with a unique, natural masculinity. It seeps into my skin and crawls straight into my veins.

In the open plan living area, my eyes rake over the obscenely attractive man currently tearing apart my house. He's ransacking every cupboard and every drawer of my magazine-worthy country kitchen.

I agonized over the décor in here for months, finally settling on grey hand-painted units complimented by an ivory granite worktop. The chrome circular knobs, which complete the style, are currently being wrenched open by the other knob in my house.

Who does he think he is?

Archie may be panty-meltingly gorgeous, but it seems his attitude still leaves a lot to be desired.

'What are you doing?' I stalk across the varnished wooden floor to hover next to him, trying not to look like I'm inhaling the deliciously scented air encircling his vicinity.

How will I survive gulping down that impossibly alluring

scent every day without throwing myself on him and straddling him like a wild horse?

He's the walking, talking definition of the word masculine. In fact, if I were to google the word right now, I'm pretty sure a picture of my new bodyguard would pop up.

'Familiarising myself with the place. Checking for bugs.'

A nervous stream of laughter rattles from my chest, echoing through the air between us. 'Bugs? You mean like the creepy cockroach kind?'

'Funny, aren't you?' Sharp bright eyes land on mine, stoking a longing in my chest so acute it burns. Confidence smoulders from every inch of him. Even snarky Archie makes my ovaries want to spontaneously combust.

It's probably a good thing he lost his sense of humour years ago because that might have tipped me over the edge completely. From the way he's practically ignored me these past few years, clearly the attraction's not reciprocated, even a fraction.

'Who on earth would bug my house?' I cross my arms, never more aware of the fact I'm not wearing a bra.

His sculpted body stiffens, in all the wrong places, I might add. Oh God, I really need to get laid. It's been too long.

'I don't know. Perhaps someone who might be looking for inside information on your family? Maybe a classmate looking to make a few quid on the side selling gossip to the tabloids? We never did find out how the media got wind of Chloe's second pregnancy. It could have been leaked from here. I assume you speak to Chloe on the phone?'

'Of course I talk to Chloe! She's my sister, for fuck's sake.' I don't like the implication I'm somehow responsible for sharing my family's secrets. Indignation surges within me. 'Or it could have leaked from one of the hundred members of staff Sasha and Ryan employ. It seems any old riff raff can penetrate the castle these days.'

Penetrate?

Talk about giving myself a visual.

I need a cold shower.

Archie backs against the granite, resting his pert backside against it as he holds his hands up. 'Look, it's not an accusation. I'm simply checking everywhere because let's be honest, Jared wasn't exactly the most vigilant of bodyguards, was he? How are you, by the way? After last night?' Concern blooms in his tone. Appraising eyes intensely rake over my body, assessing for damage.

'I'm fine. Just like I told Sasha. It was just a coincidence I happened to be there. The police said the guy who got shot was a drug dealer who'd pissed off the wrong people dealing on their turf. It had nothing to do with me personally, or this family.' I moisten my lips which feel like they're drying out with every passing second.

Archie's eyebrows furrow into a crease. 'It became everything to do with this family when your picture was splattered across every social media site known to man. What if the shooter thinks you saw too much and comes back?' That deep rough British accent. That voice. It exudes experience. Confidence. A worldliness I can only imagine from my pristine Edinburgh prison.

I fling my hands in the air with despair. 'I didn't see anything! Like I told Sasha, I was having a drink with my friends on a Saturday night, letting off some steam after a long day at the hospital. That's all.'

'But do *they* know that, though? Your picture and your name are all over the internet. It wouldn't take a lot to find you if someone thought you were a threat.' It's the longest conversation we've had in years, and I physically squirm under the intensity of his attention.

'That's ridiculous. I'm a student doctor. Trying to save lives is my job.'

'Don't be so quick to write off a potential threat. We'll keep our wits about us, for the next few days especially.' His head cocks to the side. 'Who else has a key to this place?'

'Just my cleaner, Miriam. She comes twice a week, usually when I'm at the hospital.'

'Did she get vetted?' Stern eyes bore into mine.

'Yes.' Truthfully, I have no idea but she's worked for me for four years and I've never had an issue. 'Is this really necessary?' My hands sweep across the open drawers. I dread to think what he might find in there amongst the old takeaway menus and silver cocktail shakers.

'It's absolutely necessary. I'm here to protect you, Victoria. I'll lay down my life for you if I have to. But I'd prefer not to. Please, let me do my job.'

I nod. Something about him laying his life down for me strikes a chord buried deep within. An echoing reminder of the car crash I suffered as a kid. The doctors managed to save me, but not my parents.

I've always secretly wondered what would have happened if the paramedic had pulled them out first. Would they have survived instead of me? My sisters assure me both my mother's and father's injuries were fatal. It wouldn't have mattered. Yet I can't help but wonder sometimes.

The last thing I remember about that night is my mother screaming, 'She's in the back.'

She put my life before hers.

The last thing I want is for anyone else to lay down their life for me.

Archie heads into the living room. I follow him, trying to shake off the melancholy clouding me. A huge, custom-made cream leather couch facing the ivory marble fireplace punctuates the centre of the room. Flames lick the burning logs, dancing to an inaudible rhythm.

'I thought I was the one supposed to be shadowing you?'

Archie stokes the fire with a metal poker before turning to me with a pointed look.

He proceeds to check every square inch of the property; doors, windows, wardrobes, and even the attic.

I make myself scarce and not because I'm scared of some wayward shooter coming to hunt me down.

No.

What scares me is the sheer force of longing surging through every bone in me. Fizzing and crackling beneath my skin.

Archie Mason is still as devastatingly attractive as he's always been. More so, in fact. It's just a pity it seems he can barely tolerate me.

Fuck the cold shower.

I need a hand-held shower with a very large, powerful head.

Though I doubt even that will alleviate the aching lust pulsing waywardly between my legs right now.

Chapter Four
ARCHIE

Victoria's house is nowhere near secure enough for the sister of one of the most famous women in the world, let alone one who's involved in a high-profile shooting.

It's in need of a massive upgrade. The locks require changing. The alarm system needs to be updated. There should be motion sensors on every door and window, linked to an app which is accessible remotely.

Victoria should be wearing a tracker at all times, in case we somehow get separated.

She descends the second flight of stairs from the top floor, interrupting my inventory. 'You'll take the entire ground floor,' she says in a breezy tone, as if it's a given.

Thankfully, she's put some clothes on, even if those clothes are skin-tight jeans that sculpt her shapely thighs, and a pink cashmere sweater that does little to mask those beautiful breasts lurking beneath. The only saving grace is she appears to be wearing a bra now.

My dick twitches and my brain scrambles to summon images of the least sexy women I can think of.

Margaret Thatcher.
Teresa May.

I'm sure some people have a female politician kink, just not me. Not to say I don't appreciate women in power, on the contrary. I just know women with the ability to wield any power over my dick are not the same age as my granny.

'Yeah, that's not going to happen.' I force a smile, which probably looks as sarcastic as it feels.

Slim fingers defiantly rake back her damp, chocolate-coloured hair from her forehead. Hazel eyes glare up at me, flecked with gold and insolence. 'My bodyguards always sleep on the ground floor. We share the middle floor living quarters and the top floor is entirely my own.'

Her elbow settles on top of the ornate ivory panelling, running the length of the wall at half-height as she attempts to block me from passing.

'Like I said, not gonna happen.' I nudge past her, getting a whiff of strawberry scented shampoo as I swiftly mount the stairs. If only I could stop thinking about mounting something else. *Someone* else.

If mere thoughts of Victoria send me jerking myself senseless when we live in different countries, how will I possibly survive sharing a house with her?

Victoria emits an innocence just begging to be stolen. Oh, she's no virgin. I've heard enough stories from Sasha and Ryan to verify that, but there's a naivety about her imploring me to simultaneously corrupt and protect her.

Which is exactly why I couldn't come here with her all those years ago. She was so young. Big, wide eyes used to look at me like I was some sort of war hero.

She couldn't have been more off the mark.

Light feet pound the stairs behind me.

Victoria leaps to block the entrance to one of three grey

painted doors, darting from one foot to the other. Yep, there's nothing innocent about the crimson shade on her toenails. The way her eyes roam over my torso with intent. Or the two tiny pebbles rising on her chest.

I pick a spot above her shoulder and stare at it. It's easier to control myself if I don't look directly at her.

'No one comes up here unless they're invited,' she says boldly.

How many *have* been invited?

Fuck my life. And my relentless and indecent thoughts.

Margaret Thatcher.

Teresa May.

I pause on the large landing, assessing my surroundings. Three enormous rectangular skylights in the sloping roof cast a natural brightness on a battered-looking velvet couch pushed against the far wall. It's outdated and sticks out like a sore thumb in Victoria's otherwise Instagram-worthy show home.

As though she can read my mind, she answers a question I didn't voice out loud. 'It was my mother's.'

Matching mahogany bookcases stacked with everything from Fifty Shades to Pride and Prejudice flank the couch. 'As were the books.' A slow blush crawls from the porcelain flesh on her neck to her cheek.

'Your mother had a copy of Fifty Shades of Grey?' Even the worst mathematician can calculate there's a deficit here. 'Ten years before E L James published it?'

Victoria's cheeks stain scarlet. 'Well, they're not all hers.'

'Hmm.' Victoria reading pornography is not a visual I need right now. 'I need to get into your room.' I move towards her and her eyes double in size.

'You can't go in there. That's my bedroom. There are private... things,' she stammers over the words.

My lips twitch, battling a smirk. 'Sweetheart, you and I

are going to have very few secrets, I'm afraid. But out of common decency and respect, I'll give you a five-minute head start to put your "things" away before I check your windows.'

It takes everything I have to turn on my heels and open one of the other two doors.

Images of what she might not want me to see flash through my brain.

Lingerie?

Toys?

Blood pumps furiously below. I step into an enormous bathroom.

Teresa May.

Margaret Thatcher

Camilla Parker-Bowles.

The air is still thick with steam following Victoria's shower. It clings to my skin, coating it with a damp sheen.

I gaze through the haze at a deep-seated sink unit secured to a wall with floor-to-ceiling mirrors. A double shower cubicle with a detachable head punctuates the corner. Interesting.

A marble, free-standing crab-claw bath occupies the space in front of an enormous, open sash window overlooking the city below.

An image of Victoria naked, the hot water cascading over her curves, flashes across my mind at the same time I realise there are no blinds. Anyone could look up and see her.

I take out my phone and search for a local curtain and blind specialist, once again willing my dick to return to some level of calmness.

Drawers open, then slam closed from across the corridor. Victoria's haughty tone sounds from across the landing. 'You can come in now, if you must.'

'Be there in a minute.' Shoving my phone in my pocket, I

decide to check behind the third door before visiting Victoria and her "things."

If the house plan Ryan showed me was anything to go by, this will be my room for the foreseeable future. I can't protect Victoria if I can't hear her. A close proximity is mandatory, even if it risks putting my throbbing dick in a painful danger of its own.

I nudge open the door; two sets of sash windows come into view. The room is bright, airy and utterly feminine. A wrought metal bedframe houses silver embroidered sheets, a cashmere throw, and a mountain of fluffy, pink pillows.

Photos line the walls and dressing table. Victoria, Chloe and Sasha at Huxley Castle on Sasha's wedding day.

Victoria face to face with a girl with dyed red pixie-like hair. They're both laughing so hard I catch myself grinning back at them before I can stop myself.

Another picture reveals Victoria with her arms slung round a waif-like blonde. Victoria's short smart dress reveals legs that go on forever. Not helpful.

Every time I close my eyes, images of her whizz by like a slideshow and now, every time I open them, I see a collage of her too.

Kill me now.

Victoria's head pops round the door. 'This is where my guests sleep when they stay over. Some of them anyway,' she smirks.

My gut twists as again I wonder how many men have been 'invited' up here.

'Not anymore. This is my room now.' I straighten my spine. She's tall, maybe five foot eight, but I still have at least five inches on her.

Her hand settles on her hip. 'But we'll have to share the bathroom. We'll be able to hear each other at night. You'll know when I bring someone home.' It's almost a wail.

The prospect of listening to Victoria getting banged rotten by some spotty college student, doctor or not, makes me want to wail too. 'That's not going to happen, sweetheart.'

'What?' Her lips part and form a perfect little *O*. One that I'd love to ram my tongue and other body parts into.

'You won't be bringing anyone home for a long time. Not until I've vetted them thoroughly. They've been run through a security database and signed a whole heap of non-disclosure agreements protecting you and your family's privacy.' I silently congratulate myself on how impassively the words emerge from my throat.

'You can't waltz in here and take over. It's my life.' Her slim fingers fly into the air for the hundredth time since I arrived.

'Yes, I can, and I'm going to make sure you get through your final months of college safely enough to live it.'

I fling my suitcase onto the bed and begin unpacking. Victoria continues to stare at me with genuine distress on her pretty little face.

Even without a scrap of make-up, she's easily the most beautiful woman I've ever laid eyes on. Full lips, a perfect plump Cupid's bow, and a light matter of freckles adorning cheekbones that would give the most sought-after models a run for their money. Silky chocolate hair, boasting golden highlights so subtle, they have to be natural.

But it's her eyes that dazzle. Those twin hazel pools have such depth they suck me right in. They're fucking beautiful. Good, pure, kind, sincere. But I shouldn't be surprised. Who else in her position would give up a life of tremendous privilege and luxury to become an overworked and underpaid hospital doctor? She could cruise on the back of her family's wealth forever. Instead she's an absolute grafter with a heart the size of Africa.

She finally finds her tongue. 'Look Archie, I appreciate

your concern but it's utterly unnecessary. Jared and I had an agreement...'

'An agreement which left you unprotected in a nightclub shooting,' I remind her.

'Oh, come on. It could have happened anywhere. Plenty of criminals rock up to A&E begging for someone to stitch them up.'

'I know. And that's exactly why I'll be sitting six feet away from you in the A&E waiting room for the remainder of your placement.' I pause, clutching a pair of trainers, looking for a home for them. I brought them, hoping Victoria still runs regularly. She used to be a brilliant cross-country runner when she was eighteen. I'll need to burn off my excess adrenaline somewhere.

'You can't be serious?' Her jaw falls open.

I tear my eyes away, back to the task at hand. Unpacking. 'I've never been more serious in my life, sweetheart.'

'Urgh! Don't call me sweetheart. It sounds like an affliction rather than a term of affection, from you at least.'

'Fine, Victoria.' I annunciate every single letter just to get a rise from her, like she gets a rise from me by being so fucking beautiful and infuriating.

Has she really such little regard for her own safety? Surely, she of all people should appreciate how fragile life is? How everything can change in a split second. She experienced it as a child first-hand when she lost her parents.

I attempt to appeal to her rational side. 'Surely you can appreciate how quickly things can take a turn for the worse? You must see it in the hospital, day in, day out.'

'Exactly. And that's why I'm determined to live every day like it's my last. Because it damn well could be.'

The door slams, and she stomps across the hallway to her own bedroom, banging that door, too. I'm going to have my work cut out for me.

I finish unpacking and head down to the kitchen to rustle up something for dinner for the two of us, and give her time to cool down.

I can appreciate her situation. It can't be easy having a full-time tail, especially at twenty-three. But she's not your average twenty-three-year-old.

I find the ingredients in the fridge to make a carbonara. Even though I mostly take advantage of the restaurant at Huxley Castle, I find cooking therapeutic. Especially cooking with wine, but unfortunately I'm working. And Victoria is hard work at the moment. Still, I find a bottle of Sancerre and pop it on the table in case she wants a glass.

I'm about to call her for dinner when she descends the staircase.

My jaw nearly hits the floor.

As stunning as she is without make-up, with it she's a fucking knockout. Her lips are painted a shade of fuck-me red to match her dress, if that's what you can call the satin clutching her curves like clingfilm. The V drops so low at the front I can almost see her belly button. It takes every ounce of willpower I own to not lick my parted lips.

Long, toned legs protrude from beneath the short skirt that hangs a good four inches above her knee.

Oh, mother of fucking God, please tell me there's a fire extinguisher in this house because she's so fucking hot she could spontaneously burst into flames at any second.

My Adam's apple feels like a rock lodged in my throat. It's an effort to swallow, let alone form a coherent sentence.

I turn my attention to the stove and try to gather myself. 'Interesting choice of outfit for dinner.'

'I'm going to a party at my friend Libby's place.' Her defiant tone dares me to disagree with her.

I can't stop her. Even if I wanted to.

'Fine. Can we at least eat first?'

She shrugs and I dish her up a plate of pasta, praying I won't stab myself in the eye with my fork, distracted by the vision opposite.

This job is already proving to be more challenging than I anticipated.

Chapter Five

VICTORIA

We sit at the enormous dining room table in silence, bar the occasional scrape of metal forks and the traffic whizzing by outside the window. I reach for the bottle of Sancerre, but Archie leaps to his feet and grasps it first.

He's changed out of his suit and into a pair of grey, low hanging sweats. A tight-fitting white t-shirt showcases his chiselled chest to perfection. When his arm raises to pour my wine, so does the t-shirt. I get a flash of his taut, tanned midriff and the light masculine trail blazing to his waistband and lower.

I force my eyes back to my plate and take a huge mouthful of wine.

Archie's pasta is fabulous. It's a shame I can't say the same about his social skills. We eat without uttering a single word and he looks everywhere but at me.

Am I that repulsive?

Where did we go so wrong?

We used to laugh together. Events where he was assigned as my security used to be fun. Then something changed.

What, I don't know.

I swallow the last mouthful of pasta and stand. 'Thank you. That was delicious.'

'Was that a compliment?' His head whips up, a small smile tugging up his lips.

There he is! A flash of the old Archie! I knew he was in there somewhere.

Startling azure eyes land on me for a fraction of a second before he catches himself. The smile evaporates. His expression instantly switches to stony.

Yep, I definitely repulse him.

Maybe he preferred the nerdy teenage me? The girl with the thick-rimmed glasses?

I stack my plate in the dishwasher and thank him again. He doesn't look up this time.

'I'm ready when you are.' It's a given that he'll drive. It's part of the job description. I've only driven my own black, sleek SUV about twice in my life and that's because Jared twisted his ankle and couldn't push the pedals.

'I'll get changed.' Still, he refuses to look up.

It's killing me that he can't seem to tolerate the sight of me. If we're going to be living together for the foreseeable future, we should at least try to get on.

I will make Archie Mason look at me, if it's the last thing he does.

Libby lives in the penthouse apartment in a new block near the Meadows, a gift from her parents who are super successful dentists. They founded the largest chain of smile clinics in the UK, offering lip fillers and Botox along with every dental procedure under the sun. According to Libby, they're coining it in.

Libby is their only child, their pride and joy. To say they're proud of her is an understatement. She lives a life almost as privileged as mine, but without the restrictions.

Her gorgeous long blonde locks and stunning figure may not incite envy in me, but her freedom certainly does.

Archie parks in Libby's underground car park. It's tight, but he negotiates the vehicle into the only space available with minimal effort.

That damned aftershave wafts through the confined space. It should come with a health warning. Back in his black body-sculpting suit again, he looks every bit the hot bodyguard. It's just a shame he's so unequivocally cold towards me.

Clutching a bottle of Dom Perignon pilfered from my secret supply, I turn to Archie as he unclips his seatbelt. 'There's no need for you to come up. Seriously, this is my best friend's apartment. It's very safe.'

His scoff bounces off the dashboard. 'In your wildest dreams, sweetheart.'

I can safely say Archie Mason knows absolutely zero about my wildest dreams or that he's been the star of them for years. 'It'll be full of student doctors making doctor jokes and complaining about their placements. It'll be dull. You'll be bored senseless.'

A flicker of a frown crosses his face before he catches himself. 'I'm not paid to be entertained.' He slips out of the car.

Before I can protest any further, the passenger door opens and he offers me a helping hand.

A hand which I take without thinking. My palm lands in his. Electricity sears my skin, igniting every nerve ending in my body. My vagina feels like it's been shocked by a defibrillator.

Holy fuck.

In my stunned state, I forget to put my foot on the

ground, my three-inch rockstud-embellished Valentino Garvani sandals swing in limbo.

My body is vibrating with lust. Does he feel it?

He has to.

It's powerful enough to blow fuses in every country from here to Antarctica. Not that his poker face ever gives much away.

Archie coughs, then tugs my hand in a silent encouragement to move my startled ass from the vehicle.

Our faces are only inches apart and still he refuses to look directly at me.

I hop out, yank back my scalded hand and place it on the chilled bottle to soothe the burn. Side by side, we cross the car park, riding the lift in silence. I chance a sidewards glance in his direction, but his gaze remains rigidly forward. Tension plumes through the air swirling around us.

At least I think it's tension. Unless it's all in my head?

When the lift doors ping out, he raises a large hand, halting me before stepping out.

So much for ladies first.

Billie Eilish pumps from along the corridor and I march past Archie, in desperate need of a drink, a fan or a vibrator. Or all of the above.

He's at my heels as I let myself in. At least thirty fellow student doctors are crammed into Libby's kitchen. Gauging from the noise level, there are twice as many in the living area next door.

I'm greeted by the host herself, dressed in a stunning gold, backless Victoria Beckham dress. Sasha has the exact same one.

Melanie flanks her, the tips of her crimson hair only reaching Libby's shoulder, but she looks equally fabulous, if a little more quirky, in a crushed velvet, vintage A-line mini dress. The jade colouring compliments her sparkling irises.

'Victoria! You made it!' they screech simultaneously.

'Of course I made it. Where else would I be?' My FOMO is notorious amongst my friends. They lunge forwards, pulling me into a group hug.

'We didn't know if your new bodyguard would let you out after the other night...' Libby's voice trails off as her eyes land on the brooding hunk beside me. Her hand clutches her chest as her eyes rake over him unashamedly.

Meanwhile, I remain straight-faced, pretending my underwear isn't rapidly melting with each passing second, feigning utter obliviousness to his obscenely devastating appeal.

'Oh my...' A nervous giggle rattles through Mel's pearly teeth.

'This is Archie. He's a whole barrel of fun. Once he heard there was a party, I couldn't keep him away.' My eyes slant in his direction. I swear I see a smirk, but it vanishes before I get a proper look.

'Ladies.' He nods politely at Libby and Melanie before enquiring, 'How many entrances are there?'

Libby gazes up at Archie in obvious awe. She's practically salivating. 'There's the front door you came in through, a side door which opens out to the fire escape steps, and there's the entrance to the rooftop terrace which can only be accessed from inside. I'll be happy to show you all the erm...entrances if you like?'

His eyes meet hers and I watch on in disbelief. He's got no problem looking at my gorgeous friend, but he can't bear to lay his eyes on me.

My chest constricts and a flicker of envy flutters through my gut.

Please, Libby, not him. Not Archie. You can have any man you want. Don't pick him.

I silently telepath the memo, but she doesn't seem to get

it. Her attention is focused entirely on my beautiful bodyguard.

I shouldn't care. He doesn't want me. He never did. But for some reason, the thought of him with my best friend, or any other woman for that matter, kills me.

Finally, after what seems like an eternity, he speaks. 'That won't be necessary, thank you.'

His palm settles on the small of my back as he bends to whisper in my ear. 'Shall I pop that for you?'

My breath catches in my throat.

If he's talking about my cherry, I popped it years ago with a visiting SHO lecturer from Glasgow University. My bodyguard at the time, Vince, thought he was giving me some extracurricular tuition. I suppose he was, just not in the way Vince imagined.

'I...uh...' My mouth is dry and my heart is pounding. One fleeting touch and I'm rendered a blabbering idiot.

Archie takes the champagne from my clammy hands and the second his palm leaves my spine, I miss it.

Oh God. It's been five fucking years and I'm still insanely attracted to him.

It's just a shame he can't even look at me, let alone reciprocate the feeling.

Two glasses of bubbles later, I make my way into Libby's art déco designed living area to mingle, tailed, of course, by my silent, brooding bodyguard. Every female eye follows him as we pass through the crowd. I can't blame them. His physique is one that dominates the room, demanding attention. His discernible indifference only adds to his appeal.

Libby's apartment is not your typical student party venue. A rich claret covers the walls, contrasted by bold, bright artwork above the mantelpiece. An enormous bronze sculpture of a naked man embracing a woman punctuates the vast bright space leading to the open terrace doors.

If Archie's surprised at the opulence, he doesn't express it. Then again, he never did have an eye for material things.

I recognise most of the faces swarming before me. The medical school lectures cross over with the dental school. In the early days, we shared anatomy and physiology classes at the old medical school building.

That building houses some serious history and I'm not simply talking about the anatomy museum with its fifteen thousand specimens, established in the eighteen hundreds.

No.

I'm talking about the awe-struck freshers eye-fucking each other across the Gothic-looking lecture theatre, where many a body has been scrutinised, and not just the one on the table below the circular row upon row of descending seating.

There's a reason there are so many medical shows on Netflix. All that tension, close proximity to colleagues, and long hours, inevitably ends up in drama. I've witnessed it first hand.

Libby's large dining room table is overflowing with alcoholic beverages. A champagne fountain acts as a centrepiece, bordered by crystal flutes stacked elaborately but precariously, while a huge bowl of ripe juicy strawberries nearby begs to be devoured.

For those not partial to bubbles, (apparently they do exist, go figure) there's also a professional bottle rotary optic stacked with Grey Goose, Jack Daniels, Archers, Bombay Sapphire and something green that looks suspiciously like Chartreuse or Aftershock. Shot glasses lie next to buckets of ice and individual cans of every possible mixer.

Archie lets out a low whistle as his eager eyes scan every inch of the room. Well, every inch apart from me, of course. 'You medical students certainly know how to party.'

'Libby certainly does, anyway.' I knock back the remainder of my champagne before holding my glass under the fountain for a refill.

Archie's gaze narrows on my glass. 'Do you really need another one?'

A ripple of annoyance flips through me. I muster my most sarcastic smile. 'Do I really need *you*, Archie?'

Through the throng of bodies, I spot a familiar silhouette. It's hard to miss when that dark, floppy hair has an entire personality of its own. As if he senses my eyes on his back, Harrison Hughes turns in our direction, his blackening eyes roaming flirtatiously across the front of my dress.

Phew, I was beginning to feel invisible with only Archie-I-can't-bear-to-look-at-you, for company.

Archie stiffens beside me as Harrison stalks over like a panther evaluating his prey. Harrison doesn't acknowledge Archie. In fact, he doesn't so much as look at him.

'Victoria, you're looking incredible.' Thick fingers reach out to stroke my arm as his warm lips press a kiss to my cheek.

It's hard to be certain amongst all the background noise, but I'd almost swear Archie lets out a growl.

'Thanks Harrison. You look great too.' Honestly, he looks like he's stepped out of an advert for an expensive all-boy college, modelling a pair of navy designer chinos and a pale pink shirt. All he's missing is the trademark cream v-neck sweater draped over his shoulders and voila, he's a walking advertisement for a men's magazine. Perhaps not Men's Health, though.

No, more like a golfing magazine or something. Or maybe Home and Garden.

'That dress is really something.' His eyes fixate hungrily on my chest again before he appears to remember his manners.

'Thank you.' I take another sip of champagne, purely because I have no idea what to say to Harrison Hughes. On paper, we should have a lot in common. In real life, not so much. Physically, he's striking, in that kind of preppy boarding school way, but as far as chemistry goes, there's none.

'That was really something the other night.' I gather he's referring to the nightclub incident.

'Yeah. The bullet punctured the right lung.' I shake my head. 'He didn't stand a chance.'

'You win some, you lose some, right?' He shrugs, seemingly uncaring that a man was shot dead right in front of me.

Contrary to what I told Sasha and Ryan, the whole thing really shook me. It's one thing having a patient present with a gunshot wound on the ward where there's back up, endless equipment and protocol, and entirely another when it's a Saturday night out in a club.

Harrison's fingers return to the bare skin on the back of my arm. Goosebumps rise instinctively, but not because I'm attracted to him.

'When are you going to put me out of my misery and go out with me, huh?' He inches closer, angling his face towards mine.

This time, the definite growl sounding from behind me is unmissable. I take a small step backwards at the same time as Archie steps forwards, his hand, in all its hot and heavy glory, returning to the base of my spine. Goosebumps rise again, but this time, they can definitely be attributed to an intense, albeit inappropriate, six-year attraction.

Harrison's gaze finally turns to Archie. I introduce them purely to avoid answering Harrison's question. 'Archie, this is Harrison. He's in my year at college. This is my new security detail, Archie Mason.'

'The way he's hovering over you, I thought he was your

father, or your dog.' Harrison guffaws at his own joke and while he's busy laughing, my own mind falls into a deep rabbit hole. There's only ten years between us, but if Archie wanted me to call him daddy, I wouldn't be averse.

Control yourself, woman. I blame romance novels. Who knew daddy kink was a real thing?

'If I were her father, I'd tell you to get your fucking hands off her,' Archie hisses, swiping Harrison's fingers from where they're still lingering on my arm.

Harrison sniggers, eyeballing Archie with an antagonising smirk. 'Oh, this one is definitely more protective than the last few you've had.'

Not a good idea.

I once saw Archie put down four bouncers at a nightclub in Dublin purely because they leered at Sasha in what he deemed to be a disrespectful manner.

I turn to Archie. 'I'm wrecked after the last few days. Maybe we should go?'

His thumb strokes my spine. It's a tiny fleeting gesture, but impossible to miss when every single one of my nerve endings is tuned into his touch. 'With pleasure.'

Pleasure would be the right word, if you'd be open to it.

'See you at the hospital, Harrison.'

Archie's lips curl upwards. Harrison's curl down.

Outwardly, my own lips remain neutral. Inwardly, they tingle with a longing so fierce it aches all the way to my toes.

Chapter Six
ARCHIE

The sweet, enticing scent of strawberry shampoo is inescapable in the SUV. At least while I'm driving, I have a legitimate excuse not to look at her. It's exhausting keeping up this wall between us, but that's the way it has to be for me to protect her.

It just takes one split second, one tiny distraction and it's game over. That lesson was delivered the hard way on my final tour with the British Army. I couldn't save my men. But I can and will save Victoria if it comes to it.

The journey from the Meadows is silent.

As I indicate left on George Street, heading for Victoria's house, I'm still smarting from being looked down on by that jumped up pretty-boy prick in the pink shirt and drainpipe fucking chinos. Every stitch of his clothing screamed wealth. Every word he uttered screamed self-important wanker. 'Who was he?'

'Who was who?' Victoria asks with a voice a little too innocent to be genuine.

Apparently, she's going to make me drag it out of her.

'Park here.' She gestures to a rare free spot on one of the side streets.

'Here? Why?' My foot lightens on the accelerator and the vehicle slows.

'I said I wanted to go, but I didn't mean home.' Her face tilts in my direction. I know because her minty breath brushes my cheek.

I parallel park with a sigh. This woman is going to be the death of me.

'You said you were wrecked after the last few days,' I sigh.

Her slim fingers skim over her chest. It's official, she's trying to kill me. 'Yeah, my head is wrecked, not my body.'

That body. I know exactly how to tire it out. In another life.

One where my job isn't to save hers.

'Fine. Let's get this over with. Where to now?'

'The George Hotel is just round that corner.' Her index finger points. 'The barman there looks about twelve, but he makes the best French 75 in the city.'

If she hears the short sharp grind of my molars, she doesn't acknowledge it. Slamming the driver's door closed, I stalk around to the passenger side, scanning the streets for any potential threat, but it's a lot quieter here than on George Street.

Victoria opens her own door. I offer my arm, hoping the material of the jacket is enough of a barrier to prevent that inconvenient electricity racing through my skin and straight to my dick again.

Firm fingers grip my arm as her feet meet the uneven paving. A ripple of goosebumps rip across her bare arm.

'Do you want my jacket?' My breath fogs before my face.

'No, thanks. I'm not cold.'

My delinquent eyes stray to her chest. Twin nubs

protrude beneath the flimsy material of her dress. Either she's lying, or she's horny.

It's too much.

I've barely been here a day and I'm already fucked.

Ryan will have to get someone else.

I can't do it.

My eyes betray me, flicking upwards to meet hers for a fraction of a second. Even the cold air smoulders between us. I promptly tear my gaze away before I do something really fucking stupid like kiss her.

She drops my arm and we fall into step, side by side, under the midnight sky. A group of four guys approach in the distance, shoving each other and yelling in thick, broad Scottish accents.

My hand instinctively reaches for Victoria's back, and she leans closer into me as we pass by them.

Would they mistake us for a regular couple out on a Sunday night?

Harrison's words pierce my daft romantic notion.

The way he's hovering over you, I thought he was your father.

There's ten years between us. I'm nowhere near old enough to be her father, but I am old enough to know better than to fantasise about the woman I'm paid to protect. Jesus, if Ryan had any inclination of what was flashing through my delinquent brain, he'd shoot me where I stand, and I wouldn't blame him.

Unfortunately, fantasising about Victoria Sexton is something I've been doing for years. It's a hard pattern to break, and even harder when she's standing in front of me in an outfit like that one.

I read somewhere that it takes twenty-one days to break a habit. If I can just survive the first month, establish firm, professional boundaries, maybe I can get through this without losing my job, my cabin at the castle, and the family I've come to love.

The Gothic-looking exterior of the George Hotel does nothing to indicate its sheer magnificence inside. Thick navy carpet paves the way through the wide corridors to a spacious, double-height bar area.

The walls are panelled in a rich cherry wood extending from the chunky skirting all the way up to the elaborate coving. The bar itself is in the centre of the room, an oval wooden counter, varnished and gleaming beneath the chandelier above it.

One long built-in bench lines the room, its seat padded with thick cushioning stitched beneath taupe-coloured leather. Intermittently spaced circular tables separate one seating area from another.

Soft jazz music sounds over the hum of conversation.

Victoria wasn't kidding. The barman looks twelve. His face lights up like a Christmas tree when he spots her. No wonder. She's fucking stunning in that dress.

As she slips into the nearest free bench, he practically sprints over.

'Good evening, madam.' His fresh face stains crimson.

What, am I invisible? Admittedly, discretion's part of the job, but not in this instance.

'Can I get a French 75?' Victoria crosses one long leg over the other, her dress hitching an inch, prompting the barman's pupils to double in size.

I clear my throat noisily and his head whips to me. 'And for you, sir?'

'Water, thanks,' I grunt.

'Still or sparkling, sir?'

'Whatever.' I'm scanning the room for exits, entrances, anyone who looks out of place or like they've consumed one too many and may pose a problem.

In the States, I carried a weapon. I have a sense of vulnerability without it. There are firearms at Victoria's house. I hope I never have to fire a bullet from any of them, but the woman seems to be a magnet for trouble.

The barman glances between us before leaving to fetch the drinks.

'Would you prefer me to sit over there?' I motion to the adjacent table.

A frown creases her eyebrows. 'Am I so intolerable that you can't bear to sit next to me?'

'I thought maybe you'd want a little space.' I slide onto the bench next to her. 'I didn't want to assume...'

'God forbid people might mistake us for a couple.' A loud sigh slips from her lips. 'You know, Archie, I used to like you. I even thought we were sort of friends.'

I take a deep breath. This is exactly the type of conversation I was hoping to avoid.

'I'm not paid to be your friend.' It comes out harsher than I intend, and she flinches.

I soften my tone. 'I'm trying to ensure you're safe. I get that it's hard for you having someone by your side twenty-four-seven, but it really is necessary. Sasha shelters you from the majority of threats they receive. When there's as much public interest as there is in your family, there's always going to be a risk from the media or some crazed fan.'

'I just don't get why you have to be so cold towards me.' Thick black lashes flutter against high prominent cheekbones.

'I'm not cold,' I lie.

'You can barely look at me.' Her doe-like eyes linger on my face for a beat longer than I'm comfortable with.

'I'm scanning for danger.' Another lie. I finished that within ten seconds of arriving.

'Yeah right,' she says sarcastically. 'Because there was a

real chance a crazed axe murderer was going to jump out from under the kitchen table and chop me into pieces while I was eating my carbonara?'

The barman returns with our drinks, saving me from having to answer that one.

From my periphery, I notice her lips press slowly, almost indecently, against the champagne flute. She takes a huge sip of her cocktail, staring ahead.

'Tell me about Harrison.' His smug face is still fresh in my brain. 'Are you and he...?'

'What's it to you?' she asks haughtily.

'As your bodyguard, I need to know these things. It's for your own safety.' Even if I can't bear to hear them.

She readjusts her seating position before finally answering. 'No. He's asked me out a couple of times, but I haven't accepted.' She takes another sip from her drink. 'Yet.'

The fleeting relief that initially flicked through my torso goes up in a raging pile of smoke.

She runs a mindless finger over the rim of her glass. 'Harrison's the third generation of doctors in his family. They own a huge estate in Fife.'

He's everything I'm not. Everything I'll never be. Educated and from the right social class.

A memory of goosebumps rising on her arm when he touched her sears through me. I press my glass against my lips to hide my irritation. 'And do you like him?'

Her neck cranes in my direction, a thoughtful expression on her face. 'Is that also information you require for my safety? I don't think so.'

'If his advances are bothering you, I need to know.'

'They aren't bothering me.'

So she does like the jumped-up little prick. Though he's not little, in truth. If he didn't dress like a fucking golfer, he could probably pass for a rugby player.

'I'll get some background checks run on him in case you do decide to date him.' The word date sticks like a thorn in my throat.

'Oh, I'm not thinking about dating him.' Her voice is playful, tinged with amusement. 'I'm thinking about fucking him. It's been an absolute age since I got laid and a girl has needs, you know?'

She's staring at me with those huge hazel eyes. Gold flecks dance with devilment.

This time, I can't drag my own away. They rake over her prominent chest. Follow the dip of that indecently low V that reveals creamy, silky skin that I'm dying to run my tongue across.

What I wouldn't give to slip my hand under her dress and take care of those needs for her. Kiss every inch of her body until she forgets her own name.

Blood pulses below. My cock is rock solid, straining so hard against my tailored suit pants they're in danger of ripping.

I've barely been here twelve hours and already my self-control has evaporated into the Edinburgh night air. 'Needs?'

'Yes. I am a healthy, red-blooded woman, you might notice now you're finally looking at me.'

I am looking at her. A rare, risky indulgence I'm granting myself. 'You need a man to take care of those needs. Not a preppy boy-band reject. That guy we met tonight couldn't meet those needs if you gave him a map, a torch, and a million quid.'

'And you could, I suppose?' A single dark eyebrow rises to challenge me.

'Sweetheart, if the circumstances were different, we might have been allowed to find out.'

She swallows hard. Glassy eyes smoulder straight to my soul.

For fuck's sake.

I drag my eyes away from her again.

Teresa May.

Margaret Thatcher.

Camilla Parker-Bowles.

I take a sip of water. I could pour the whole damn lot over my head and it wouldn't make the slightest bit of difference. I'm as hot for Victoria Sexton as I've always been.

'Harrison seems like a total creep,' I mutter.

She shrugs nonchalantly. 'Like I said, I'm not thinking about dating him.'

Damn right you're not.

Not if I have anything to do with it.

Chapter Seven

VICTORIA

With three days off before I'm due back at the hospital and a mountain of studying to do, the time passes pretty uneventfully. If there was supposed to be some comeback on that nightclub shooting, there's been nothing. Not that I expected there would be. I knew I was never personally in danger. It was my family who needed reassurance.

Still, Archie hasn't let me out of his sight, bar bedtime, worse luck.

I've replayed our conversation in the bar over and over in my mind.

If the circumstances were different, we might have got to find out.

Maybe he doesn't despise me after all? But if not, then why is he so cold?

We left the George shortly after that and I haven't brought it up since. Mind you, I haven't had four glasses of champagne plus a French 75 since either.

We've fallen into a routine very different from the one Jared and I had. Archie insists on following me absolutely everywhere, including on my morning runs. Back in my school days, I was a cross-country champion.

Archie is one of the few people who can keep up with me. And more to the point, he makes it look effortless.

I throw on a pair of black Nike compression tights, a black sports bra, and tie my hair up in a tight ponytail. My morning run used to be my alone time. Time to think, process, and reflect. For the past couple of days, the only thing I can think about is the magnificent man who runs beside me.

It grates on me that he doesn't joke with me like he used to. That he doesn't even pretend to want to be my friend. I understand he has a job to do, but I wish he could do it with a fraction of the warmth he used to express when I was a teenager.

The only time he opens up slightly is when we're running. Which means I've been running every day. Using the time for my own personal mission to get Archie to lower his guard around me again. The more resilient he is, the more determined I am.

Why can't he be my bodyguard and the guy I used to consider a friend?

Though friends aren't supposed to imagine each other naked, I've been doing a hell of a lot of that the past few days.

Sharing a house with him is a brutal form of torture. That damned aftershave wafts through every room, stirring up old longings and new hopes. Ridiculous hopes, given he can barely look at me.

I have a lot less freedom.

But would I have Jared back now?

Not a chance.

Even the moodier, more serious version of the carefree man I used to know rouses an appeal so addictive I'll pound the pavement from here to Glasgow if it means he might open up to me.

This morning, Archie beats me to the kitchen. A grey

running vest hugs his torso. Smooth, sculpted pecs poke from beneath the thin cotton. Black running shorts showcase that perfectly toned backside.

He glances up as I enter the room before quickly reverting his attention to his coffee.

I grab a bottle of water from the fridge. 'You up for fourteen miles this morning?'

A half-smile tugs at his lips, and I get a flash of the old Archie. 'I'm up for however far you can go.'

'Careful, Archie, that almost sounded like you were flirting with me.' I bang the fridge door closed but it does nothing to ease my growing frustration.

'I meant on the roads, Victoria.' The frown is back, but it looks as if it's taking every facial muscle to keep it there.

We step out into the chilly morning, using the front wall as a prop to stretch our hamstrings before taking off.

We cut up the Royal Mile, past the castle, and loop back through the old town. It's one of the most scenic routes in the city, even if it does mean negotiating the traffic.

Archie's by my side every single step of the way. We run the first three miles in silence.

'Do you miss Dublin?' I ask as we bump elbows for the hundredth time.

He inhales before blowing out a long, slow breath. 'I miss Huxley Castle. My cabin. Ryan. And I miss the kids.'

My head whips to look at him and I nearly collide with a woman furiously stomping towards us. 'You miss the twins? *My* niece and nephew?' I didn't have him pegged as the sentimental type.

That rare smile flashes across his face again, revealing strong white teeth. The front tooth slightly overlaps another on the lower arch, a perfect imperfection. 'Yeah, they're so cute and cool. Like, how could they not be?'

'You're kidding, right? Blake's the devil himself in the

body of a four-year-old and Bella is a bigger diva than Mariah,' I scoff.

Archie sniggers. 'They're not that bad.'

'Huh! Last time I was home, Blake put twenty bugs from the garden in my bed and Bella used my Charlotte Tilbury lipstick to draw on not only her face but the freshly painted wall of my bedroom.'

Archie's laughter cuts through the air and my heart sings a song of triumph.

He *is* in there, after all!

'I miss the kids too,' I admit, 'Even if they are a handful. I miss Sasha. And even Ryan. But I don't miss living in their shadows, being fussed over like a fragile child, and wrapped up in cotton wool.'

'I can understand that,' Archie nods, darting between passing pedestrians.

'It's a first world problem, but I never signed up for this life of fame and fortune. All I've ever wanted is a normal life since I was a little girl. To be a doctor. To do some good in a world that's overflowing with badness.'

'It's really admirable,' he says between ragged breaths.

It's the closest he's come to issuing a compliment since he arrived.

'Is it though? Or is it self-serving in some ways?' I have no idea why I'm opening up to Archie right now, but it all pours out. 'Is it that I need to prove to myself, and the entire world, that my life has a point? That I'm something? Like, am I really trying to save lives, or am I trying to save myself? Do you know what I mean?'

He probably thinks I'm crazy. Hell, maybe I am. I just haven't quite found my place in this world yet. My curious brain is as interested in the human psyche as the human form.

Archie's pace quickens and my legs burn trying to keep up

with him. 'Yeah, I know exactly what you mean. Like, was me signing up for the army honourable? Or because I wanted to be seen as honourable? My dad always said I didn't have what it took to make it as a soldier. In the end, he was right. But either way, whether it's honourable or self-serving, the outcome is the same. You *will* save lives, Victoria.'

'Just like you did in the military.'

His eyelids press closed for a beat and when he opens them again, he ups the pace once more, leaving me struggling to breathe, let alone talk. I'm not naïve enough to think it's a coincidence.

When we finally get back to the house, panting like we've done twelve rounds in the boxing ring... or bedroom—a girl can dream, right?—my next-door neighbours are hovering in their doorway, laden with more designer bags than I can count.

I raise a hand, clutching the wall as I catch my breath.

Kristina and Marissa moved in last month. Glamorous, elegant and eternally in heels, I've yet to see either of them without a full face of make-up, their matching blonde bobs perfectly coiffed by a professional volumizing blow-dry.

Together they own a high-end women's lingerie boutique on the corner of George Street. Their chic style and class would be intimidating if they weren't both so lovely.

I've been meaning to invite them over for drinks, but between college and my placement, I keep missing them.

'Fair play to you.' Marissa assesses my running gear with awe. 'I don't know how you do it every day.'

'It's addictive,' I confess, tightening my ponytail. The running, *and* spending time with my sullen security guard.

'So is sex,' Kristina snorts, lasciviously eyeing Archie as he stretches against the wall next to me.

Huh. I wouldn't know. It's been so long I think my vagina has closed over. I wasn't entirely joking about sleeping with

Harrison. Even if I would have to pretend he was someone else. Someone who would be across the corridor listening to every subtle bang of the headboard.

'So is champagne,' I add. 'I've been meaning to get you over for a few glasses.'

Kristina stares at Archie like he's the last cream cake on the baker's shelf. I can't blame her, but it still irks me.

'Oh, that sounds heavenly.' Marissa's bright blue eyes dance with delight. 'We'd love to, wouldn't we, Kris?' She nudges her friend, who is still unashamedly ogling my bodyguard.

'Are you going to introduce us?' Kristina finally manages to drag her tongue back into her mouth.

'Oh, sorry. This is Archie. He's my...' I trail off, not knowing what he is. Bodyguard? Friend? The man I've been obsessing about since he walked into my house three days ago?

Archie finishes his stretches and steps between us. 'I'm Victoria's bodyguard.' The way he annunciates the word *bodyguard* implies there's way more to it than that.

'Lucky bitch,' Kristina whispers with a wink. 'I was envious when I found out Ryan Cooper was your brother-in-law but, oh my God, this guy right here.' She talks about Archie as if he can't hear her, exhaling a low whistle while pretending to cool herself down with an imaginary fan.

Archie's expression remains neutral as his palm settles on my spine again, nudging me towards my front door. That potent desire blazes through every cell again. Heat creeps into my cheeks as I wave goodbye to the girls. 'I'll let you know about that party.'

Kristina's voice carries through before my pink front door fully closes. 'They are definitely sleeping together.'

I fucking wish.

'Don't invite them over, Victoria,' Archie warns.

'Why not?' I kick my runners off at the door.

'Inviting absolute strangers into your home is a breach of security.'

'They're not strangers. They're neighbours. Are you trying to piss on all my bonfires or what?'

'Just the ones that put you at risk. Now, I need a shower.' Archie excuses himself.

I head up to my bedroom to wait for my turn. I could use the downstairs bathroom, but my shampoo and conditioner are up here. Peeling off my clothes, I wrap a fluffy towel around my body and wait.

Archie's going to be the death of me. Death by desire. Or death by boredom because he won't let me do anything that remotely resembles fun.

A door creaks open and I step out onto the landing.

Archie exits the bathroom wearing nothing but a silver army dog tag chain, complete with what looks like a battered St. Christopher pendant, and a tiny, turquoise towel around his ripped, sculpted midriff. Steam emanates from his torso. And my vagina.

The man is ripped like a Greek god, just begging to be worshipped. Smooth, defined planes that would give He-Man a run for his money, beg to be touched. Mottled scars splay across his left shoulder and disappear down his back, making him look like a warrior. His right pec is inked with scrawled text interwoven with an eight-inch cross. It's an effort not to reach out and run my fingers over it.

A smattering of light fine hair dusts below his flat stomach before disappearing beneath the towel.

He's the textbook definition of sex on legs.

A toothbrush hangs from the side of his full, luscious lips, which are coated with a light rim of toothpaste. Lips that are meant to do unspeakable things.

It would be polite to look away, but my manners have

been misplaced. Having this prime example of the male species living under my roof is tipping me over the edge.

He's so close, yet so far out of my reach.

His eyes flick over my own towel before settling somewhere to the left of my ear. Anywhere but at my face.

'I'm nearly done. Just need to grab my razor.' His words slur around the toothbrush as he disappears into my guest room, then darts back, clutching an electric razor.

Silently willing his towel to fall to the floor, I watch in disappointment as his broad back disappears back into the bathroom.

I collapse onto my mother's worn-looking velvet sofa while I wait. None of the scenes in romance novels have a patch on what I'd do to Archie Mason if he'd only drop his guard. Or his towel. My nipples stiffen and my hands automatically seek to soothe the hard sensitive nubs that seem to jump to attention whenever he is near.

The door opens again. The toothbrush is missing. He freezes momentarily. His gaze falls to watch my fingers mindlessly stroking over my breasts. It's fleeting, but it's unmissable. The lips that were wearing a delicate layer of toothpaste are now wearing a look of longing.

A shiver of pure desire rips through me as a bulge rapidly forms beneath Archie's towel. He stands like a rabbit caught in the headlights, blinded by shock.

Or maybe lust, if the rising towel is anything to go by.

'Victoria.' His voice rings with a warning.

'Sorry, I...' I shrug, letting my hands fall to my side. I stare at him, silently challenging him. 'Those needs again.'

'A cold shower. That's what you need.' His Adam's apple bobs in his throat. He's not convincing either of us.

My eyebrows arch defiantly at his groin. 'Care to join me?' He did say I needed a man, not a boy.

'I knew you were going to be trouble, Victoria.' He shakes

his head as he steps out of the doorway, as if to say the bathroom is mine.

His body can't lie. There was no hiding that bulge. Perhaps he doesn't still see me as a silly teenager after all, though clearly he hasn't got the memo that I don't need to be wrapped in cotton wool.

A tiny smile plays on my lips.

This attraction isn't entirely one-sided. I'd bet my last pound on it.

Trouble? Archie Mason is about to discover the meaning of the word. I'm going to bulldoze down his walls and peel off those sublime grey sweats, along with the tough guy act he wears around me. And I'm going to enjoy every second of it.

By the time I've finished with him, it won't be a case of not being able to look at me, it will be a case of not being able to look away.

Chapter Eight
ARCHIE

My cock is harder than a steel pole.

This is bad.

So bad.

So why is there a stupid fucking smirk playing on my lips?

She's ten years younger than me. An absolute knockout, with brains the size of Broadway. And she's attracted to me? "Archie, the fuck up." Go figure.

Still, as flattering as it is, it's really not helpful.

We can never act on it.

The shower starts in the bathroom again. Has she taken the head off the wall? Is she using the water to touch herself? Lathering soap all over her satin-like skin? Over those full, pert breasts? Between her legs? My hand wraps around my rigid cock and I pump three times before my phone rings.

Fuck. It's Ryan. It's a quick cure for my raging hard on.

'Hello?'

'Archie, how's it going, buddy?'

'Good, man. All good.' More lies.

'I'm just checking in to see how everything is going over there.' His gravelly voice resounds across the miles.

'Everything is fine.' *Apart from I was about to wank myself senseless over your little sister-in-law, and believe me, it could have been a lot worse.*

It took every modicum of willpower I had not to jump her in the shower.

'Is Victoria okay? She has a habit of attracting trouble.' The twins screech in the background, fighting over whose turn it is with the TV.

'I noticed.' My mind wanders to the party at Libby's.

Harrison, and Victoria's confession about her needs.

That invitation.

'I've ordered a new security system for the house and the locksmith is coming tonight to upgrade the locks on the doors and windows.'

A low whistle of relief sounds directly into my ear. 'Good. Thanks, Archie. I knew you were the right man for the job.'

Guilt pricks in my chest. 'Honestly, Ryan, I don't know if I am.' My resignation is on the tip of my tongue. But I could never give an adequate reason why. Not without losing my sacred position in the family I've come to love.

'What are you talking about? You're perfect for her.' Genuine surprise rings in his tone.

Yeah, my dick thinks so too, that's the problem. It was a problem before I got here and now it's a fucking catastrophe.

He continues, not waiting for a response. 'You're the only bodyguard she's not complained about.'

'It's early days.' I scrape my fingers through my damp hair.

'She complained about Jared within ten minutes. Little did I know they swiftly came to an agreement shortly after.'

'Hmm.'

'Has she tried to proposition you?' Ryan asks.

'What?' The colour drains from my cheeks. Are there cameras in here? Not five fucking minutes earlier, that's exactly what she did.

'Has she tried to cut a deal with you?'

Oh.

'No.'

Not like that, anyway.

'Probably because she likes having you around. It's perfect.'

'Hmm.' I keep my mouth shut because the truth is, I like being here. More than I should. Even the runs have been rewarding.

'Has there been any blowback from the nightclub shooting? Do you have any reason to believe Victoria's presence was anything other than a coincidence?'

'I'm pretty sure that was random, but I won't let her out of my sight, just in case.'

'Good man.' Ryan exhales heavily.

If only you knew...

'I'll keep you updated,' I promise.

'Right, well, look after her. And yourself.' He disconnects the call.

Victoria struts around the kitchen wearing a dress that can only be described as fit for the beach. It's white, see-through and buttons up the front like an oversized shirt. She hums along to a Bastille song blaring through the retro-looking radio as she chops an onion.

'Are you hungry?' she asks.

I'm fucking starved. For sex, that is. It's been a long time since I even attempted to date anyone. Coming here has only served to reinforce why.

'Yeah, I'd eat.' I avert my eyes from the clear outline of the thong wedged between her peachy ass cheeks, but not before she catches me looking.

Does she have to wear such a provocative outfit to make dinner? My balls are already blue and burning.

Teresa May.

Margaret Thatcher.

Camilla Parker-Bowles.

'I'm making fajitas.' Since I made her carbonara, she's cooked for me twice. Tomorrow, I'm going to make her something sensational. After twelve hours on A&E, she'll need it.

'Sounds good.' I check my phone. It's easier than trying to stare past Victoria's shoulder. Or pretend not to stare at her bum.

The screen lights up with an incoming call. It's my sister, Andrea. I reject it, but she calls again immediately. I reject that too, unable to deal with the same question she will inevitably ask.

I know she wants me to visit the farm, but the longer I leave it, the harder it is to go back.

'Everything okay?' Victoria hovers next to me, a glass of white wine in her hand.

'Yeah, it's just my sister, Andrea.'

'I didn't know you had a sister.' She perches on the couch next to me. The dress hitches up further, displaying inch upon inch of creamy smooth legs.

I'm hard *again*.

She's going to be the death of me, I swear.

'We don't see much of each other. She lives in England.'

'What about your parents?' She takes a sip from her drink.

'They're...' How are you supposed to articulate that I'll never be good enough for my own father? 'My mother died in labour birthing me and my father worked away for most of my childhood.'

'Wow. I'm so sorry, Archie. I had no idea.' Hazel eyes cloud with compassion.

The doorbell sounds, saving me from answering any more questions.

As I jog down the stairs, I glimpse the silhouette of a large man. The locksmith.

I open the door, wedging my foot behind it just in case.

The tweed suit is the first eyesore. The second is the stupid smirk carved onto Harrison's face.

What the fuck?

Is she wearing that shirt dress for him?

'I didn't say I was going to date him.' Oh, please.

Did she invite him over because I turned her down? Are her needs so strong she'd seriously contemplate shagging the campus creep?

I don't yet have the results of Harrison's background check, even though I made the call the morning after the party. Jayden and Ryan have a guy who can find out almost anything about anyone. The information Declan obtains isn't strictly legitimate, but it's always accurate.

But even if Harrison's check comes back clean, I can't tolerate him near Victoria.

Mind you, I'd find it hard to tolerate any guy sleeping with her.

Harrison's heavy hand rests on the door, trying to shove it open, but my foot and knee hold it firm.

'What do you want?' He might scream old money, but he also screams entitled wanker.

'I came to see Victoria.' Two-day-old scruff lines his jaw. Does nobody teach these toffs how to use a razor these days?

'Is she expecting you?'

'No, but...' I slam the door in his face and disconnect the doorbell. He can press it a million times and she won't hear it. I pull out my phone and text the locksmith to call me when he's outside.

Just because I'm in no position to aid Victoria Sexton and

her needs, I'm damn well not going to let anyone else in to do the job. No fucking way. I'll die before that happens.

'Who was that?' Victoria asks as I return to the room. She's stirring a sizzling pan of chicken coated in peri peri seasoning.

'Just someone selling something. I told him you weren't interested.' My eyes fall to her ass again. This time when she catches me looking, I don't even attempt to tear my eyes away.

Chapter Nine

VICTORIA

The clock on my bedside locker tells me it's time to get up. I'm due at the hospital in an hour and the buzz of what might arrive at A&E is enough to propel me out from beneath the duvet.

Following yesterday's nearly naked encounter in the hallway, Archie is nowhere to be seen this morning. I heard the shower at five-thirty, a full hour before my alarm was due to go off. Clearly, he's not taking any chances, even if he did ogle my ass last night.

I shower, then throw on a pair of yoga pants and an oversized sweater. My Converse are downstairs.

'Good morning.' I head straight for the Nespresso machine.

'Morning.' Archie barely glances up from his phone. Note to self: wear the shirt dress again tonight. 'Do you know your rota for next week yet? There's a company coming to fit a new security system. I want to be here when they arrive.'

'Even if I'm working, you can still be here. Jared used to drop me and go. The hospital has its own security guards.

There are cameras in all the corridors.' Even as I say the words, I know it's futile.

Archie's looking good enough to eat in another tailored black suit. My stomach flips and not because I'm hungry. Not for food, anyway. Why, oh why couldn't any of the boys I met before have this effect on me?

'Cameras aren't going to protect you, sweetheart.' His cool conviction only adds to his appeal. 'I will, though.'

The steely determination in his hard-set jaw only serves to reinforce his promise.

When we reach the hospital, Archie follows me up three flights of stairs and into the women's changing rooms. 'You can't be here.' I glance around, glad we're half an hour early or there'd be a lot of half-dressed, unhappy women wondering what the hell he's doing.

Archie checks the shower area, the toilets, and every corner of the locker room. I grab my scrubs from the space on the shelf labelled with my name, pulling them up to my nose to inhale the familiar fabric softener. Thank the laundry fairies. They really are amazing.

Seemingly satisfied for now, Archie stalks to the changing room door. 'I'll wait outside.'

Probably a good idea. Though if he wanted to watch me undress, I wouldn't have a problem with it.

Three minutes later, with my hair twisted into a crab clip and my identification pinned to the pocket of my scrubs, I step into the hospital corridor. Two nurses walk towards us. 'Doctor Sexton.' They acknowledge me with a brief smile before turning their attention to Archie, elbowing each other in the less than discreet way in which women wordlessly convey, '*Fucking hell, he is hot.*'

I can't argue with them.

'Wait outside, if you insist on hanging around the hospital all day.'

'Outside? You must be joking.' He takes a seat in the waiting area, which is already overflowing with people waiting to be seen.

'You can't be serious.' Blood flames my cheeks. 'Do I look like I need a babysitter?'

His head cocks to the side as he stares me down. 'Do I look like a babysitter to you?'

This is mortifying.

Does Peter Andre's wife have this problem when she goes on shift?

'Doctor Sexton.' Doctor Dickson's greying temples pop out from behind a curtain, followed by the rest of him. 'I expected to see you in my office the other day.'

'Sorry, Doctor Dickson. There was a bit of an incident. A shooting.' *And even if there wasn't, I still wouldn't have landed in your office.*

'I saw. Are you okay?' He uses his concern as an excuse for his beady roving eyes to check out my body.

Archie tuts from six feet away. Him staying was a bad idea. I'm well able to fend for myself here. Plus, he's a distraction. My eyes refuse to stay away from him.

'I'm great. Not a bother on me. Thank you for your concern.' I nod towards the curtain Doctor Dickson emerged from. 'What do we have in there?'

'A suspected fractured femur. I've administered IV pain relief and the patient's heading to radiography shortly. Would you like to take a look?'

'Please.'

Nothing feeds the ego more than being observed by someone less experienced.

Does that work the same in the bedroom? Archie must have a lot of experience, given he has ten years on me. Would he like to be watched? Or would he prefer to be worked?

'Doctor Sexton?' Doctor Dickson's voice snaps me back from my illicit daydream.

'Coming.'

If only.

All hell breaks loose at lunchtime. A three-car motorway pile-up results in two ambulances arriving at the hospital simultaneously, each with patients in critical condition.

The next eight hours are a blur of blood and bodies.

When I finally get time to run to the loo, Archie follows me.

'What a day.' I shake my head.

'Did everyone survive?' He hands me a cup of coffee from the vending machine and I swig it gratefully.

I shake my head, tucking a stray strand of hair behind my ear. 'The husband didn't make it. He lost too much blood. His wife is in an induced coma, but hopefully when the swelling on her brain goes down, she'll make a full recovery.'

'Shit. That's intense. I don't know how you do it.' Earnest, awe-filled pupils meet mine. Finally.

Perhaps now he might see me for the adult I am. For the woman who can't forgive herself for the patients we don't manage to save. Entering the family waiting area and breaking the news that a loved one has died never gets easier. I'm beginning to realise it never will.

I exhale a weary breath. 'It doesn't matter how many people we save, at night when I close my eyes, I only see the ones we lost. It's a constant reminder to live life to the full every day,' I confess, handing him the cup back. 'Don't follow me into the toilets. That would be one step too far,' I warn him.

I wash my hands, glimpsing my reflection in the mirror above the sink. My skin's flushed with the rush of adrenaline that circulates in a permanent stream on duty. For all that Doctor Dickson might be, he's a brilliant doctor. What will it be like when I'm the one in charge? When I'm the SHO on duty? The thought sets another swift jolt pulsing through me.

Archie's waiting outside, clutching a chocolate orange protein bar. 'Here.'

Chocolate orange is my favourite. It always has been. Did he remember that from when I lived at Huxley Castle?

Or is that a pure coincidence?

'Thank you.' A hit of warmth spreads through my chest. 'There's no danger of gaining an ounce in this place.'

'I noticed.' We walk the length of the squeaky lino flooring back to the ward, side by side.

I unwrap the orange wrapper and sink my teeth into the thick, gooey protein bar. 'Did you also notice there is absolutely no danger to me here, unless you count the risk of starvation, of course? You don't need to hang around. I'm fine.'

Startling blue eyes land on mine. He's definitely conquering his aversion to looking at me. 'I'm not going anywhere.'

'Fine, but if you collapse from boredom, don't expect me to revive you. Apart from the fact we have no free beds, it'll be ages before Ryan and Sasha notice you're out of action. Imagine how much fun I could have, footloose and fancy free for a few days.'

He snorts. 'Huh. Imagine how much trouble you could get yourself into, more like. Some people just seem to attract it. Flock to it, even.'

'Whatever. Excuse me while I put my underwear on the outside and go save some lives.' I stuff the empty wrapper into his palm, my fingers brushing across his rough, calloused hands. Electricity sears across my skin again. My heart rate doubles between my ribs. I can safely say I have enough adrenaline to keep me going for another twelve hours straight, but this time it has nothing to do with the rush of the job.

One heart attack and a broken hand later – neither mine, thankfully – I've almost finished my shift. The prospect of a long bath and something hot to eat hovers at the forefront of my mind.

One of the receptionists marches into the cubicle where I'm observing Doctor Dickson suture the top of one unlucky carpenter's finger.

'Just had a call from the prison. A fight broke out. An ambulance is on route with three injured prisoners.'

Doctor Dickson continues to skilfully thread the needle. 'We have no beds. See if you can discharge someone or transfer them to another ward.'

'I'll do my best.' There goes my dinner.

The prisoners arrive, two of whom are in a bad way. Harrison is shadowing another SHO and between them, they're bearing the brunt of it.

Doctor Dickson and I are left to examine the third prisoner, a tattooed tank-like type, who reeks of tobacco and stale sweat. Outwardly, he doesn't look too bad, bar a superficial stab wound to his abdomen.

Two prison guards wait on the other side of the blue curtain while we assess his injuries.

My own personal guard paces the waiting room, clearly unhappy with this turn of events, but prisoners are entitled to the same level of care as anyone else, no matter what they've done in the past.

'Where's Jen?' Doctor Dickson looks around for the nurse who assisted us earlier. 'I need forceps. There appears to be a piece of metal still inside the wound.'

Doctor Dickson sticks his head out from between the curtains and in that same brief second, the prisoner lurches from the hospital trolley and wraps his huge bulging bicep around my shoulders, pulling my neck up in a vice-like grip.

The tightness around my throat is suffocating. I manage to choke out a gasp, and Doctor Dickson's head whips around.

Something sharp and cold presses against my clavicle. A scalpel.

'Don't make a sound, or I'll kill her,' he hisses with a broad Scottish twang, pressing the scalpel further into my skin.

I can't see if I'm bleeding. I can't feel anything past the crushing of my windpipe. My life flashes before me.

My sisters.

Huxley Castle.

The car accident that shaped my entire life.

Archie. He'll never forgive himself.

'We don't want any trouble.' Doctor Dickson raises his hands, his whispered words cracking with fear. 'We can help you. What do you need?'

'Get me out of here. And give me your wallets, watches and phones.' He tightens his hold on my neck. 'Or she gets it.'

Starved of oxygen, my vision blurs. I can't breathe. I can't hang on like this much longer.

'Let her go,' Archie's deep masculine voice demands from behind us. The choke hold on my neck releases. My knees buckle and I hit the lino, my palms splayed out across the floor.

Archie wears an expression I've never seen before. Nor ever want to see again. His jaw is set so tight it could pop, but it's his eyes that stand out the most. A storm swirls in those steely pupils, promising death and destruction to anyone who crosses its path.

He looks every bit the trained killer.

The prisoner's face contorts in agony, his arm twisted so far up his back his wrist must be broken.

'Guards,' Archie calls.

They charge into the cubicle and cuff the prisoner's wrists to the bed.

A minute later, and they'd have been too late. My fingers go to my neck, massaging the skin that's surely bruised. I glance down. Blood drips from a cut on my clavicle, fusing with my dark scrubs.

Archie sweeps me up off the floor, straight into his arms. His heart races furiously beneath his chest, thudding against my own.

'Are you okay?' Archie's wild eyes sweep over me before he presses a kiss to my temple.

Doctor Dickson glances between us, his mouth hanging open in shock.

I nod, unable to find the right words to express my relief. Or gratitude. If it wasn't for him... Fuck, it doesn't bear thinking about.

Doctor Dickson ushers us out of the cubicle, leaving the prisoner to bleed where he's firmly cuffed to the bed, a guard on either side of him. 'Let me take a look at you.' His slim smooth fingers take me by the wrist.

'I'm fine. It's fine. Nothing a few stitches won't heal.' Blood pounds in my ears and my legs feel like jelly.

'We'll get you fixed up. You'll have to make a statement, but then I want you to take the rest of the week off to recover.'

'I'm fine, really.' My protest sounds feeble, even to me.

But my trembling hands don't lie.

If it wasn't for Archie...

He places a strong arm around my shoulders, and I press my cheek against his chest.

And I thought I was the only one going to be saving lives today.

Chapter Ten
ARCHIE

Victoria sprawls across the couch in front of the roaring open fire wearing nothing but those tiny shorts and *that* cami vest top again. Her long legs stretch out over the leather futon. Even in her shaken state, she's stunning.

The bandage covering her wound is only small, but a significant reminder of how quickly a situation can escalate.

What happened today was an abomination.

Thank God I was there. If Jared hadn't been relieved of his duty, the entire shit show could have had a very different ending.

I swept her into my arms like a fucking caveman, refusing to put her anywhere but on my lap while Doctor Fucking Dickhead stitched the cut on her clavicle. The man was about as useful as a condom in a nunnery. How could he turn his back? Leave her so vulnerable like that?

And why wasn't that prisoner cuffed, for fuck's sake?

Heads will roll for this.

Victoria's glazed eyes gaze forwards, her attention focused far, far away as she sips neat whiskey from a crystal tumbler.

It's good for shock, so my sister used to say. That's precisely why I'm having the same.

Bolognese bubbles on the stove. My own blood bubbles in my veins. How could security be so fucking lax?

Patient confidentiality, my ass. I don't care about those prisoners' rights. My priority is Victoria's safety.

The idea I could have lost her has haunted my every moment since. Imagine being mere metres away, clueless that the life was being squeezed out of her.

And it's not because I'm paid to protect her. It's because a world without Victoria is inconceivable.

If I was obsessed with her before I came here, I'm utterly enamoured with her now.

Her laugh.

Her smile.

Her not-so-subtle flirtation.

The way she tries so hard to win me over.

Her attempts at bulldozing my self-preserving walls, asking seemingly innocent questions designed to penetrate my boundaries as we lope through the streets each morning.

I might not be able to have her, but I can't live in a world where she doesn't exist.

She's going to have to start wearing a tracker. Maybe a watch with a heart-rate monitor that I can link to an app on my phone. One that will flag any suspicious spikes or changes.

Huge hazel eyes flick to me. 'How did you know?'

Her question is ambiguous, but I know exactly what she means.

'I just knew.' It's true. My gut instinct fired like a cannon. A silent alarm sounded from her body, straight to my soul.

The air in the room changed.

Like my breath was stilted along with hers.

Like there was an invisible thread tying us together, and it was in danger of snapping. But that's not something words can explain.

'But how?' she presses in a gentle, curious voice. 'You couldn't see behind the curtain.'

'I had a feeling something was off. Call it a hunch.' I turn the heat down on the stove and let the Bolognese simmer, resting my backside against the countertop.

'I dropped to my knees to look for your feet beneath the rim of the curtain. I saw his feet flanking yours and I knew right away.'

She swallows hard, continuing to stare at me. 'Thank you.'

'It's my job.' A flashback of my lips pressing against her temple reminds me not all of my actions were part of the job description.

Against my better judgement, I grab my glass and stride across the room, dropping onto the couch beside her.

The need to be near her is primal.

For a man who couldn't stand to look at her, I can't seem to tear my eyes off her now. That's what happens when you think you might lose somebody. The events of this evening have flipped my perception of the world on its head. And I'm struggling to flip it back again.

Thick glossy hair falls loosely over her shoulders in unruly waves. Toffee-coloured highlights shimmer through the dim firelight. The urge to wrap it in my fist and drag her plump, parted mouth to mine eats me alive.

I extend a hand to offer comfort, support, even friendship, but the second her soft skin grazes mine, that immense explosive chemistry crackles between us.

Her backside writhes involuntarily on the leather beneath her, the new position sending her bare thigh to rest against mine.

She grabs my other hand and tugs until I twist to face her

fully. Dark smouldering pupils burn me through to the core. A longing swells like a rising spring tide.

A sultry breath slips from her chest. 'Finally, he looks at me.' She addresses an imaginary audience.

Thank God there's no one actually here to witness this because I'm teetering dangerously close to the edge of doing something there's no coming back from.

'I was beginning to wonder if my name was Medusa, the way you've been avoiding me. Like one look would change your life forever.'

I swallow the saliva pooling in my mouth. 'One look *did* change my life forever, but that was a long time ago.'

She edges closer, as if sensing my rapidly depleting willpower.

'Looking at you is...' I search for a word with enough significance to express what I'm trying to convey. The one thing I shouldn't express. '...distracting beyond measure. You are the definition of stunning.' I swirl the whiskey around my glass.

Her lips curl into a triumphant smile.

'And off-limits.' Am I reminding her? Or myself?

The shock of almost losing her earlier has done something to my rationale. My fingers trail up her arms, chasing and creating goosebumps in their wake. 'I want you, Victoria. More than is healthy for either of us.'

A sigh of pure, unconcealable longing echoes between us. Did it come from her or me?

'I thought I was the doctor. Let me be the judge of what's healthy.' She prises the glass from my fingers and sets it on the coffee table next to hers.

When she turns back to face me, there's a potent desire in

her eyes I can't ignore. I can't deny her or myself any longer. The tension between us detonates like a bomb. Our lips crash together in a hot, desperate frenzy of sliding lips and gnashing teeth. There's a raw carnality between us that I've never experienced with anyone else. My tongue plunders into her mouth, tasting, exploring, and devouring her from the inside out.

It's not enough. Nowhere near it. The need to be inside her is overpowering.

She climbs onto my lap, a smooth, creamy thigh balancing either side of my hips. My hungry hands slip beneath the silk of her top, skimming the soft, taut skin of her stomach. Skirting beneath her breasts. She grinds her pelvis on top of me in response, communicating exactly how urgent those needs she mentioned are.

I need to stop this.

I have to.

But while she's dry-humping the rock-hard bulge beneath my sweats, it's fucking inconceivable.

Nothing else matters in this moment. It's just her and me. The rest of the world bleeds away.

Kissing Victoria Sexton is every bit as explosive as I knew it would be.

Impatient hands grip mine, urging them upwards to tease those firm twin peaks beneath the cami top. I lift it up, exposing her full, round, perfect breasts and take one in my mouth.

'Oh, Archie.' She grinds harder against me.

I've never wanted anything more in my life.

I flip her onto her back, pinning her onto the couch. My lips trace over the bruise emerging on her neck. Peppering tiny kisses across her throat, I ask, 'Do you have any idea what you do to me?'

'I know what I'd like to do to you.' Her short nails scrape

across my spine. Lust rages from every pore of her beautiful body.

The unmissable chime of an incoming call sounds from the phone in my pocket and instinctively I leap to my feet. Caught doing something inconceivable.

Ryan's name is etched across the screen. Shame cascades over me. If he knew what I was up to, if he knew how badly my cock aches to penetrate his little sister-in-law, he'd kill me.

Fuck. What am I doing?

'Ignore it,' Victoria pleads, but I can't.

The spell is broken.

I'm broken.

I never should have kissed her.

Touched her.

Thank fuck we were interrupted.

Victoria bites her lower lip, silently willing me not to take the call.

I answer it. I have no choice. 'Hello?' My voice echoes like I'm on speakerphone.

Ryan's velvety voice sounds through the receiver. 'Archie, how are things?'

'Everything is under control.' Except me, and my disobedient dick, of course.

I need to tell him I can't do this job. I can't protect his sister-in-law because I'm obsessed with her, and it drives me to the point of insanity.

But then if I go, who will take my place?

Will they be good enough?

Will they care for her like I do?

That's the whole point, though. They're not supposed to.

'Was there an incident today? One of Victoria's lecturers called Sasha to say she'd been involved in something upsetting and that she should probably check in on her.'

That tool, Doctor Dickhead, no doubt. Sticking his nose in where he shouldn't.

Perhaps that's not fair. Maybe he was genuinely concerned.

Ryan coughs an awkward sort of sound. 'He also expressed concerns about you and your presence on the ward.'

No, definitely not concern. That fucking asshole. Rage seethes inside my chest. 'If I hadn't been on that ward, who knows what would have happened.'

Victoria shakes her head furiously, begging me not to say anything.

'There *was* an incident today. Several prison inmates were brought to A&E. One grabbed Victoria. I intervened. She's fine,' I say. 'Shaken, but fine, not thanks to Doctor Dickhead.'

Sasha shrieks in the background, 'Put her on the phone, Archie, please.'

I pass the phone to Victoria, who can now barely look at me as she pulls on her cami top, adjusting it over her perfect mounds. I pad across the floor to stir the Bolognese.

It takes Victoria half an hour to reassure her sister that she's fine. When she finally hangs up, she stalks across to me.

I keep my back turned and my eyes on the cooker, adding some diced chillies to the sauce for extra flavour. As if things aren't spicy enough around here.

'So what, are we just going to pretend like that didn't happen?' Her hand rests defiantly on her hip and the strap of her top falls down her arm. My stomach twists with a longing so excruciating it throbs through every single cell.

'I'm so sorry, Victoria. I never should have lost control like that.' I keep my eyes firmly focused on the pan. 'It won't happen again.'

It takes every single drop of determination not to throw her over my shoulder and drag her to my bed for the night, and every night after that.

We eat at the table, shoving our food around our plates in silence like the first night. The atmosphere is fraught with tension. Awkwardness.

And on my part, at least, a heavy sense of regrettable longing.

The second we finish cleaning the kitchen, Victoria excuses herself to bed.

She doesn't come out of her room for the rest of the night.

Chapter Eleven

VICTORIA

The wound on my clavicle is improving. It's just a shame my wounded pride isn't healing as fast.

Archie's rejection stings deeper than any physical cut. I offered myself on a plate to him, well, the couch at least, and he shut me down.

Mortified doesn't cover it.

Clearly, he wasn't as invested in our sizzling hot make-out session as much as I was. Because the Taoiseach himself could have rung and I wouldn't have answered the damn phone.

Although the way his body met my every grind with a promising thrust of his own begs to differ...

Ugh. I'm like one of Huxley Castle's dizzy pheasants staggering around, blinded by need in mating season. Archie Mason consumes my every waking thought. And most of my sleeping ones too. The way I feel about him is unlike anything I've ever experienced before. Grabbing his attention is becoming an obsession. I want him more than I've ever wanted anyone or anything else in this world. And I'm driving myself insane.

I'm going to have to invest in a vibrator at this rate.
A text pings on my phone. It's Libby.

> How's the patient getting on?

Ugh. I hate being the patient.

> I'm in agony.

I'm not talking about my injuries.

> Your neck?

> No, my vagina. I've got it bad for my bodyguard.

> No wonder, the man is like your own personal 007, but even hotter. And I saw the way his hand rested on your spine! What are you waiting for?

> This 007 has the willpower of steel, unfortunately.

> He's mad in the head. I'd ride you if I had the equipment.

> It's getting so bad, I might have to buy some equipment of my own.

> Bring him to Ann Summers. Let him see what he's missing.

> That, my friend, is a wickedly cruel idea. I LOVE it!

I breeze through the living area. It's overflowing with a huge array of sweet-smelling bouquets, plus get well wishes from Sasha, Libby, Melanie, Harrison, and even Doctor Dickson. I'm not due back on the ward for another five days, and for the first time since I started in A&E, I'm glad of the break. Instinctively, I rub the spot on my neck where the prisoner gripped me.

'Are we going somewhere?' Archie asks, eyeing my running tights and sports bra. He sits at the dining table, a thick slice of buttery toast pinched between his finger and thumb.

A palpable tension hangs in the air between us.

'I was going to go for a run.' It comes out sharper than I intended. Like I'm daring him to stop me.

'What about that?' His gaze travels to my bandage. 'You might set it bleeding again.'

I hate to admit he's right, but I'm going stir crazy trapped in here for days on end. There's only so much studying a person can do.

'We could go for a walk?' he suggests.

I shrug, imagining a million more satisfying ways of burning off the restless energy plaguing me, but I already know from his stance that it's not going to happen.

'How about a drive to Portobello?' he offers. 'We could walk the beach and grab a coffee? The fresh air might be good for you.'

'Fine. Just as long as you don't plan on spending the entire trip avoiding looking at me, because it makes me feel like utter shit.' I seem to have no filter around this man. I don't know if it's a blessing or a curse.

Genuine anguish crumples his face. The corner of his eyes crinkle in a wince. 'I'm so sorry, Victoria.'

'So am I. Sorry we couldn't finish what we started.' Could I be any more desperate?

'Victoria, I told you, it's highly unprofessional. I'd lose my job, my cabin at the castle, my place with Ryan and Sasha, and the kids. My whole life as I know it, and worst of all, I risk losing you, too. What if something happened to you because instead of focusing on danger, I'm focusing on the perfect swell of your hips and ass? I can't protect you if I'm perving on you.'

'So, you didn't leap off me because you were horrified by my touch?' He's so much older. I'm sure he's had women with much more experience than me. Women who are way more sexually sophisticated than my clumsy hands clawing his shirt off. Dry-humping him like a horny teenager. Shame flushes up my neck and heat colours my cheeks.

Thick neat eyebrows furrow into a frown. He throws his toast onto the plate on the table, shoves back the chair with his powerful thighs and strides towards me.

'I'm going to say it one more time, Victoria.' He cups my chin with his fingers, forcing my face upwards to meet his. 'You are fucking stunning. I want you more than is healthy. But what I want and what I can have are two totally different things. We can't go there. But for the love of fucking God, don't think it's because I don't want to. It's all I've ever wanted.'

His words are a cool, soothing balm to my battered ego, but they do nothing to soothe the throbbing in my underwear.

Frustrated isn't the word for it.

'I don't need to tell you the feeling is mutual. I'm pretty sure you got that memo while I was dry-humping your leg. Classy, right?'

'Victoria.' That one word is weighted with warning.

His hand falls from my face and he takes a step backwards. Clearly, if I want him to crack, I'm going to have to play the long game.

'I hate this atmosphere between us. This huge wall you

insist on driving between us. Your rejection hurts. Can we at least try to be friends?' I reach out to touch his bicep and the familiar surge of electricity circuits between us, buzzing and vibrating with desire.

'It's self-preservation, not rejection.' He rubs a palm over the stubble dotting his chiselled jawline.

'It amounts to the same thing.' I retract my hand.

'Fine, I'll try to keep you safe without being quite so uptight.' He exhales heavily.

'Thank you.' It's a start, I suppose.

'Now, to the beach,' he says.

We walk four miles side by side across the length of Portobello beach and back. The chill blowing in from the North Sea does nothing to cool the inferno blazing inside of me every time Archie's arm bumps against mine. He scans the horizon as we walk, but true to his word, while we sip Americanos and make small talk in a beachside café, he maintains eye contact as the world passes by us.

I watch as a young couple kiss on the pavement outside the café window, imagining this is what people who don't have a day job do. People-watch, observe their surroundings.

Looking in from the outside has never been enough for me. It's one of the reasons I devour romance novels. I love glimpsing the world through someone else's eyes, even if they are a fictional character. Hoping to shed some light on why people behave the way they do. Why, when they fall in love, they often lose all sense of rationale. Why they forsake their careers, families or anything else they may have dreamed of along the way.

There has to be so much more to it than attraction, but even as I'm beginning to experience these new overwhelming feelings for the first time, I'm no clearer on the subject.

Words can't explain why I crave Archie so much. Why I can't control my tongue or the rest of my body around him.

I've always wanted a partner, and not just because of the urges I teased him about.

I want to find that innate bond I can't live without.

Sasha has it with Ryan.

Chloe has it with Jayden.

I have a sneaking suspicion if Archie drops his walls completely, I could find it with him. Though that could just be wishful thinking on my part. Perhaps the lingering of my silly teenage crush.

But then why does it feel as if we're teetering on the verge of something so much more?

He admitted the attraction is mutual, but it's so much more than that. Long before I even thought about Archie romantically, we formed a friendship. I was still a kid then. He accompanied Ryan, Sasha and me on a trip to the Winter Wonderland. Then he accompanied us on several European dates of Ryan's farewell tour.

He was funny, sunny and kind. Effortless to be around.

He still is, when he drops the armour.

When Sasha insisted a bodyguard accompany me to Edinburgh, initially I was devastated, fearing I would be robbed of the usual student experience. Then I began to wonder if it was a gift in disguise.

I begged her to let Archie be the one to come with me.

It didn't occur to me that he'd turn it down.

When he did, I felt foolish for even suggesting it. He was this mature, muscly mountain of a man and I was a silly girl with big dreams of saving the world.

My biggest fear is that's how he still sees me deep down. Even now. A senseless girl. Is that why he won't cross the line with me? The 'I can't protect you if I'm perving on you' line is bullshit.'

Surely if we were intimately involved, he'd want to protect me further? It doesn't make sense.

I'm twenty-three years old, about to qualify as a doctor. And somehow I get the feeling I'll always be 'Little Victoria' to Archie, just as I am to my sisters.

Doctor Dickson, however, doesn't seem to see me as childlike in any way. My phone vibrates on the chequered tablecloth in front of me.

Archie squints to read the screen upside down. 'Is that your teacher again?' He pronounces the word teacher like it's the dirtiest word in the English language.

'Yeah.'

'Do you think he offers his other students the same attention he showers on you?' Archie's fingers flex into a fist on the table.

Is that jealousy in his tone? Hope sparks inside of me. 'The other students didn't get held hostage under his supervision, even if it was for a fleeting moment.'

'Huh. You want to keep an eye on him.'

'And there was me thinking that was your department,' I tease.

'Oh, believe me, I'm on it,' he says grimly.

> Come to my office if you want to talk about what happened. My door is always open.

Yep, and so are the flies of your corduroy trousers, by all accounts.

It's one offer I'll decline.

I might be desperate, but I'm not that desperate.

Chapter Twelve
ARCHIE

Sprawled on my back, I alternate between staring at the ceiling and the digital clock. At two thirty in the morning, there's still no sign of sleep. A lustrous full moon glares through the half-open new blinds, but that's not what's keeping me awake.

I haven't slept well since my final military tour. If I get three hours, it's a good night.

Every time I close my eyes, my brain replays technicoloured images of my men blown across a dusty dirt track when that bomb went off at the side of the road. Those pictures will haunt me forever.

And if my brain gives me a brief reprieve from tormenting me, my body starts, hyper-aware of Victoria's across the hallway. My skin tingles as I recall her smooth skin beneath mine.

Shame and a burning longing simultaneously wash over me. She's my client. Ryan and Sasha's little sister. And even if she wasn't, she's still too young for me. And too good. We're classes apart.

Thank God Ryan interrupted us. It's like he has a sixth sense where I'm concerned.

An email pings through on my phone.

It's from Declan. Ryan and Jayden's guy who carries out the background checks. Harrison has come back clean. Not that I'm going to willingly offer up that information to Victoria. Even if she threatens to extract my teeth one by one.

It's unequivocally unfair of me to keep her away from other men. She's entitled to live her life, but accepting that and putting it into action are two very different things.

The thought of having to guard her, hovering five feet away while she dates another man, is unbearable. Watching helplessly as someone else gets to press their lips against hers. Take her out to dinner or the movies. And even worse, bring her home afterwards.

Acid churns in my stomach. If that happens, which it will at some point because I can't expect her to remain single forever, I'll have to conjure up some weird and wonderful illness that will excuse me from my position.

It's hard enough being here, aching to touch her. There's no way I can sit back and watch while someone else does.

A high-pitched scream from across the landing sends me hurtling out of bed. It's weighted with sheer unrestrained terror, and rips directly through my heart.

Grabbing the gun from my bedside drawer, I dart to the landing, blood pounding in my ears.

I scan for intruders, but it's clear.

Kicking open Victoria's door, I charge into her bedroom, adrenaline propelling me faster than a bullet. Her door swings back, slamming against the inside wall with an almighty crash.

Victoria is lying face-down on the bed, writhing between the sheets. Her fingers clinging to the cotton like her life depends on it.

The screams continue as if she's utterly petrified.

But there's nobody here.

There never was.

Whatever's haunting her is in her head. I can relate more than she'll ever know.

My chest sinks with an exhale of relief.

I creep closer to the bed as quietly as a fourteen-stone man can. Although, if the door crashing didn't wake her, I'm not likely to either.

She's thrashing around, pounding something imaginary on the sheets, wriggling closer to the edge of the bed. Any second now she's going to slide off completely and hit the wooden floorboards.

'Shh, Victoria, it's okay.' My smooth voice sounds way calmer than I feel.

She whimpers, but the thrashing begins to slow. The urge to comfort her is utterly compelling. I slip into the bed next to her, fingers lightly sweeping her thick, silky hair from her clammy forehead. I uncurl her fists with murmured reassurance that everything is okay. That I've got her.

But really, it's she who's got me.

By the heart and by the balls.

She turns in her sleep, the whimpers fading. Shimmying backwards, her back settles against my chest into the spoon position. Tucking my arm around her waist, my palm splays across her bare stomach where her cami top is hitched up.

I have no idea where her shorts are, but I'll never complain they're tiny again because compared to the lacy pants sculpting her lush peachy ass cheeks, they're enormous.

The delicious scent of strawberry shampoo clings to the pillows.

Victoria's breathing settles into a calm, even, peaceful rhythm. It's over. She's okay. I should get up. Go back to my own bed. I have no business being here while she sleeps, but I can't seem to entice my legs to comply.

I might never get another chance to hold her like this.

And seeing as I'm already here, why not just spend five more minutes to make sure the night terrors really are over.

Who am I kidding? Even one more minute here is purely for my own benefit, but being an insomniac has to have some benefits. I'll creep out before she wakes. She won't remember, and given her advances, I'm pretty sure she wouldn't object, anyway.

It was me who stopped our liaison before it got out of control. Me, who's supposed to know better.

My palm travels over her taut skin, revelling in the sensation of the swell of her hip beneath it. She might be young, but she is ALL woman.

She repositions her arm, resting her hand on top of mine with a soft sigh. 'Archie.' It's little more than a whisper.

Her breathing pattern hasn't changed. She's still asleep. She's thinking of me in her dreams. My heart swells in my chest and I rest my chin on the top of her head, nuzzling in closer.

'I'm here, sweetheart. I'm here.'

Weak morning sunlight peeps through the slatted blinds and, for the first time in years, I wake weighed with happiness.

Oh fuck.

That weight on my chest isn't happiness, it's Victoria.

I never sleep more than three hours. And drifting off pretty much always involves three meditations, two bloody sacrifices and a partridge in a pear tree.

Yet, last night, of all nights, had to be different. Fuck. My. Life.

And I'm not the only one awake. Blood furiously floods to my rock-solid dick, sheathed only by a thin layer of cotton boxer briefs. But is it any wonder, when her cheek is resting on my bare chest, her left leg slung across my waist, and those flimsy lace panties directly grazing my hip?

Shit.

Margaret Thatcher, Teresa May and Camilla Parker-Bowles naked and offering a threesome isn't enough to quieten the steel-willed monster throbbing against Victoria's inner thigh.

I glance guiltily around, looking for a way to extract myself, when Victoria's cheek peels slowly from my chest. Heavy eyelids flutter open, confusion clouds her eyes, and she blinks hard.

'Archie?' Her voice is thick with sleep.

'You were having a night terror.' I shift beneath her in a really feeble attempt to move because, even though I know I should go, it's the last thing I want to do.

Her thigh pushes down a fraction. It's subtle, but she's definitely trying to hold me in position.

She groans and winces in embarrassment. 'I'm sorry. I've had them since I was a kid.'

If anyone should be embarrassed around here, it should be me and my unruly dick.

'It's fine. I thought someone was in the house.' A stray strand of hair flops across her forehead and it takes every ounce of self-control I have not to tuck it behind her ears in a gesture that oddly seems even more intimate than my erection pressing against her.

She must have noticed it beneath her thigh. Clearly, she's too polite to mention it.

She wriggles further on top of me, balancing her sex deliberately on top of my shaft. 'Is that why you brought a super-sized gun into my bed?'

Or maybe not.

'Victoria...' The name emerges from my throat like a low guttural growl.

Amorous eyes sparkle with unconcealed glee, roaming across my torso before returning to my face. 'Archie, I'm only human...'

'So am I.' I might have survived four military tours, but this assignment is definitely going to be the death of me.

'That's exactly what I'm counting on.' She grinds herself against me.

How I would love to rip that lace straight from her. 'Don't start something we can't finish.'

'Oh, I always finish what I start. Remember those needs I mentioned...? Waking up to this...' She grinds again. '...certainly doesn't do anything to extinguish them.'

It's every man's fantasy, waking up with the woman they've been obsessed with for years straddling them. But to me, it's a nightmare. It's a line I can't cross.

Her head drops to my neck and she inhales my scent in a show of raw animalistic appreciation. Her tongue darts downwards across my pecs, tracing the lines of my tattoo. Pressing tiny kisses across my scars.

'Victoria.' Desire rages through every vein and artery. But so does duty.

I rock upwards into a sitting position, grab her bum and lift her sideways, placing her on her own side of the bed.

Huh, her own side? Check me out. I've only been here a few hours and I'm staking a claim on her bed. Talk about being presumptuous.

Her face falls as I leap from beneath the covers.

Huge, heated eyes rove over my chest and directly down to my underwear. She looks as though she's in physical pain. 'You want this as much as I do.'

'Sweetheart, believe me when I tell you I want it *more* than you do. I have for a long time. But it's one line I can't cross.'

'Why not? We're both consenting adults.' The silk cami

does nothing to hide the erect nubs beneath it. A visceral desire rolls from her in waves.

What I wouldn't give to be able to pin her down and lick her like an ice cream.

'There are a million reasons why not, the first of which is it's a breach of my contract.' My mouth's saying no, but my feet still haven't got the memo, rooted to the floorboards as if they're part of the furniture.

Her breathing is heavy, ragged. Passion emanates from every single one of her pores. 'Don't leave me to take care of myself again, Archie.'

The visual she's creating is almost enough to make me blow in my pants.

'Victoria...' I should walk away. Step under a freezing cold shower. But it won't help. Victoria has ignited an inferno in my underwear that five thousand cold showers couldn't put out. But that doesn't change the facts.

Finally, my feet receive the message and I'm at her doorway. 'I'm sorry. Please don't think it's because I don't care about you. If anything, it's because I do.'

She flops back lazily onto a plump pillow with an exasperated huff. Thick tousled hair fans out around her head. Shooting me a flirtatious wink, she says, 'We'll see about that, Archie.'

I might have survived this battle, but Victoria looks as if she's about to embark on a war that might actually kill me...

Chapter Thirteen
VICTORIA

Waking up with Archie's strong arms around me easily earned this morning the title 'the best of my life.'

If the content of his underwear was anything to go by, I no longer have to worry he still thinks I'm just a little girl.

No, those blazing black pupils eyed me like I was all woman. I just have to convince him it's okay to mix a little work with pleasure.

I crave his attention like a drug addict craves her next hit. And I'm going to get my fix one way or another.

Something dangerous sparks inside me. Hope, fused with a lust so powerful, it has the potential to spontaneously blow at any second.

It would seem the reason none of these college boys have been able to hijack my heart over the years is because it's been with Archie the whole time.

Even at the castle when he'd get up and leave the room the moment I'd enter, and when he rejected the offer to come here initially, and all the times he pretended he could barely look at me, somewhere deep down I held a torch for him that burnt so brightly, no other man could hold a candle to him.

Having him here in my bed only confirmed what I've been denying all these years.

I am deeply obsessed with Archie Mason.

And from the tender way he held me so protectively in his arms this morning, I'm certain he feels the same way, but a misplaced sense of honour forbids him to act on it.

Flashbacks of his lips on mine, pinning me to the sofa the other night, cause me to actually moan. *'Sweetheart, believe me when I tell you I want it more than you do. I have for a long time.'*

He has willpower made of iron.

But even iron melts at twelve hundred degrees.

Time to crank up the heat.

Bodyguard or not, he will be mine. He just needs a little persuasion.

Running water from the shower ceases suddenly and I bounce from the bed to take my turn, buzzing with my newfound purpose. To blow up the heat to over a thousand degrees.

Archie barely looks up when I enter the kitchen.

So, we're back to this again.

No harm. I'm ready for him. The air is charged with sexual tension so taut, the tiniest spark could set the place on fire. It's a battle to keep the smirk from my face.

I grab a banana from the fruit bowl and peel it seductively as I breeze over to the table where Archie's mindlessly flicking through yesterday's newspaper. I say mindlessly, furiously might be more accurate. One page flips after another, too quickly to read a headline, let alone anything smaller.

Resting my bum on the table next to him so his head is in line with my breasts, I take a bite from the banana. Archie glimpses up warily, but for the first time I'm confident in the knowledge it's not because he can't bear to look at me, but because he likes what he sees.

He sucks in a short sharp breath, raking over my wet-look leather leggings and fitted cashmere jumper, which stretches a little too tightly across my boobs to be decent. Libby calls it my wolf-in-sheep's clothing outfit because it covers everywhere but clings tight enough to showcase every asset.

I take another bite of the banana. He shakes his head, but the side of his lip curls in a reluctant smirk.

'Victoria.' Another warning.

I fake nonchalance. 'What? You're safe, Archie, don't worry. I'm not going to throw myself at you. You made your feelings quite clear this morning.'

He clasps his fingers together and lets out a low, rumbling chuckle. 'What is this? Reverse psychology now? The oldest trick in the book.'

'No, it's not. It's me respecting your wishes.' *The wishes of your raging erection, at least.*

'So, what's the plan for today? Your last day of freedom before it's back to the hospital.' Huge, clear eyes bore into mine. I had hoped they'd be drawn lower, but at least he's ceased avoiding looking at me entirely.

'I want to go to Princes Street to do some shopping.' Libby's evil plan lingers at the forefront of my mind.

Archie's shoulders relax slightly. He probably envisioned me bringing him to a sex club and making him watch. I might have to if he doesn't get the memo before then. Drastic urges call for drastic measures.

'Okay, sound. But I have someone coming to upgrade your alarm system this morning, so can it wait until after that?'

'Sure.' I slip off the table and switch Alexa on at the wall. 'I'll just listen to my audiobook while I wait. I'm at a really good bit.'

Archie shrugs and returns to flicking through the paper.

As I bring up my Audible app on my phone, it's a battle to suppress my laughter. Poor Archie. He doesn't stand a chance. And the best bit is, he has no idea. I haven't had this much fun since Freshers' Week.

Alexa's voice booms across the kitchen, reading the kinkiest book I own. I turn it up as loud as it will physically go.

His hand skirts beneath the hem of her dress, fingering the silk of her crotchless underwear. Desire beats between them like a drum. A low moan of appreciation exits her crimson lips as his fingers penetrate her centre, sinking into her hot, tight pussy.

Archie's head jolts up. The expression of sheer horror on his face is fucking hilarious.

'Okay, Victoria, you've had your fun.'

My facial muscles twitch as I battle to keep them in straight lines. 'Shh, they're just getting to the good bit.'

"You dirty, dirty girl. Look at you, dripping for me. Everyone in this room is watching us. Watching you. But you know that. It's the reason your pussy is pulsing beneath my fingers. You're wound so tight, just desperate for a release."

'They're in a sex club,' I explain to Archie, who is staring straight ahead with a stony expression on his face.

'I know what you're doing, Vic —'

'Shh!' I wave my hand in the air, silencing him. 'He's about to go down on her in the club while everyone watches.'

"Alex, please." She writhes as his fingers pump her slowly.

"Bend over the table and spread your legs like a good girl and I'll think about letting you cum."

The legs of Archie's chair scrape forcefully over my varnished floorboards and he stalks towards me, pushing his washboard torso, clad in one of those tight white shirts he favours, right against mine.

Could it really be that easy?

I didn't have him pegged for an exhibitionist, but if the hard length currently pressing against me is anything to go by, the prospect of my main character getting eaten out in a sex club definitely did it for him.

Torrid dilated pupils blaze into mine, blistering like an inferno. His hot breath brushes my lips, and his raw scent surrounds me.

A hand reaches towards my breast and I inhale a breath, trembling at the prospect of his touch, but instead of landing on me, it brushes past to the switch on the wall behind me to silence Alexa.

'Is this how you respect my wishes?' His pelvis remains pressed against mine. 'Do you know how hard it was to walk away from you this morning? How hard it is to pick duty over desire, when I've thought about you day in and day out for the past five years? Rubbed myself senseless in the shower, imagining the feel of the walls of your sex.'

My stomach somersaults as a million butterflies flutter through it.

My hands gravitate to his broad, strong shoulders before sliding downwards across the hard muscle of his pecs.

Our lips are millimetres apart.

'I want you so fucking badly, it's unbearable. But I won't risk anyone else I care about with my own selfish desires.' He tears his body from mine, leaving it bereft and aching.

Who else did he risk with desires?

An ex?

The doorbell sounds before I can summon the courage to ask. 'That'll be the guy about the alarm.' He readjusts his dick in his pants and breezes out of the room as if nothing happened.

Which I suppose is about right.

But I'm nowhere near close to giving up yet.

In fact, I'm only getting started.

His lips might refuse me, but every molecule of his body vibrates with a heated promise.

Chapter Fourteen
ARCHIE

It takes a full hour for the guy to upgrade Victoria's security system, and equally long for my semi to subside.

As much as I resent her trying to drag me over the edge, I can't help but respect her resolve. And her ploy was fucking hilarious. Playful, tempting, and such a fucking tease. I can only imagine how fucking good the sex would be. Every sexually neglected fibre in me thrums to life, desperate to hear her *'low moan of appreciation exiting her crimson lips as MY fingers penetrate her centre, sinking into her hot, tight pussy.'*

Seriously, can you die of desire? Because I'm this fucking close to exploding. No wonder with those wet-look leggings leaving nothing to the imagination, and that jumper under so much pressure from the swell of her tits. I was waiting for it to pop open in front of my eyes.

Not helpful.

'Are you ready?' she calls from the front door.

'Coming.' *If only.* I slip into my suit jacket, remembering how it never fails to draw her eye. Two can play her game. Just because I refuse to cross the line, it doesn't mean I can't enjoy dangling myself over it. As long as I don't fall.

'It's a nice afternoon. Shall we walk?' Victoria pulls on a fitted knee-length woollen coat that ties at the waist. She's also wearing thigh-high boots over those leggings. Fucking hell.

'Sure.' Beats trying to get a parking space. Plus, I wouldn't put it past her to play her audiobook in the car.

We stroll companionably to the West End, admiring the city's resplendent architecture. The February sky is grey but with intermittent patches of blue. A chill carries on the wispy breeze, but it does nothing to cool the heat prickling my skin.

The tension thrums between us like a live wire. Not awkward tension. Sexual tension. Like even the tiniest of sparks could set the entire city on fire.

It would be all too easy to give into it. Whisk her up into my arms, spread her out on my bed and explore every inch of her soft, inviting skin.

But then what?

Where would that leave us?

Compromised, that's where.

But truth be told, we're already compromised because I can't see straight for thinking about her, even when she's standing right in front of me. *Especially* when she's standing right before me.

I was intrigued by her five years ago. That stubborn, stunning teenager determined to leave her life of luxury to become a doctor. Now she's almost achieved it, she's flourished into this formidable force, exuding the same stubbornness and determination, with a newfound supreme sexuality. A sexuality which she is unafraid to use to get what she wants.

And apparently, what she wants is me.

Why though? Because to her, I'm a bit of rough? Classes below her in every way. Or because she thinks she can't have me? Taking a taste of the forbidden apple always seems more alluring.

She's probably never been knocked back in her life. Any man would have to be out of their mind to say no to that.

Hell, I said no, and I've been out of my mind ever since.

'How are you healing?' I nod towards her stitches.

'I'm fine, thank you.' She runs her fingers over her throat. The bruising has faded to a yellow tinge. My chest tightens.

When we bypass Harvey Nichols, and several other high-end boutiques on George Street, I have to wonder where we're going. 'What exactly are we shopping for?'

'You'll see.' Victoria links her arm in mine and pats my hand. It could be viewed as a patronising gesture, but it's every bit as provocative as this morning's advances, even if it's a million times more subtle.

Subtle I can probably deal with. Just about. That's why I don't pull away. Plus, the paving can be a little unstable and she's liable to break her neck in those heels. That's what I'll keep telling myself, anyway.

I scan the streets, assessing for potential danger. A skill so finely honed, it's automatic.

A homeless guy approaches and I steer Victoria out of his way, discreetly slipping him a twenty pound note.

'You're softer than you look, you know.' Those stunning lash-framed eyes don't miss a thing.

'Huh, you weren't saying that this morning.' There I go, testing that line again.

'Archie Mason, lo and fucking behold, did you actually just crack a joke?' Her face lights up as if I've given her a shiny new toy.

'I am actually quite funny when I want to be.' For a long time after I returned from the Middle East, humour was my defence mechanism. People find it hard to pity someone constantly smiling and cracking jokes. 'Though not nearly as funny as you and your stunt with Alexa this morning...' I deliberately flex the bicep she's gripping.

'Your face.' Her saccharine smile would dazzle the devil. 'But seriously, that scene was so hot.'

'Never mind my face. My poor dick.' Is it still crossing the line if I don't plan on acting on it? 'Would you be into that type of thing?' The need to know crushes my sternum.

She slows to a complete stop halfway along Princes Street and pivots to face me.

'Why the sudden interest in my sexual preferences, Archie?'

The rushing traffic fades around us. All I see is her.

I inhale the plume of air she exhales deliberately. I've got it so fucking bad for this woman. 'I need to know if you're going to drag me to a sex club one day. I'd hate to have to pummel every man in the place that looked at you, but I would, you know.'

'I quite believe it. But it's not entirely fair though, is it? You don't want me, but you don't want anyone else to have me, am I right?' She's so close, the tips of our toes touch and her breasts rest against my chest.

'I never said I didn't want you. In fact, I specifically remember telling you, even showing you, how much I do want you.' My lips graze against the sensitive skin of her ear and she sucks in a short, sharp breath.

'But you're not willing to take the plunge, so to speak.' Twin hazel pools glint as she baits me. The air crackles between us.

'I can't.'

'Which is precisely why we had to come here.' She points to the black fronted shop front behind me, a mischievous laugh pouring from parted lips.

The Ann Summers sex store.

My jaw locks with a crack.

She's determined to make me combust with lust. 'You're not serious.'

'Deadly. Or would you rather we find that sex club tonight?' Swaying hips strut through the automatic doors. I briefly contemplate doing a Jared and waiting outside, before reluctantly following her in, half intrigued, half horrified and entirely turned on.

Row upon row of lingerie to suit every fantasy imaginable hangs in the store. High-waisted ebony g-strings, hot pink crotchless lace panties, suspender belts and stockings taunt me. Images of Victoria's beautiful body in all of them, or none of them, infiltrate my delinquent brain. Blood rushes to my crotch again. I'm worse than a horny fucking teenager. But of course, that's what she intended. I'm going to make her pay for it, one way or another. Just as soon as I work out how, without compromising my relationship with Ryan, my home and just about everything else I care about.

Victoria stops at a dominatrix outfit, thumbing over the sheer, translucent mesh.

Fuck. My. Life.

Margaret Thatcher.

Teresa May.

Camilla Parker-Bowles.

It's not helping.

Those thigh-high fuck-me boots sashay all the way to the back of the store.

I keep my focus trained on her, not the Aladdin's cave of multicoloured, weird and wonderfully shaped vibrators she's leading me into.

What will she pick?

Watching Victoria pick out something for her own pleasure is hot as fuck. Imagining her touching herself, thinking of me. The thought alone is enough to make me dizzy.

Groups of women in twos and threes snigger and glance my way. I step closer to Victoria and pull my phone from my pocket just to do something with my hands. It's official. I'm as bad as Jared. Next, I'll be downloading Tetris.

'Can I help you?' Just when I thought things couldn't get any worse, a shop assistant appears. She can't be more than twenty, but she wears an expression of a woman with much more experience than her years. Black Doc Martens match the exact shade of her thick, blunt fringe.

Victoria beams back at her. Oh my god, has she no shame?

'Yes, please. I'm looking for something, but I'm not quite sure what.' Victoria's fingers glide over a lifelike dildo complete with actual veins, stroking it from base to tip. It even has a slit on the shaft.

I can't tear my eyes from her hand, imagining her gripping my cock.

My trousers are strangling my dick.

It's too much.

'Well, I can guarantee you, you'll find something in here to cater for every type of need.' The assistant proffers Victoria a wink before turning to the wall behind her mounted with sex toys.

'Are you looking for clitoral stimulation?' She motions to an array of smaller devices which could be mistaken for mini massagers, which I suppose is precisely what they are. Just not ones you'd gift your granny on Christmas day.

'Or penetrative?' She points to a display of enormous fake dicks which makes even Victoria flinch.

'Or both?' The Doc Martens pivot and the fringe bobs as the assistant nods directly over my shoulder. I turn around, my eyes half closed in apprehension of what the fuck else they might be assaulted by, and with good fucking reason.

A huge assortment of U-shaped toys are boxed, one on top of the other.

'What the fuck?' It's out of my mouth before I can stop it.

'Meet our Rampant Rabbit range. These are our best sellers. This part is for penetration.' She unboxes one and switches it on. The biggest part begins to rotate with a whirring noise. 'This part, the rabbit ears, so to speak, are for the clit.' She hits another button and the smaller side of it bursts into a low but powerful vibration.

Victoria bites her lower lip as if she's really intrigued.

I'll give her intrigued. She can't seriously be thinking about purchasing one of these monstrosities?

'I'll take two,' she announces with glee. 'Give me the biggest one you've got. And I'll take this small discreet one too.' She picks up a three-inch silver gadget named *The Bullet*.'

How fucking ironic.

Would it count as touching her if I used that on her instead of one of my own body parts?

'Great choices.' The sales assistant grins knowingly before reverting her attention to me. 'What about you, sir?'

'What about me?' I scowl.

'Perhaps you'd like something for your pleasure? We stock an array of cock rings strap-ons —'

I cut her off before she can continue. 'That won't be necessary, thank you.' Not that I'm averse to spicing things up a bit, but as it stands, I shouldn't even be seasoning anything, let alone spicing.

'Righty-o-then.' Taking Victoria's items to the till, she asks, 'Would you like some extra batteries and lube to go with these?'

'Why not?' Victoria laughs, handing over her credit card.

I shake my head.

She thinks she's pulling out the big guns.

I've a good mind to take that bullet from her.

I am her bodyguard, after all.

And I know exactly what to do with a weapon like that.

Chapter Fifteen
VICTORIA

Archie tugs at the shiny black bag swinging from my arm, offering to carry it for me. Even while I'm doing my utmost to rile him, he's still the perfect gentleman.

'Now you've had your fun, can we go home?' he asks.

I link my arm through his again, revelling in the sensation of his muscles. He is *all* man. Those toys in the shop had nothing on the firm length pressed against me this morning.

'As much as I can't wait to try out my new toys, we have one more stop to make.' Glee rings in every single syllable. This is too much fun. Libby will die when she hears about this.

Archie's lips purse tightly. A jolt of satisfaction jumps inside my chest.

If the roles were reversed, and he was in his room pleasuring himself and thinking of me, I'd be so hot I'd beat the door down with my bare hands to get to him. But then again, he is Mr Iron Will. Which is precisely why we need to make a second stop.

I wasn't joking when I said I always finish what I start.

The toys are mostly for show. Sure, they might come in

handy, but the toy I really want is in Archie's pants, and he knows it.

Kristina and Marissa's lingerie boutique is a three-storey sand-coloured building on the corner of Fredrick Street. Thick dark carpet lines the concrete steps to the frosted glass-fronted doorway. The boutique's name, Sublime Secrets, is etched in bold gold italics against a midnight blue background.

I nudge Archie up the steps, biting back my smirk.

'What is this place?' He scans the sign warily.

'Marissa and Kristina's lingerie shop.'

Inside, the low-ceilinged room is filled with a slow, sensual electro music. Dim, violet lighting illuminates an ornate display of lingerie opulence. There are no racks or rails here.Instead, stunning-looking lifelike mannequins display the exquisite range of designer lingerie for sale. High end, quality silk cut in every shape, style and colour line the room. There are cute, chic baby doll outfits. Stylish, sublimely sexy bodysuits. Hold ups, pinned with sheer suspender belts.

I feel like I've died and gone to lingerie heaven.

Ann Summers was a bit of fun, but this is a sophisticated, next-level sensual selection. Every item is stitched with class, style and luxury.

I brought Archie here with the hope of turning him on further. Driving him mad with desire. Mad enough that he'll act on it. But it's me who's turned on. The thought of trying on some of these stunning pieces while Archie watches is as hot as hell. After all, he's the one who insists on being five feet away from me at all times.

Maybe I'm no better than one of those flashers on the Tube. I want him to see me. I want him to *want* me.

Desire races through my blood, fuelling every cell with a primal lust.

His grip on my arm tightens, but I don't look at him.

A stunning lace bodysuit catches my eye. The ivory material is virginal, but there's nothing pure about the high-cut leg and the way the front dips to the navel in a V.

It speaks to me.

Archie's eyes blaze over the same item, mirroring the exact same desire I feel.

'That one.' We utter the same two words at the exact moment. Our pupils lock in an unspoken agreement.

What we're agreeing on exactly, apart from our mutual outstanding preferences of lingerie, is beyond me.

Is he finally giving in to me?

If so, I need to move quickly, before he changes his mind.

I catch a glimpse of Marissa, who's dressed immaculately in a tailored burgundy pencil dress that showcases her hourglass figure. She's instructing two equally pristinely- dressed cashiers on how to do something at the till.

As if sensing my attention, she glances up, a warm smile of recognition extending all the way to her heavily winged eyelids.

'Victoria, welcome. It's lovely to see you.' She appears at my right, while Archie hovers at my left with a pained expression on his face. 'Like what you see?'

I finger the ivory lace. 'I love this one.' A tiny discreet label is pinned to the shoulder with the price. It's more than most people earn in a month, but I need it.

'That's actually from our bridal collection on the second floor. Why don't you go on up? It's not limited to brides-to-be, but the entire floor is dedicated to virtuous-looking pieces.'

She offers an encouraging nod towards the wide white painted staircase at the side of the room. 'Take as many pieces as you like, bring them up to the third floor. The girls will set up a dressing room for you. Take your time up there. I'll organise some refreshments to be sent up.'

The second floor is every bride's wildest dream. I point out the lace bodysuit and five other pieces to one of the assistants, including a silk balconette bra with matching thong and a suspender belt dotted with tiny Swarovski crystals, which blows the original lace bodysuit straight out of the water. I think I'm in love. There's a first for everything, I guess.

The assistant weighs me up with one swift, unobtrusive glance. 'I'll bring your size up.' One slim finger points to another set of stairs, which Archie and I climb silently, arms still interlinked.

Heat blazes between us. I want him to hold on to me forever.

I'm barely breathing. He's barely touching me, and I'm more turned on than I've ever been in my entire life.

Another assistant greets us at the top with a professional smile. She leads us along a navy carpeted corridor to one of four doors. Archie pauses for a split second, as if he's unsure whether to come in.

'You're supposed to be within five feet of me, remember?' My whisper comes out like a plea. If there's a hell, I think I've just booked myself a one-way ticket.

Thankfully, he indulges me.

Inside the large rectangular dressing room are floor-to-ceiling mirrors lining each of the four walls. A flutter of anticipation soars through me. Archie has a front-row seat to examine *every* angle. Let's just hope he likes what he sees.

A frosted folding screen separates a small area from the main part of the room opposite a large, pearlescent chaise lounge. Adjacent is a small glass table bearing an ice bucket containing a bottle of Taittinger champagne.

'Help yourselves to a drink while you wait,' the assistant says.

A heavy door clunks shut. And we're alone.

The air is electrified with an invisible circuit. Archie finally drops my arm and turns to face me. Azure irises smoulder into mine from above. I press my body against his huge physique, but not my lips, in case I scare him off again.

His arousal is evident in his trousers. Mine is less obvious, but there nonetheless.

'Victoria.' The same old warning is getting tedious, but it's definitely waning in its resolve.

He steps away from me and opens the champagne with a delightful pop, pouring it into one of two long stemmed flutes.

'Won't you join me?' I motion to the other empty glass.

'I'm working.' Somehow, his expression remains neutral.

Two sharp raps on the door cause me to jump. Archie takes the lingerie from the assistant and closes the door behind her.

'I should wait outside.' His gravelly tone is weighted with wanting. Torn between doing what's right and what he desires. His hand goes to the silver pendant he wears around his neck, finger and thumb pinching his St. Christopher. I'd never have pegged him as the religious type, but he seems to do that any time he's in doubt, so maybe he believes in something.

I believe in something too. That I might actually wither and die if he doesn't touch me soon.

'You're my bodyguard. You're paid to watch me. So do exactly that.' I knock back the contents of my glass for Dutch courage before taking the garments behind the frosted screen.

I slip off my coat, hang it on a chrome coatrack and undress with shaky fingers. The same electro beat plays through the speakers. It's low enough for me to hear Archie's heavy feet pad across the room. Is he going to slip out?

The chaise lounge decompresses.

Boom! It appears he's staying for the show. A hit of heat bursts through my veins.

I start with my favourite. The balconette bra. It fits flawlessly, lifting my cleavage and accentuating the swell of my breasts. The Swarovski encrusted thong sits perfectly on my hips and between my ass cheeks. I pull on a pair of silk-topped stockings and pin them in position with the matching suspender belt.

An array of high-heeled shoes has been assembled behind the screen and I slide my feet into a pair of ivory satin courts before daring to look at myself in the mirror.

I don't recognise the woman staring back at me, but I like her. A lot. She's sexy, sophisticated, empowered, and about to burn a tonne of plastic.

I take a deep breath, summon my inner brazen whore, and strut out from behind the screen with my pulse hammering in my throat.

Archie's eyes meticulously absorb the view in a painfully slow examination.

His silence is killing me.

My stomach levitates. 'What do you think?'

Blue sapphires blaze hot enough to incinerate me where I stand.

'I think I need a closer look.' In one swift leap, he's on his feet. Hooded slits narrow and darken, as those powerful legs strut across the room with a firm purpose. In this moment, he looks every bit the hot, off-limit bodyguard he is.

But this man is on the edge of doing something neither of us can come back from. And he knows it.

Good.

Now he can appreciate what it's like for me watching him strut around like an Adonis under my roof, twenty-four-seven.

There's something so fucking arousing about being so exposed while he's fully clothed in that body-moulding suit that I love so much. His poised posture screams strength, authority and control.

I stand rigid as he circles me like a hungry lion.

If only he'd devour me.

'Spread your legs. I want to see how that thing sits between your gorgeous ass cheeks,' he commands.

My mouth dries as my thighs part six inches.

'Wider,' he demands, staring at my lower half.

For once, I do as I'm told, watching in the mirrored walls. He bites his lower lip before whistling lowly.

A hot finger trails across my stomach, fingering the silk of the suspender belt from front to back, tracing the material backwards, trailing over my thong as it slips between my cheeks and lower.

For one magnificent, fleeting second, his index finger brushes over my sex before he yanks it away.

I wanted to tease him.

I was a fool.

He's the one calling the shots here.

Who am I kidding? He has done since he got here.

I'd do well to remember it.

Warm fingers trace lightly across my bare bum, leaving goosebumps in their wake. They dip closer to my sex with maddening circular sweeps. 'You wanted me to see you like this.' It's an accusation, dare, and invitation rolled into one. 'So, show me. Bend over.'

I obey, dropping forwards so my nails graze the carpet in front of me, keeping my eyes intently adhered to his in the mirror.

If I hadn't planned on buying the lingerie, I'd be left with no other choice. The material is destroyed by my desire.

'You want to drive me insane with lust, so I'll risk everything to be with you.' A thick, decadent finger slips inside the thong, swiping through my slick arousal.

He's right. I wanted this. I wanted to bring him to his knees. 'Yes.'

His finger slides upwards, circling my sweet spot, teasing me for another millisecond before he tears it away again. It's the worst and best form of torture.

Well, it would be if I knew he might eventually make me come.

'You know I want you. But you're not mine to take. You're determined to push me over the edge. My job is to protect you. To serve you.'

He drops to his knees behind me, running his tongue across my ass cheek. I watch on in the side mirror, utterly transfixed as his face approaches my silk-clad sex from behind. Between peppered kisses, he says, 'Today, and today only, I am going to serve you.'

His hot breath brushes my inner thigh as he removes something small and shiny from his pocket.

The bullet.

It vibrates in his hand, and a wolfish grin rips across his face. 'This weapon is definitely safer in my hands.'

He pushes the cold metal inside the silk and yanks us both to a standing position. Rippled abs flank my back as he wraps one arm around my waist to support me. We watch our reflections together with ragged breaths.

His impressive length digs into my butt from behind. I try to grind against it, but he stills my hips with one hand.

With one strong yank, he tugs the bra down so my breasts spill over the top. 'So fucking beautiful, Victoria,' he murmurs against my earlobe. Fingers pinch my nipple and a moan bursts from my lips. The vibrator buzzes powerfully against my clit and my core clenches. I won't last a minute like this. I was ready to blow before it even touched me.

It's too much.

It's not enough.

Expert swipes drive the bullet over the most sensitive parts of me. Up and down and around. Over and over and over.

My thighs tremble, battling to support my weight as his lips curve at my utter undoing. He's devouring me alright, it's just a shame it's with his eyeballs.

'Archie, I...'

'You what, sweetheart?' His tone is knowing, arrogant, borderline cruel.

He ramps up the voltage on his weapon and it takes every bit of concentration to keep upright. 'You are a bad influence on me, Doctor Sexton.' His fingers tease the plane of my stomach before darting up to circle my breast. 'Did you do this with your other security guards?'

He blows a gentle breath over my shoulder to my nipple, watching as I arch in pleasure.

'No.' It comes out like a cry.

'Is this why you wanted me to come to Edinburgh with you all those years ago?'

'Yes. I need...'

'You and those needs, sweetheart.' His tongue grazes the sensitive skin of my earlobe. 'What do you need? Tell me.'

He won't kiss me. It's so impersonal. But so fucking sexy.

A tiny click is the only warning I get for the increase in voltage focusing intensely on my sweet, sensitive nub. I don't stand a chance. I never did.

My orgasm detonates, my insides liquify, and a hot burst of stars blind me. Strong arms support me while I shake and shudder in his grip, riding wave after wave of ecstasy before eventually returning to earth.

He presses a kiss to my temple, breathing in the scent of my hair. Our eyes lock again in the glass, his expression is one of resolve.

'I'm buying you the lingerie. All of it. But this can't

happen again, okay? Please don't push me. It's not fair on either of us.' There's a detached look in his eyes.

He's pulling himself back from me again. Robbing both of us of any type of intimacy.

On some level, I understand his rejection. This is the way it has to be. But it still hurts like hell. Especially after that earth-shattering orgasm.

A devastating despair chases away the remnant of the ecstatic high, kindly delivered by the same man. Tears prick at the corner of my eyes. I blink them back hard and fast.

He's taken my power. I've become powerless.

I might have procured a release, but my needs are nowhere near close to being met.

Because what I really need is *him*.

Chapter Sixteen
ARCHIE

The tables have fully turned. It's Victoria avoiding looking at me since our encounter in Sublime Secrets yesterday. She's also avoiding eating with me. Or breathing the same air.

An appropriate name for a lingerie shop coincidently, because if anyone discovers our ephemeral encounter, our rendezvous will cost me everything. My place in Ryan's family. My job. My sense of purpose. My home.

What happened between us was as inevitable as the rising sun.

I barely laid my hands on her, but I'm under no illusion that getting your client off with their own vibrator is a sackable offence. Not to mention what Ryan would do to me if he found out.

I torpedoed over the line. The worst thing is, it did nothing to relieve this thing between us. Instead of closure, I got captivation.

Addiction.

Victoria's shaking pelvis, fevered shudders and hooded hazel fuck-me eyes are the only images I see every single time I shut my eyes. The feel of her slickness on my fingers. What

I wouldn't give to watch Victoria spiral into ecstasy in my arms again and again and again.

That lingerie scenario was more transcendent than any personal fantasy I've concocted over the years.

The same items, delicately wrapped in glossy boxes, remain untouched on the kitchen table. Abandoned amongst the million bouquets of flowers she received after her attack.

Is she mad at me? Or mad with herself for allowing things to escalate like that?

None of my relationships ever lasted long enough for me to decipher female body language. Well, out of the bedroom anyway.

I glance at my chunky Swiss watch, a Christmas gift from Ryan five years ago. If Victoria doesn't get a move on, she'll be late for her first shift back.

Cutting it to the last second, she stomps down the stairs two at a time in her usual white Converse. Wearing a pair of faded skinny jeans and an oversized jumper, she looks equally as stunning as she did in that dressing room yesterday.

A fleeting closer inspection reveals tell-tale puffy shadows beneath her eyes.

Clearly, the orgasm did nothing to help her sleep.

The two I gave myself in the shower furiously afterwards did nothing to help me switch off, either.

Desire licks at my soul, a flame that rises fiercer and higher and increasingly out of control with each passing day.

It's inescapable. It's all consuming. I should resign, but the prospect of not seeing her is even worse than the prospect of being near her and not being able to touch her.

'Coffee?' I offer. Maybe a peace offering will soften her mood. Break this weirdness between us.

'No.' She adds, 'Thank you,' in a pained tone. Like she'd rather do anything than utter another word to me, but her impeccable upbringing insists upon excellent manners.

We head out to the SUV. That strawberry scent pollutes the car like the most delicious poison.

'Victoria…' It's impossible to articulate the right words.

'Don't, Archie. Just don't.' She flicks her hair from her shoulder.

'I'm sorry.' I grip the steering wheel tightly to stop my tingling palm reaching out to touch her.

'Sorry? For what exactly? Sorry you took pity on me and let me convince you your job title involves serving my needs?' Victoria buries herself deeper into her oversized coat like she's willing it to swallow her whole.

A snort erupts from my chest. 'Pity? Is that what you think? A pity sex scenario?'

'Wasn't it? I practically forced you into that dressing room with me. What else could you have done without embarrassing me?' She drags her hair into a ponytail, securing it with a hairband.

'The only person I pity is me. I wanted to fuck you so badly my balls are blue even after two self-awarded handjobs.' My fist bangs the dashboard hard enough to make her jump.

'What I wouldn't give to be with you, Victoria. You're the most magnificent woman I've ever come across. Or will ever come across again. Not only are you absolutely stunning on the outside…' My hand gestures to her beautiful body, '…but I've never met anyone with a heart like yours. Someone so selfless. You could be living the highlife on the back of Ryan and Sasha's fame, but here you are, tending to others, doing a job that constantly puts you at risk.'

'And you and I getting involved is another risk, right?' Her gaze remains forwards the entire time.

She was right. It's horrible when someone you care for avoids eye contact. I'll never do it to her again.

'If your family didn't employ me, and I didn't think so highly of them, it would be a different matter altogether.'

I negotiate the rush hour traffic to the university hospital without uttering another word.

When we get inside the building, Victoria changes into her scrubs and I escort her to A&E where Doctor Dickhead is already waiting like a slimy predator.

'Ah, Doctor Sexton. I trust your injuries are well improved?' His grubby hands brush over the pale, almost faded bruising on her neck. If he touches her clavicle, I'll rip them from his wrists.

She offers a curt nod and a tight-lipped smile. 'Yes, thank you.'

Narrow eyes darken, holding hers for a beat longer than is comfortable. 'The offer stands if you want to talk. My door is always open.'

She knows. We all fucking do.

I step forwards, towering over him. 'Speaking of open doors, the Sexton family is insisting on an open door, or rather curtain, policy, as it were.'

Unless we're in Sublime Secrets, of course.

'Ryan and Sasha would hate to have to file a claim and complaint against the hospital, and whoever was in charge last week.' My pointed stare ensures there's no mistaking I know exactly who was supposed to be in charge last week.

Doctor Dickhead freezes, the full enormity of my words washing over him. 'I'm afraid it's not up to me to change hospital policy. It's a matter of patient confidentiality.' He coughs.

'It will be a matter of front-page news if it's not rectified immediately.' I remove my phone from my pocket, pretending I'm about to call Ryan or Sasha or any other member of Victoria's famous family.

Doctor Dickhead raises his hand in protest. 'Fine. I'll deal with it.'

'I need a clear view of her at all times. I don't give a crap about patient confidentiality, especially when they're convicted criminals.'

If looks could kill, I'd be stone dead, abandoned in a heap of blood and guts, the favourite bits of my anatomy severed from my bruised and bleeding body.

Thankfully, looks *can't* kill.

But if this punk steps a foot out of line with my girl, then *I* will.

Victoria's arms fold across her chest as she glances between Doctor Dickhead and me, like she's watching a tennis match.

When Doctor Dickhead finally nods reluctantly to my demands, I swear I see a flicker of relief cross her fabulous features. She's bound to be shaken after her last shift in here.

My girl.

If only it were a remote possibility.

Even if I resigned and took another position before telling Ryan and Sasha, it would cause war. Even if I could somehow get Ryan and Sasha to accept a real relationship between Victoria and me, if we were to take the chance, try to make a go of it, it doesn't change the fact she's twenty-three and probably nowhere near ready to settle down.

It's too risky.

She's too young.

She might think she wants me but she doesn't really. Not the way I want her, at least.

It would probably be great for a while. Yesterday proved what my dick has suspected for years. Physically, we are an explosive combination.

Who knows, if we were to go down this road, I might even end up being her first love. But that's not enough for me. I want to be her last love, too.

And that isn't something a twenty-three-year-old party girl could ever commit to. Not with someone like me. She needs someone with the same IQ as her. Someone from the same social class. I don't doubt I can equal her in the bedroom, but if her friends and acquaintances are anything to go by, we are worlds apart.

I wish she'd talk to me.

Though why would she, when I played her body like the sweetest instrument and then the second it sang, shut her down?

Victoria's shift passes without incident, unless you count my numb backside on these shitty metal hospital seats. A few broken bones. One stroke victim. An anaphylaxis. Several cuts requiring stitches.

I remain within eight feet of her at all times. My eyes don't leave her for a second, bar her brief toilet trips.

So there's no chance of it escaping my attention when Harrison fucking Hughes and his stupidly coiffed dark hair rocks up next to her, ducking inside the cubicle where she's writing up her paperwork.

'Victoria, I'm so sorry about the other day. What a scumbag.' His rugby player physique slants into her slim one, way too close for comfort. My comfort, that is. Weirdly, she seems okay with it.

'Yeah, thanks, H. It wasn't my best day.'

H? What, are they fucking BFF's now? The guy's a fucking creep.

My blood boils but I deliberately gaze over her shoulder, like this entire fucked-up scenario isn't unfolding helplessly before me.

Her chestnut hair falls across her forehead and he sweeps it out of her eye in a gesture that's WAY too familiar.

'Did you get the flowers I sent?' The creep moves in

closer. The famous *Jaws* music plays on repeat in my head. My pulse ticks furiously in my neck.

'They're gorgeous, thank you. I meant to call, but I was knocked off kilter for a few days.'

'No wonder.' He shakes his head in exaggerated sympathy.

Seriously? Fuck off, toff boy!

All Harrison's interested in is getting into Victoria's knickers. If he cared about her at all, he'd have beaten down the front door with his bare, bleeding fists to check she was okay.

That's what I'd have done, anyway.

His voice drops to an audible whisper. Narrow, black pupils shoot me a look of sheer unconcealed malevolence.

'I've been so worried about you. I've made no secret of my...' He swallows hard in a cringeworthy show of faux coyness, 'intentions towards you.'

What is this? A fucking nineteen-forties romance novel? Spit it out, you dick, and let her turn you down - again.

Victoria pats his arm in what looks like an appreciative gesture. She's about to blow him off. She has to. There's no alternative.

'I know, Harrison. Your uncomplicated attention is actually refreshing.' The glare she shoots me smashes through my sternum.

'It is?' His tone sounds as shocked as I feel. Each and every tiny fine hair on my neck and body prick up in an inaudible alarm.

'Yes. You've been unwavering in your affection...' Her lips rise in a forced, breezy smile.

'So, will you go out with me?' He takes her hand in his like he's making a goddamn marriage proposal instead of proposing to stick his dirty dick in anywhere he can.

Victoria glances in my direction. I don't look, but I don't need to. An acute awareness bristles over every bone in my body. And I mean EVERY bone.

She pauses for a second. She's searching for the words to knock him back gently, because she's got such a huge heart and she even cares about hurting a douchebag like Harrison.

One word ends my life as I know it. 'Okay.'

'Okay?' At first I'm not sure if *I* shrieked out at her offensive acceptance, or if Harrison did. The pads of my fingers press against my lips. They haven't moved. It's one small saving grace.

'Yeah, why not?' She offers a half-hearted smile.

'Sugar, you are not going to regret this, I swear.' He drops a kiss on her cheek before moonwalking backwards out of the cubicle like the jumped-up little prick he is. 'Tomorrow night? I'll pick you up at eight, okay?'

Victoria nods, shrugging her shoulders in casual acceptance.

But Harrison's forgotten one thing. It's not her he's picking up. It's both of us.

And I intend to make his night downright miserable.

If he even gets that far.

'See you tomorrow, dog,' he hisses snidely, with a contrasting effusive sneer.

In the car home, Victoria rubs her weary eyes, crossing and uncrossing her legs in a bid to get comfortable.

'You can't be serious?' I blurt out. Anger meshes with hurt in one sickening, swirling mess of acid eating the lining of my stomach.

'Serious about what?' She adopts an air of boredom, but she knows. She fucking knows.

'Going out with the campus creep.'

She sighs heavily, staring out of the passenger window at the streetlights whizzing by. 'I've decided to only pursue what I can have, instead of torturing myself with what I can't. I intend to start the way I mean to go on. Harrison's a good fit for me, on paper at least. I intend to give him a chance.'

A chance?

Over my dead, fucking body.

She's just goading me. Testing to see if I'll crack. It's another one of her games, just like the stunt with Alexa and the trip to Ann Summers.

It has to be.

He might be socially a better fit, with his third level education and fancy family. But she's not seriously going to let him put his filthy hands anywhere near her.

Is she?

Chapter Seventeen
VICTORIA

The doorbell chimes at exactly one minute to eight. Harrison is punctual. It's a good start, whatever happens next.

I run a hand over the sleek midnight blue silk of my dress, a stunning Evangeline Araceli number gifted from Sasha. It's deceivingly conservative-looking from the front, midi in length with a high neck. It radiates class and elegance.

The back of the dress, however, screams something else altogether. The silk is cut low enough to reveal my entire spine, leaving no option but to go braless.

Silver Manolo Blahnik sandals give me extra height I don't need, but love. Even when I'm in heels, Archie towers above me.

Whoops, I mean Harrison, because that's who I'm supposed to be impressing, right?

Maybe it's cruel, agreeing to go out with another man, but I have to do something. As my dad, God rest him, used to say, shit or get off the pot.

After tonight, one way another, I'll know if Archie will ever give in to this thing between us.

If dating Harrison doesn't tip him over the edge, nothing

will. And if not, perhaps dinner with Harrison won't turn out to be as dull as I initially suspected. Doubtful, though, doubtful.

Harrison's polished accent carries up the stairs as he addresses Archie. 'Good evening, dog.'

Anger simmers in my blood at his disrespectful greeting.

Any remorse I harboured for using him to make my bodyguard jealous just evaporated. If I thought there was even a slight possibility Harrison and I might actually have as much in common in real life as we do on paper, that single statement blew that foolish notion straight out of the water.

This might be a tough night for Archie, but sitting through Harrison regaling me with stories that paint him as some sort of hero could be equally painful for me.

Still, no pain, no gain, right?

Harrison exhales a low whistle as I strut into the hallway, my coat draped over my injured arm and my clutch bag tucked under the other. 'Victoria, you look stunning.'

He doesn't look too bad himself, in that posh boy tweed suit way, apart from the fact his trousers are so tight he probably had to jump off the wardrobe to get into them. He's the epitome of what his family stands for - generations of old money, titles and elitism.

Not to put too fine a point on it, especially given the way he spoke to Archie, he's a snob.

Harrison's lips press a greeting against my cheek at the same time his palm lands on my bare spine. His aftershave swamps me. It's not awful, just completely overpowering.

Dark eyes light with approval. 'Wow.' A finger trails across my bare flesh, giving rise to goosebumps across my skin, but there's not a single butterfly in my stomach, let alone a swarm of them, like when Archie touches me.

He's towering a few feet away, glowering thunderously at the wall. Dressed in his familiar black Armani suit that hugs his pert backside and moulds his muscular chest, he's every bit the hot, brooding bodyguard.

My stomach flips. The soles of my stilettos are rooted to the spot.

This feels so wrong.

Every part of me wants to scream, *'I can't do this.'*

But I have to.

Archie has to understand I won't sit around and wait for him forever. I can't waste the next ten years pining for him, like my sister Sasha did with Ryan. If he really won't claim me, I'd rather know now.

'I have a car waiting outside.' Harrison guides me to the front door, nudging me back to reality. A sleek black limo with tinted windows is double-parked on the kerb outside.

A smartly dressed driver stands ready to open the back door for us, but Archie shoulders past and dismisses him. 'I'll be driving these two tonight.'

That wild Rambo look glints in his eyes. I swoon and sigh simultaneously.

It's his job. I get it. But he could try to be a little less intimidating. His disdain for Harrison isn't the driver's fault. He takes three good steps back, gawking open-mouthed, then hops back into the car.

'Is this really necessary?' Harrison runs a palm over his day-old stubble.

'You didn't seriously think I was going to entrust my client's safety to a child, did you?' Archie's voice is dangerously low.

'Oh, this *child* knows exactly how to take care of Victoria.' Harrison drops a hand on my back in what I'm sure is a deliberate attempt to antagonise Archie.

He's brave. Or stupid. I'm not sure which. This was a terrible idea. What the hell was I thinking?

Archie's sporting the same dangerously cold expression he

wore when he took out the four bouncers in Dublin. 'Doubtful, boy, doubtful.'

'Fine,' Harrison finally shrugs. 'Drive, dog.'

Annoyance whips through me. 'H, please don't call him that. Archie's the best there is.'

'Is that so?' Harrison helps me into the back seat before sliding onto the leather next to me.

Archie reaches across to strap me in with a large, calloused hand attached to a huge defined arm, and shoulders that make Harrison's rugby player ones look insignificant in comparison.

Then Archie slips into the driver's seat, switching on the engine before Harrison has even closed his door.

'Woah, what do you think you're doing?' Harrison snarls, righting himself as Archie swings the car round a corner at high speed.

'Where are we going?' Archie barks, avoiding glancing in the rear-view mirror to where Harrison's attempting to slide a little closer than I'm comfortable with.

'The Witchery.' Harrison's superior tone makes my skin crawl.

Archie stares straight ahead, clasping the steering wheel tight enough to crush it.

Harrison straightens his back, puffing out his chest like a pigeon.

'The Witchery?' I smooth a hand over my dress and try to feign some enthusiasm. 'Don't you have to book like a year in advance to get a table?' It's hard to be enthusiastic when I'm hyperaware of Archie's proximity. Of the sheer masculinity he radiates. Of the chemistry swirling in the air between us.

I'm supposed to be torturing the man, like he tortured me with that vibrator, getting me off, then blowing me off. My cheeks sting at the memory, still so fresh and raw.

Harrison's lips curl into a victorious smile. 'Most people do.'

Ugh, that ego. It probably needs a reservation of its own. I take a deep breath, trying to focus on anything other than the tantalising scent of bergamot.

It's just a crying shame it's wafting from the thick, powerful neck of my bodyguard, and not the guy I'm on a date with.

The Witchery is notoriously the most spectacular and atmospheric dining destination in Edinburgh. The food is legendary. The décor is rich, baroque and screams romance with a capital R. I've never been here before. I've never had anyone to go with.

A waitress wearing a crisp, brilliant white shirt and black pencil skirt shows us to a table tucked away in a private alcove. Chunky church candles cast little light on the original oak wood panelling tracking across the dining room walls and on Archie's stoic expression as he perches on a stool in the corner.

He hasn't uttered a word since we arrived. Not even a flicker of emotion has crossed his deadpan face.

A wave of sadness washes over me.

He's prepared to put up with this. With me dating someone else. Which means he can't have even a fraction of the feelings I have for him. I'm not a violent person, but if the roles were reversed, and he was sitting across from a woman who looked as though all she wanted for dinner was him, I'd gouge her eyes out with my spoon.

'Would you like to order something to drink? Perhaps some champagne to start?' The waitress suggests, draping my napkin across my lap.

'Yes, please. And bring the bottle.' *I'm going to need it.*

Harrison grins at me. 'That's the way to do it.'

Throughout dinner, Harrison drones on about his family's estate. How much it's worth. His trust fund. The influence of his family on their community. He's every bit as egotistical and lacklustre as I suspected.

Thankfully, the food is every bit as sumptuous as the restaurant's reputation claims.

To start, we order Pacific oysters to share. They're drowning deliciously in mignonette sauce, tabasco and lemon.

Harrison leans across the table, squeezing my hand roughly. 'You know, oysters are an aphrodisiac.'

So is the sight of my surly, silent bodyguard in that indecently tailored suit, even if he's refusing to look at me again. Whatever he's looking at on his phone has to be more interesting than listening to how many tries Harrison scored for the college rugby team last season.

I knock back another two glasses of champagne and force my attention on my date, and not my defender.

For my main, I order lemon sole meuniere with cucumber and caviar butter sauce, each mouth-watering morsel like a religious experience. At least the food means the night's not going to be a complete write off.

Archie isn't prepared to step up. He'd rather see me with someone he hates than risk his job. It's not as though he even needs the damn job. Chloe told me Archie is comfortable enough. Being a bodyguard isn't about the money for him. It's about honour. How the heck can I compete with that?

To dull the throbbing ache in my chest, I drink too much champagne.

'Would you like dessert?' Harrison leans across the table, his question dripping with subtext as his hand grazes my skin.

Archie stiffens, mid scroll in my periphery. Boom! It's not over 'til it's over.

'I've been known to be tempted, now and again.'

Archie's head turns so fast he's in danger of giving himself whiplash. Finally. But it's still not enough to reassure me he's going to do what it takes to stop it.

That he's ready to claim me as his own.

Harrison's booming laugh echoes off the low ceilings.

'I always knew you'd be game for a good time, Victoria. You have a certain...reputation.' He raises his glass in a toast.

'Do you know I've had thirteen different bodyguards since I arrived in this city?' I say, trying to change the subject. 'Apparently, being on the frontline is preferable to babysitting me.' I take another sip of my drink, willing Archie to intervene, or give me some sort of sign.

Harrison rests an elbow on the table, gazing pointedly at my chest, before finally lifting his eyes back to my face. 'You're only young once.'

'Let's skip the sweet stuff. I'm full.' I motion for the waitress to fetch the bill.

'Don't even think about it.' Harrison's cheeks blaze with embarrassment.

'You're not the only one with a trust fund.' I hand my credit card to the waitress with a finality. 'Take a forty percent tip for yourself, too.'

Paying is the least I can do when I've shamelessly used him, but emasculating Harrison, in his mind at least, has been one of the highlights of the evening.

As the maître de bids us farewell at the door, Harrison's lips brush against my earlobe. 'Fancy a nightcap at mine?'

A polite refusal rests on my tongue, but then a low growl erupts from behind me.

Progress, at last!

My soul silently rejoices.

'One drink, okay" I eye Harrison firmly, making sure he's in no doubt that a drink is all I'm agreeing to, and nothing else..

Even if I was attracted to him, I never put out on the first date.

'Yes, ma'am.' He links his arm through mine. The cold midnight air fogs in front of our faces as we stroll along the Royal Mile to where the car is parked on one of the flatter side streets.

I can't see Archie, but I'm acutely aware of his presence behind me. The way his eyes burn into my back. His anger. His desire.

He needs one final push.

And I'm going to give it to him.

Camera flashbulbs light up the darkness. 'Victoria! This way. Give us a smile. Just a couple of pictures.'

'Who is your boyfriend?' someone shouts.

'Move.' Archie steps in front of me, sheltering me from the blinding lights until I'm safely back in the car.

'Is it always like this?' Harrison asks, looking shocked and slightly dishevelled.

'It's usually worse.' My shaky hands clasp my clutch. I wasn't cut out for this life, although it's something I've had to get used to since Ryan returned to Sasha's life.

'That's so cool.' Harrison's awe-filled tone is a further reminder of our incompatibility.

It's about a ten-minute drive to Morningside, where Harrison lives.

The car slows to a stop. 'Victoria,' Archie mutters a warning and a plea rolled into one.

I don't want to do this, but I have to. One drink. Long enough to make Archie sweat.

Let him hang like he left me hanging in the dressing room at Sublime Secrets.

He needs to understand that if he's not willing to step up for me, to give me what I need, to give me himself, then one day someone else will.

And that will be a shame for all of us. Because he's the one I want. And I'm pretty sure he feels the same. If only he'd give into this thing between us.

Stop this.

Show me you're ready.

Claim me.

'Wait outside, dog,' Harrison hisses.

Archie's huge blue eyes shoot daggers through the moonlight. 'Are you really going to do this?' he asks, his voice sharp, cool and utterly disapproving.

The time for questions is over.

He shouldn't be asking.

He should be acting on impulse. I'd throw his date out of the moving vehicle if the roles were reversed.

'It's one drink. I won't be long.'

Archie's knuckles are whiter than fresh snow as I step out of the vehicle and follow Harrison into his house.

Chapter Eighteen
ARCHIE

Harrison's front door slams shut with a bang loud enough to wake the entire street.

Adrenaline furiously soars through every artery and vein, and my heart hammers in my chest. I hop out of the car in a fit of rage. My foot connects with the back wheel, but no amount of kicking will resolve my anger. 'Fuck it.'

What the fuck is Victoria playing at?

Is this some sort of punishment for the other day?

Because I wouldn't take it further between us?

Doesn't she realise I already broke my own moral code for her?

I'm teetering on the edge of doing something that will ruin me, or her, or potentially both of us, and it's taking every modicum of my willpower to stop myself. I'm desperately digging my claws into something concrete before I slide off the edge for good.

My rejection wasn't because I don't want her, but because I do. Because I care for her so fucking much, I'd willingly die for her. I signed a fucking contract to prove it.

Every cell in my body hums with irrepressible anger. I

vowed not to take another life unless absolutely necessary, but tonight, that promise means nothing to me.

Horrifying multicoloured images of what might be occurring behind that front door flash through my mind like one of those super-sized digital photo frames with a million pixels.

Harrison's filthy, clumsy hands on Victoria's bare, silky skin.

His blundering lips plundering hers as she grinds herself into him, the way she did to me.

She wouldn't, would she?

Bile burns the back of my throat.

I stalk across the street, pacing the uneven garden pathway with the intention of dragging Victoria out of there. Claiming her as my own. Taking her right here in the street just to show her exactly who she belongs to.

Despite her little show, it was painfully obvious she has no interest in Harrison. She's trying to rile me. And even though I see through her little charade, I can't see past it. Anger simmers in my blood. With him. With her. And with myself for caring.

My fist is hovering an inch away from the door, ready to bang the damn thing down if need be, when a twig snaps brashly under my boot, triggering a memory so fucking tangible it transports me straight back to my final military tour. To the desert. To that landmine. To the day I led my men to their deaths on my selfish jaunt.

My skin pricks with heat. Every fine hair stands to attention on my body. The sensation of dry, dusty sand grazes my face, my hair, and stings my eyes.

I crossed the line. Bent the rules once in my life. *Once.* And it left three of my best friends dead.

It should have been a simple mission.

We were withdrawing. The town we'd been assigned to protect was secure. The risks reducing with every day that passed. A few of us took a spin in a Land Rover to the nearest town. It was my idea. Totally against protocol. We weren't supposed to leave the base unless it was a matter of life or death, but I bent the rules.

How was I to know rebels had planted a landmine on a dirt track near one of the small roads?

When the back left wheel of the Land Rover hit the mine, it blew Brady and Hanson to bits. Jones, who was in the passenger seat next to me, survived the initial blast, but died in my arms minutes later.

I survived physically. Mentally, I doubt I'll ever be right again.

It was the worst day of my life.

The worst year of my life.

Victoria isn't the only one who suffers from night terrors. The faces of my comrades, my friends, still haunt my dreams.

I sanctioned the unapproved trip.

I risked my men for my own selfish desire to prove to my father I was a hero. That I *was* cut out for army life.

How can I compromise Victoria's safety for another selfish desire?

Albeit it a very different one - the desire to make her mine.

If I get distracted, her safety could be compromised. I can't risk losing anyone I love again.

And risk losing Ryan and Jayden and the entire Cooper family in the process.

My clenched knuckles hover against the door, torn between what I want and what's right.

Victoria in there with that creep definitely isn't right, though. It's a fucking travesty. This whole situation is killing me.

'No, Harrison! I told you, I agreed to a drink and that's

all,' Victoria screams, those few snatched words coming from inside the apartment making the decision for me.

'You want it, you slut. You know you do.' Harrison's deep booming voice is the final straw. I ram my shoulder against the door hard enough to take it off its hinges and send it crashing into the plasterboard behind it.

I fly through the narrow corridor and into the first door on the right, a deep dark kitchen with a cherry wood worktop which Harrison has Victoria rammed up against.

'What the...?' Harrison has Victoria by the wrist, his fingers digging into her skin tight enough to make it blanch.

At the sight of me, he releases her. 'Dog.' Cruel, low laughter rumbles from his throat as I grab it, squeezing his windpipe.

Now *he's* shoved against the worktop. Let's see how he likes it.

'If you ever touch her again, I'll snap your fucking neck in a heartbeat.' Flexing my fingers, I tighten my grip to show him exactly what I'm capable of. 'Got it?'

Harrison's eyeballs bulge in their sockets, his complexion going a deeper shade of purple with every passing second. Satisfaction flows through me. Witnessing the life drain from him is positively thrilling.

'Archie.' Victoria's voice yanks me from my fantasy of killing Harrison. Reluctantly, I release him. He's not worth the jail time.

He crumples to the floor. 'I'll fucking sue you for this. Do you know who my family are?'

On jerky legs, he lurches upwards, swinging his fist. My elbow connects with his face. I may be the only non-medic in the room, but you don't have to be a doctor to work out I've just shattered his nose.

'I know exactly who you are. It was impossible to miss the

three hundred times you name-dropped "Mummy and Daddy" tonight.'

'Then you won't have missed how influential they are.' He clutches his nose as blood pours down the front of his shirt, soaking through the fabric.

'Oh, shut up, you spoilt little prick. I'll have you arrested for sexual assault on my client.'

My attention turns to Victoria, who's wide-eyed and trembling. Shock, no doubt. 'Are you okay?'

She nods, staring at the blood pouring from Harrison's nose.

'Get the fuck out of my house,' he snarls.

'Gladly.' I sweep Victoria into my arms and carry her out into the street and back to the car. I place her gently in the passenger seat and strap her in before slipping round to the driver's side.

She doesn't speak until we arrive back at her house.

'I'm sorry,' she says, resting against the kitchen counter.

'You should be, Victoria.' I help myself to a whiskey from the crystal decanter on the worktop.

The first rule of security is never drink on the job, but with the front door locked and Victoria only a foot away from me with her tail between her legs, I feel justified bending it just this once.

'I had no idea he had that side to him.' She bites her lower lip. It's still trembling.

'Here.' I offer her my glass and she sips the alcohol thoughtfully.

Remnants of carefully applied make-up are smudged under her huge, sorry eyes. I reach across and wipe it with my thumb while my other hand steadies her hip.

Her scent assaults my senses, strawberries again, but tonight it's mixed with a rich, sensual perfume. My eyelids close as I breathe her in.

My palm remains resting on her hip. I should tear it away, but I can't. After watching her with another man all evening, the urge to claim her, to take her and teach her who she belongs to, is overwhelming. 'You know I have a good mind to put you over my knee and spank your ass for your behaviour tonight.'

My hand hums, desperate to explore what lies beneath that navy dress.

A sharp gasp slips from her lips and her hip jolts like she's been electrocuted.

'If you'd only done that in the first place, we could have avoided this entire damn evening.' Hazel-hued eyes rise to meet mine, heavy with a hunger that no fancy dinner could satiate.

'Victoria.' I swear I should record that warning and play it on repeat. It's all I seem to say around her. Not that either of us is paying any heed to it tonight. I'm itching to touch her. To kiss her.

Technically, I've already made her come once.

Would it be so bad if I did it again?

The familiar internal duel between what I want and what is honourable recommences in my head.

The faces of Brady, Hanson and Jones force themselves to the forefront of my mind and I'm reminded of the need to live for today, because tomorrow is promised to none of us.

Guilt bubbles in my stomach, along with an overwhelming sense of longing. My fingers go to the ever-present pendant hanging from my neck as I swallow back the emotion rising inside my body.

'Give into me,' Victoria urges, gently setting the whiskey glass down on the countertop.

Her pelvis arches forwards, closing the remaining few inches between our bodies. Amorous eyes gaze upwards, while gold flecks dance like a devil wielding fire, tempting me to do something wicked.

Something selfish.

Something I've obsessed about for a very long time.

There are so many reasons I should shut this thing down. Not least because Ryan might actually murder me. And rightly so.

But I'm in too deep. We've gone too far.

I can't stop this now if my life depended on it.

Chapter Nineteen
VICTORIA

Nothing else matters in this moment other than Archie's huge hot hand resting on my hip. Anticipation flurries like a thousand starlings in my stomach, and lower. He's thinking about it. Contemplating giving into this thing between us.

And that knowledge alone is enough to ruin my underwear.

'After tonight's stunt, you need to be taught a lesson.' His excitement presses against me. Long, hard, and powerful. The need to feel him fill me up is unbearable. If he's going to get me off and fuck off again, I might not actually survive.

I hold my breath, frightened to move, or even breathe, and break this moment.

He might work for my family, but there is no mistaking who's in charge tonight.

'It won't happen again.' My breath comes in ragged, shallow bursts.

'You're damn right it won't happen again, Victoria. Because you are mine,' he growls, gripping my wrists and pinning them against the counter.

Is this for real?

Because it's like he's tapped into my own personal dominant alpha fantasy.

Urgent, fevered lips seek my throat, pressing hard, but with contrastingly tender kisses across my jugular. In this second, I'm reminded of his power. His capability. He's a soldier. A trained killer. And the knowledge he's about to break his own moral code for me is kryptonite.

'Yes, Archie. I'm yours.'

'And I take care of what's mine, Victoria, right?' Bergamot and sweat hang heavily in the air between us. I suck it in, revelling in his carnal scent.

'Are those needs getting to you again?' His grip on my right wrist relaxes and his finger sweeps over my spine, sending goosebumps rippling over my entire body. My nipples are like bullets beneath my dress. Bullets that are begging to be fired.

I nod, unable to trust myself to speak.

With one short sharp tug, he unties the bow at the base of my neck. My dress slithers down my body, revealing my breasts in all their braless glory.

He takes a step back, his gaze chasing the fabric as it slides past my hips and all the way to the floor, leaving me in only a navy silk thong and the Manolo Blahniks.

'So fucking beautiful, baby.' His tongue dips out over his lower lip and the bulge in his suit trousers doubles in size.

Since forever, the word 'baby' has been a source of discontent for me. Being the youngest of three sisters, I've always been babied.

But from Archie's lips, it sounds like 'welcome home.' It rolls from his tongue like the most erotic endearment.

'But you do need to be taught a lesson so you never forget who you belong to ever again.' He swipes a finger over the silk of the thong. 'Nobody else touches this, okay?'

I nod again, swallowing the saliva flooding my mouth.

'Open your legs for me, there's a good girl.' I do as he asks, praying I don't combust with lust while he slips off his suit jacket, slinging it across one of the dining room chairs.

This entire scenario is hot as fuck and he's barely laid a finger on me.

I'm under no illusion he's about to torture me again. To make me beg. I'll do it shamelessly. I don't care. The entire world fades to nothing when he's in front of me like this.

Deft fingers roll up the sleeves of his white shirt, revealing enough thick veins on his tanned forearms to mark out a road map.

He radiates promise, expertise and power, circling me, eyes searing a blazing path across my bare skin, over my breasts and right the way down to my stilettos and up again. But he doesn't touch me. My nipples ache with longing as he blows a long, slow breath over them and watches them tighten further.

Firm, fiery lips finally reach my skin, trailing over my neck and collarbone.

'Kiss me.' Did I mention I wasn't averse to begging?

'No.' Calloused hands grip my waist and my head rolls back as he presses himself against me. 'I'm going to drive you to the edge, the same way you have done to me since I got here. Then I'm going to tip you over that edge until you shatter into a million pieces. And even when you finally manage to put yourself back together, you'll never be the same again. You'll be mine.'

My sex clenches in anticipation. I could grow to like this kind of punishment.

'Then I'm going to do it to you again. And again. Until you don't know anything but my name.'

Archie drops to his knees and tugs the silk scrap to the side, laying me bare for him.

How is this god-like creature on his knees for me? It should be me kneeling for him, trying to make up for tonight. With any luck, I'll get to that shortly.

Our eyes lock as his face inches towards my sex. It's the hottest thing I've ever witnessed. His tongue darts out again, but instead of licking his own lips, he licks mine slowly and deliberately before pulling away once more. My greedy hips buck, desperate for more.

'You're in for a long night, baby. The exact same duration you made me suffer through that toffy twat pawing all over you.' A wicked grin curls at his lips before his flat, wide tongue swipes across me again.

It's heaven.

It's hell.

It's everything.

'Like that, do you?' Big blue eyes mock me.

'You know I do.' My thighs tighten beneath his grip and, as if in reward for my honesty, his tongue extends, this time offering several long, slow strokes.

His hot breath rushes against my clit as he inserts a finger inside me. 'Oh, baby, you are so wet. It's taking every bit of control I have not to slam my cock into you.'

Another moan gurgles from my lips as he retracts his finger, popping it into his mouth and sucking like it's the sweetest lollipop he ever tasted.

'So sweet. So sexy. I'm going to need more of that.' His tongue finds me again, sweeping up and down the length of my sensitive spot, driving me closer and closer to oblivion. My release builds inside, thighs clenching and tightening, wave upon wave of pleasure cresting on the horizon, but seconds before I crash deliciously over the edge, he stills and stops.

My cry is animalistic. 'Archie, please.'

His chuckle vibrates against my sex. 'Who do you belong to?'

'You.' I can't get the word out quickly enough.

'You're learning.' His tongue resumes those delicious strokes, igniting every nerve ending I own.

The world as I know it spins, tilting on its axis, turning everything inside out in blistering, chaotic glory. Hot white tingling sensations blaze through every cell as blood roars through my ears. I convulse and writhe, delirious with desire, shattering spectacularly in a hot, rushing shower of relief before finally breaking.

When my legs buckle beneath me, he catches me, lifting them up around his waist and cradling me against his chest.

'You are so fucking beautiful, baby,' he murmurs, pressing his mouth against mine.

I slump into his huge torso. 'Can we go to bed now?'

'No chance.' His palm slaps across my bare butt cheek. 'I told you, you're in for a long night. That barely covered the time you took to eat that starter. How do you think it made me feel, watching Harrison paw all over you?'

He carries me to the dining room table like I'm a bag of sugar instead of a ten stone woman. 'You still need to pay for that, lady.'

Placing me gently down onto the smooth, cool wood, he nudges me backwards until I'm flat on my back and my bum rests on the edge. Tugging my saturated underwear down to my ankles, he spreads me open, positioning my legs either side of him. Admiring the curve of my calf, his thumb hooks under my stilettos. 'You can keep these on for now.'

I'm still pulsing down there, recovering from the first earth-shattering release. There's no way I can hack another right now. 'Archie, I can't. It's so fucking sensitive down there. It's too soon.'

'I warned you, baby. You're not even halfway through this lesson yet.' Decadent lips blaze over my inner thigh and my treacherous vagina jolts to life again at the prospect of another blinding orgasm.

'I don't know if I can go again.' Even as the words tumble out, blood rushes below.

'Trust me to take care of you. It's my job, after all.' Those magnificent shoulders shrug and in this single fleeting moment, I know he's going to give me everything.

Fuck the rule book. He's composing his own after tonight. Enduring Harrison's less than gentlemanly behaviour was worth every second, because it led to this.

I trust Archie. With my life. With my body. With everything I am.

'Time for the main.' Sapphire twin pools rove over my clit before he captures it in his mouth. My pelvis jolts from the table. It's beyond sensitive. But his mouth doesn't leave me for a second.

I exhale hard, forcing my body to relax. If he's shown me one thing already, it's that the ten years he has on me have provided him with experience.

My stomach flips, imagining him doing this to others before me.

It won't happen again.

He's right. I am his. And he is mine.

I tilt upwards, allowing him easier access, vowing to take whatever he's giving. To enjoy every sensitive second. I've imagined him down here so many times, to watch his dirty blond hair bobbing up and down in his quest to tease and please me. It's almost enough to set me off again.

'So fucking responsive,' he murmurs against my swollen clit. 'I've imagined doing this to you so many fucking times.'

He's a mind reader.

That tongue flattens again, dipping across my entrance

and all the way up again. 'I'm probably going to hell for this, but I'm pretty sure I was going, anyway. How can something that feels so right be so wrong?'

My thighs tremble as my climax builds once again.

This time, he doesn't stop. He stretches his mouth wide across me and devours me like a man who hasn't eaten in weeks.

A million stars cloud my vision before bursting in front of me as I come harder than a freight train, calling out the name of the only man with the ability to do that to me.

I pant, floating back down to earth for the second time. 'You're unbelievably good at that.'

Archie presses a kiss on my inner thigh, fingers skimming my breasts.

'Is it time for dessert yet?' I inch off the table, straight onto his lap, undoing his shirt buttons one by one.

'Hungry little thing tonight, aren't you?' Rough hands catch mine, stilling them. 'Remember who's in charge here.'

'Let me make it up to you.' My fingers flutter over his forearms.

'No. I haven't finished with your lesson yet. Get back on that table so I can bang some sense into you.'

A thrill of anticipation shivers over my spine as I inch backwards on shaky legs, watching as Archie prises open the thick leather belt on his suit trousers. The zip practically flies down by itself beneath the swelling pressure of his huge thick cock, which bursts out.

He's beautiful. Enormous. Engorged. And mine for the taking, finally.

My greedy hands reach out for him, stroking, caressing, admiring.

'You're gorgeous, Archie. Please take the shirt off. Let me see you,'

I plead, pumping his length with my hand. His head rolls

backwards as his fingers reach for the buttons of his shirt, undoing them one by one.

He slips the white cotton from his shoulders but hesitates before fully removing it.

A flash of vulnerability flickers across his face.

His scars.

Archie Mason, the most stunning example of masculinity I've ever laid eyes on, is self-conscious?

I've seen them all before, but that morning when he slipped into my bed when I was having a night terror, he was more concerned with trying to hide his boner than his burns.

Maybe I'm not the only one who needs teaching a lesson tonight.

I nudge his shirt down further, exposing his sculpted pecs and the perfect planes of his stomach. My fingers trace the trail of italic writing inked across his chest. Jones. Brady. Hanson. I don't dwell on the meaning of it, but I instinctively know it's not a happy story.

The guy could pass as a goddamn male model, and it seems as though he's the only one who doesn't know it.

As my lips fall to the fibrous scar tissue, he flinches. I give him a second to adjust to the sensation before trailing kisses across each and every mark on his perfect torso.

'Victoria.' That warning tone again. He pushes me backwards onto the table, his fingers finding my sweet spot again.

'Archie, I need you.' Desperation hangs on my every word.

'There are condoms in my room,' he says, but neither of us moves to get them.

'I'm on the pill. How are you fixed?' Does everyone ask in a roundabout way if the person they're about to let inside their body has had a recent sexual health screening or is it a doctor thing?

'I'll tell you exactly how I'm fixed.' Archie rubs the tip of his cock against my slick entrance and a moan caresses my throat. 'I've been fixed on you for years, so much so that there hasn't been anyone in my bed for over two years.'

'Really? And there was me thinking you couldn't stand the sight of me. Every time I walked into a room at Huxley Castle, you got up and left.' He nudges into me but nowhere near deeply enough, pausing to observe my utter undoing from above.

'I had to leave. Sitting through dinner with your family with an enormous erection was inappropriate.' He gives me another inch. 'Think anyone would miss this? It's pretty hard to ignore.'

'But why didn't you come here with me all those years ago?' It's the one question I promised myself I wouldn't ask him, but all the cards are on the table, spread wide like my shaking limbs.

Earnest eyes glint as he looks down to where our bodies join in a decadent display of exactly why. 'I didn't trust myself.'

'And you do now, clearly?' My walls clench around his length and he groans.

'You're older now. Old enough to know what you want, even if we both should know better.'

'I know exactly what I want, Archie Mason. The question is, will you stop talking and finally give it to me?'

He drives into me, over and over again as my nails pierce the skin of his firm, toned backside. Slam after slam assaults me in the most exhilarating experience of my life. I've never known sex like it.

Our bodies mould as one, eyes lock, speaking our own silent language as we give each other everything we've got.

The world crashes to nothing around me as I peak for the third time, free-falling into the most addictive oblivion.

Archie grips my hips, pinning me on the table as he finishes seconds after me.

Ragged panting fills the air between us.

'Well, that was certainly worth the wait.' He scoops me from the table and carries me upstairs.

Chapter Twenty
ARCHIE

I wake in Victoria's bed for the second time in my life, just as well rested as the first time. The only item I'm still wearing, other than Victoria herself, is my dog tag, chain, and platinum St. Christopher pendant.

Warm, wandering fingers flutter over my pecs, pausing for a second on the metal. 'Do you always sleep with this on?'

'Yes.'

'Does everyone in the army wear a St. Christopher?' Victoria asks.

'No. It was a gift from my sister when I enrolled.'

Her fingers stroke the misshapen metal. 'No offence, but it looks like it's seen better days.'

'It was bent by a bullet. It saved my life.'

'What?' Victoria props herself up onto her elbow.

'A few months into my second tour, we were drawn into a frenzied fire fight. One of the corporals was badly injured. I scooped him up and carried him seven kilometres back to camp, still under heavy fire. I took a bullet, but I was saved by my St. Christopher. Call it luck or fate, but I wouldn't be here today without it.'

'Wow. My hero.' She swoons exaggeratedly. 'So, is this like a lucky charm now?'

A shiver of unease ripples over me. 'No, it's actually supposed to be a reminder not to break the rules.'

She arches a questioning eyebrow. 'How's that going for you?'

'Not as well as I'd planned, clearly.' A heaviness weighs on my chest and I'm not talking about Victoria's lithe body. Still, I can't bring myself to regret what happened between us. That woman is so far under my skin, there's no way it could ever have ended any other way.

She snuggles further back into me, wriggling that perfect naked ass over my morning glory.

'Careful, you're about to start something you might not be able to finish.' My lips brush against her ear. In response, she reaches round, grabs my cock and squeezes it.

'Oh Archie, I told you before, I always finish everything I start. You don't ever need to worry about that.' She flips round, pushing me onto my back. Long, toned thighs slip either side of my hips as she straddles herself on my cock.

She glides over the length of me, taking every inch like a goddess. 'You're soaking.'

'Tends to happen when you're close by.' Thick lashes dance over her cheekbones.

This time it's slower. Less frantic. Languid. Loving. Familiar. And still so fucking addictive.

My fingers can't stay away from those pert, round breasts. I can't get enough of her. I'll never be able to get enough of her. Hooded eyes gaze down at me, glassy with pleasure. She ups her pace, grinding me, working me until her walls clench and we shudder together. She flops onto my chest, clammy and satiated, for now at least.

My lips press against her forehead. 'What a way to start the day.'

'Thank God I'm not on shift.' She snuggles in tighter.

I wrap my arms around her and exhale a heavy sigh. It's one of satisfaction.

Sleep has been an issue since my final tour, but with Victoria wrapped in my arms, her heart beating against mine, it's no longer a problem.

Two weeks pass and we create a new routine, one that seems to satisfy both of our needs. Sex, sleep, hospital shifts, classroom lectures, dinner, more sex, more sleep and the occasional glass of wine.

The long days she's on shift, I cook, draw her a bath and wash every inch of her silky skin. It's the least I can do when she takes care of people all day, but that's not why I do it. I do it because I've got an increasing suspicion I've finally found my true purpose in this life. What I was born to do. Worship Victoria Sexton.

I'm living out my own personal fantasy and every time the shame creeps in, I remind myself of Victoria's motto. Tomorrow is promised to none of us.

Do I feel guilty for being paid to be here?

Yes, of course, even though I haven't touched a penny of the salary Ryan wired to my account. I've never slept with a ward before. It's the most unprofessional thing a bodyguard can do.

But even with our illicit relationship, if that's what it even is (we've yet to put a label on it), Victoria is in less danger than she would be if she was traipsing around every bar and nightclub in Edinburgh looking for someone to quench her "needs."

She's never out of my sight.

Her house is more secure than it was before I arrived.

She's excelling at her assignments and thriving in her practical work at the hospital.

At this precise moment, our relationship isn't affecting my ability to do my job.

Would Ryan and Sasha see it that way? Probably not. But I'm trying not to dwell on it. The Irish Sea between us is particularly helpful in that respect. If they knew how much I cared about her, how serious I am about her, maybe they could be persuaded our union isn't the worst thing in the world. Maybe.

It's essential we're careful how we act around each other in public because of the ever-present paparazzi, though lately things have calmed down simply because she's not out partying as much. It seems she's found a superior form of entertainment at home.

Harrison is avoiding both of us at the hospital. He wore a surgical mask for the entire week after our encounter, but even that failed to hide the purple bruising beneath his eyes.

Doctor Dickhead continues to be a little overfamiliar for my taste, but after the prisoner incident, I keep my eye on him at all times. A fact he's only too aware of.

Victoria breezes into the living room where I'm lighting a fire, her hair still damp from the shower. 'I'm cooking for you tonight.'

'Is it my birthday?' The kindling bursts into orange flames, along with my insides, every time she's near.

What we have is the real deal. It is for me, anyway.

'Yeah, your fiftieth, isn't it?' Two firm fingers pinch my bum as I load another log onto the pile.

'Very funny. I'll have you know that's next year,' I joke.

Seriously, I'm thirty-four. Most of my friends, the ones I didn't accidentally lead to their death on my final tour, are married, or settled at least.

I never gave my own future much thought, but the idea of

actually having one that involves settling down is beginning to crop up more regularly.

Which is ludicrous, because apart from the fact we've only been sleeping together for a couple of weeks, Victoria is at a totally different stage of her life entirely.

I suck in a deep, smoky breath.

One day at a time.

My phone rings in my pocket. I silently will it not to be Ryan. He checks in once a week, and Victoria speaks to her sisters almost daily. None of them suspects there's anything going on between us, as far as I'm aware.

We haven't lied, but we're not being honest, and that's not something I'm comfortable with. Right now, though, my own selfish desires outweigh anything else, and thankfully Victoria appears to feel the same.

Pierce's name pops up on the screen.

Ryan's senior security guy has been with the family even longer than me. Big, broad and as bald as a coot, he bagged himself a wife last year, marrying the manager of Huxley Castle, Sasha's childhood friend, Meghan.

I press my finger over my lips to silence Victoria, who pretends to zip her mouth closed.

'Pierce, how's it going, man?'

'It's going great, thanks. How are things in bonnie Scotland?' His American drawl seems more obvious over the phone than in person.

'Oh, you have no idea. I have my work cut out with Victoria Sexton.' My shins receive a short, sharp kick, wiping the smirk straight from my face.

'I heard she's a wild one, alright. You'd want to be in the best of health to keep up with her,' he sniggers.

'You can say that again. Still, there have been no more nightclub shootings, so I guess that's one plus.'

'Look, I know you weren't keen on taking the job in Edinburgh in the first place, so I wanted to give you a heads up. Ryan's employed three new security staff. They came highly recommended by Jayden. If you want to come home, it would be the perfect time to voice it.'

A frown flickers across Victoria's face for a split second before she collects herself.

'Thanks for thinking of me.' I hesitate, acutely aware Victoria is listening to every word.

'I know it's a bit awkward with Victoria being Sasha's little sister. Do you want me to say something to Ryan?' he offers.

Victoria swallows hard, eyes trained on the floor.

'You know, Pierce, we've kind of settled into a routine here. It seems a bit unfair to rock the boat, you know?'

'That's good.' Pierce clears his throat. 'I just wanted you to know there are options. I know Ryan feels bad for forcing you into the position. If you approached him now the immediate threat is over, he'd definitely reassign you back here. Huxley Castle isn't the same without you.'

I pause for a beat, trying to gather the right words. 'Maybe it's exactly what I needed. To be forced out of my comfort zone.'

'Well, don't get too comfortable over there. There are two tiny four-year-olds robbing me blind with their fucking swear jar,' Pierce grumbles good-naturedly.

A familiar high-pitched voice shrieks in the background. 'I heard that! You owe us a fiver,' Bella demands.

My heart constricts in my chest. I love those little douchebags. But not nearly as much as I love their aunty.

Love? Fuck, yes. Who am I kidding? I was half in love with her before I even got here. Not that I'm going to tell her that. She'd probably run a mile, or twenty, knowing her athletic capabilities.

While we're perfectly compatible in the bedroom, the couch, the shower, and the dining room table, I'm still aware of our major differences in social class. Okay, financially, I'm comfortable, but I wasn't raised in a damn castle. My family has zero fame or influence and I don't have a single GCSE, let alone a fucking degree in medicine.

Would she be prepared to introduce me to her doctor friends as her boyfriend and not her bodyguard? I don't know.

'Is that Archie?' Blake's voice cuts across in the background.

'Yep. Want to talk to him?' Pierce offers.

'Archie?' I imagine Blake snatching the phone out of Pierce's hand.

'Hi buddy, how are you getting on?' My pitch changes totally, enough for Victoria to arch her eyebrows in surprise. Peeping at me through those thick ebony eyelashes, relief floods her face. Apparently, she's not tiring of me just yet. Thank God, because I'm nowhere near tired of her.

'I miss you,' Blake whines. 'But we make more money out of Pierce. He says loads of bad words. Even more than you. Also, he's no good at baseball. When are you coming home?'

How can I explain that here with his aunty, I feel more at home the last few weeks than I've ever done in my life?

'I'll be home in the summer, okay?' I look at Victoria and raise my hands in a question. She nods.

'Aww, summer is ages away,' Blake huffs.

'Think how much money you'll have made off Pierce by then.' Fingers roam over the stubble dotting my jawline. Summer. Will we come out as a couple? We'll have to. I need this to be okay with Ryan and Sasha. I don't want to live in the shadows. Even if it will cause untold amounts of ructions at first.

How are we going to play this?

The funny thing is, I'm not playing at all.

Is Victoria?

Blake contemplates for a minute. 'Hmmm. Okay. Will you bring me back a present?'

Got to admire the kid's ability to say whatever's on his mind. Maybe the world would be a simpler place if we all did that.

Or maybe it might cause another war.

'I think I can arrange that. Want to speak to your Aunty Vic?'

'Sure, is she there?' His voice ricochets with excitement.

'I'll find her for you. She's here somewhere.' I press a kiss to Victoria's lips as she takes the phone. Cooing over the line, she lashes a mountain of praise and encouragement on her nephew, then her niece, promises she'll play baseball with them in the summer, then returns the phone to me.

After bidding Pierce and the twins goodbye, I hang up and check the fire.

'So,' Victoria hovers behind me.

'So?' My fingers grip her waist, pulling her against me.

'You looking for a reassignment?' Her tone's teasing, but there's an undercurrent of concern.

'The only assignment I'm looking for is between your legs.' My palms roam over the swell of her hips and across the Lycra leggings.

At least these days we don't have to run fourteen miles to strike up a conversation.

'You didn't want to come here.' It's not a question.

'You know that. And you know why. It's not because I didn't want you, it's because I did.'

She nods, like she still doesn't fully trust it. Trust what we have. Like she's looking for validation. Those three little words swirl on the tip of my tongue, itching to fly off and out into the world where they can never be taken back.

Is it too soon?

A sigh slips out in their place.

Taking her wrists, I place her hands on my shoulders and tilt her chin upwards, forcing her to look at me. A vulnerability lurks in those gold-flecked eyes.

'Victoria, I told you I didn't sleep with another woman for two years before I got here. If that doesn't tell you enough, I don't know what will.'

'It's just you're so sophisticated. You're savvy enough to read a room the second you walk into it. You even cook better than Gordon fucking Ramsay himself, and you manage to ooze masculinity in the process. I can barely make it through a day in A&E without flopping on the couch...Whatever this thing between us is, I just hope I'm...' She swats the air between us.

This thing between us is everything. That's what it is. To me, at least.

'What do you want this thing to be?' She has to call it, not me. She's ten years younger than me. She has her whole life ahead of her. The reality is, she probably won't want to be tied to me. Not long term. I might be a chapter in her romance novel. She's my entire book.

I search her face for whatever it is she's trying to tell me. For a man who can read the room, I'm not doing very well reading what's right in front of my eyes because I'd nearly swear this goddess before me is exhibiting signs of insecurity, but that can't be right. 'Talk to me, Vic.'

Her voice is barely more than a whisper. 'Sometimes I worry I'm not enough for you.'

'Not enough? You're kidding, right? You're everything I ever wanted. All I've ever wanted.'

I lift her up and she wraps her thighs around my waist. Now is not the time to hold back, clearly. 'I'm falling head over heels in love with you.'

Her hot lips crash against mine and she kisses me like she's drowning. Our mouths tear frenziedly against one another. Her tongue strokes mine, devouring, consuming, cementing our connection.

She pulls back all too soon. 'You're not the only one falling, Archie. Don't ever dream of getting reassigned anywhere, okay?'

'Yes, ma'am,' I mutter into her mouth.

Her hands palm the back of my neck. 'So, summer at the castle?'

'Well, where else were you planning on spending the holidays? I presume you have to wait for registration after graduation or something?'

'Yeah, then I have another two years' residency to do as a junior.'

'Here?' An image of my cabin at Huxley Castle flashes through my mind.

'Not necessarily. Maybe Ireland. I'll have to put in my applications immediately after graduation and see what I get offered. It'll be a long summer waiting at Huxley Castle.' Pearly white teeth capture her lower lip, nibbling on whatever she's about to say next. I gather it's not about work. 'I hate lying to my sisters, Arch. Like, if this thing between us is serious, as I hope it is, perhaps we should just tell Sasha Ryan we're together?'

Hazel pools swirl with longing before me and my instinctive reaction is to give this woman whatever she wants. Everything she wants, whenever she wants. But I'm not sure this is her best idea.

'Then the reassignment might be taken out of my hands.' The thought of another man living here with Victoria is too much to bear. 'You only have a few more months before graduation. Let's do it after the graduation ceremony. That extra time will give us a lot more credibility when we do come out. Plus, they can't be mad at us on your grad, right?'

They probably can, but at least they'll have to hold their

tongues until the next day, which might leave a few hours to recover from the shock.

Her gaze zeroes in on my mouth. 'When? Not if?'

'When.' My tone is staunch, but even as I say the word, I feel the weight of it. I refuse to fully contemplate the repercussions telling Ryan might bring. He's become like a brother to me these past few years.

Will having the woman I want cost me my place in her family? The only family I've ever really known. Or if I can keep her safe until graduation, and then prove how much I love her, will that be enough?

Chapter Twenty-One
VICTORIA

'Sherri Fitzpatrick?' I call the next patient in from the waiting area. We're short-staffed. Three nurses called in sick with a stomach bug, and the place is overrun with patients. Even more so than usual.

A red-haired woman stands, a distant look in her olive eyes. With a grimace, she motions for a little girl next to her to get up. The child has her mother's eyes and the same bone structure. Her strawberry blonde hair is plaited into two neat braids that drape across her pink duffle coat.

She's about the same age I was when I lost my parents, which is the last thought that pops through my head before Sherri Fitzpatrick's body hits the floor.

Archie leaps from his position a few feet away to assist me. 'Doctor Dickson!' My voice is fraught with emotion. I've never seen this mother and daughter before, but I'm already overly invested in their well-being.

'Mum? Mum?' the child screeches, dropping to the floor and shaking her mother's shoulders.

'Stand back, sweetheart.' A maternal instinct I didn't realise I possessed kicks in, overriding my usual instinct to tend to the wounded. I reach for the little girl, pulling her to her feet and in the direction of a private family waiting area. Doctor Dickson and another SHO are more than capable of attending to her mother.

The child's small hand slips into mine, but her neck cranes over her shoulder. 'Don't look, pet. The doctors are helping your mammy.' I send up a silent prayer that I'm right. The sudden vacant look in her eye appeared pretty final to me. Aneurism? Head trauma? Fuck.

'What's your name, sweetheart?' Archie asks, flanking the other side of the child's tiny body.

'Lily-May.' It's little more than a whisper.

In the family room, I find Lily-May a book to read while Archie fetches her a bar of chocolate and an apple juice from the vending machine.

Within minutes, Doctor Dickson appears in the doorway.

He looks at me and then at Lily-May, and bows his head, a look of resignation in his eye. Sherri Fitzpatrick is gone.

The waiting room is overflowing with patients, many of whom are understandably distraught at what they've just witnessed. I have no choice but to go back to the ward. But I can't bear to tear myself away from Lily-May. I feel her pain so acutely, as if it's my own. It was my own once.

Archie's fingers brush across my spine. 'I'll stay with her until a family member comes,' he promises.

'I'll get one of the nurses to check her over. I think she's in shock,' I whisper in his ear before kneeling and enveloping Lily-May in a tight embrace. 'I'm here if you need me, sweetheart. The receptionist is contacting your family. Someone will come soon, okay?'

My legs weigh a tonne as I force them to walk away.

. . .

That night, I lie on the couch, my conscience torturing me with what I should have done. Could have done. Sherri might still be alive if A&E hadn't been so busy, and she'd been seen quicker.

Archie pulls me onto his lap, cradling me like a baby. 'There's nothing you could have done.' He's uncannily good at reading my mind, as well as the room.

'I don't know. Maybe if I'd...'

A strong hand cups my chin, tilting my head upwards to face him. 'Look at me, Vic. It wasn't your fault.'

Lily-May's cries for her mammy repeatedly ring through my ears.

My palms cup a tumbler of whiskey, rolling it between them. 'I just wish...' I can't even articulate what I wish.

'I know, believe me, I get it. More than you'll ever know.' Archie swirls his whiskey around his own glass.

Physically, I'm here, but mentally, I can't leave that ward. 'Who came for Lily-May?'

'Social services. They're still looking for a relative.' His eyes flicker with understanding. He knows. 'You were seven when your mother passed.' It's a statement, not a question.

I nod, lifting the glass to my lips. It burns, but nowhere near as much as my heart burns for that child.

'It was at that exact age I decided to become a doctor. Even though they couldn't save my parents, they saved me. It changed me forever. Inspired me. What have I inspired that child to do? Nothing. That's what.'

'You can't save them all, Vic.' His tone is full of compassion.

'Says the war hero.'

He knocks back the remnants of his drink in one large gulp. Glassy eyes stare into the distance. 'I'm no hero.'

'Of course you are. You even have medals to prove it.'

They might be tucked away in his bedside locker, but they're his.

'I should have handed them back. I don't deserve them.' Nudging me from his lap, he crosses the room and returns with the whiskey bottle to top us both up.

'Archie, why would you say such a thing? Everyone speaks so highly of you. Says how amazingly well you coped with what happened when you were in the army. Positive. Hopeful. Unscarred, mentally at least.' He flops back on the leather beside me. My fingers instinctively trace over the mottled skin lining his left shoulder.

'Is that what you think?' he snorts, brushing my hand from his body. 'Those are nothing compared to what's on the inside. I just hide it better than most, Vic. We all have our demons. Smile often, crack a few jokes, and most people don't notice.'

The doorbell rings. We exchange a wary look.

Archie pulls up the security camera linked to his phone, and a whiskey-scented sigh whooshes from his mouth. 'You've got company.'

He angles the screen so I can see. Libby and Mel stand, hopping from foot to foot, at the front door, their faces barely visible behind an enormous bouquet of flowers and a bottle of wine.

Archie goes to the door and my friends traipse up the stairs like a herd of noisy elephants. I don't get up, instead, simply pat the couch next to me. The spot Archie just vacated.

'We heard what happened on the ward today.' Libby dumps the blooming lilies on the coffee table and throws her arms around me.

'The whole campus is talking about it,' Mel sympathises.

'It wasn't your fault,' they say simultaneously.

Archie fetches two wine glasses and pours from the bottle they brought. 'That's what I've been trying to tell her.'

Libby's head whips round quick enough to snap her neck. Sharp blue eyes volley between Archie and me.

'Oh my God. You two have had sex.' Her fingers fly over her mouth like she can't believe she said the words out loud.

'What? No.' It's a battle to muster the energy to deny it. My cheeks singe and, despite the harrowing horrors of the day, a small smile tugs at my lips. I bite it back, but not before they notice.

'So this is why you've been refusing my invitations to party!' Mel's index finger pokes me directly in the sternum.

Archie is suddenly intrigued by the contents of his glass.

'You want to practice your poker face, guys. I can only imagine what Sasha will say when she realises her baby sister is banging the bodyguard.' Libby slaps my thigh gleefully. 'Tell us everything.'

'Is he as capable as he looks?' Mel squeals, running her fingers through her scarlet spiky hair and sloshing wine over my leather couch.

She speaks about my boyfriend as if he isn't standing his allocated five feet away.

Boyfriend.

The word doesn't do justice to what Archie is to me. He's become my closest confidant. My best friend. Running partner. And lover. All in a matter of weeks. Well, I suppose there are the last five years we unknowingly pined for each other to take into consideration too.

'Girls, I thought you came here to comfort me, not interrogate me.'

'We came to distract you, sweetie, but clearly someone beat us to it.' Libby raises her glass in a silent cheers, flicking her long blonde ponytail from her shoulder.

Archie shrugs and makes himself scarce while I share a couple of drinks with my amazing girlfriends.

Today's loss doesn't leave me, but the company of my two favourite friends eases my sorrows, for a short while at least. Listening to their shared experiences, the patients they've lost, helps to bring home what I already know. What Archie said. We can't save them all.

But the lives I can't save always mentally morph into my parents. And today, I morphed into that little girl, Lily-May.

Mel and Libby leave just before midnight. I'm exhausted, mentally, emotionally and physically, but it still takes an age to nod off. Lily-May's face is the last face I see before I fall into a fitful sleep, and it's the first one I see when I wake up to my own screams ricocheting around the room.

Archie's comforting arms are wrapped around my thrashing, sweaty body. 'It's okay. It's okay. I've got you.' Strong hands smooth back the hair that sticks to my face.

'I'm so sorry.' The night terrors have plagued me for as long as I can remember. In my dreams, I'm falling into an endless darkness. Oblivion. Like the car I was in when it plummeted off the side of a cliff.

It was a miracle I survived. Though I don't have outward scars like Archie, I can definitely relate to the inner ones he talked about.

Turning on the crumpled sheet, I nuzzle my cheeks against the smooth ridges of his bare chest, the pads of my fingers returning to the uneven scars lining his shoulder. 'What did you mean earlier when you said you should have given back those medals?'

He exhales, running his fingers through my hair. 'I've never really spoken about it before.'

'Do you want to?'

'Not particularly. It's not something I'm proud of, but I

don't want any secrets between us.' His sombre words float above my head.

Taking comfort in his arms, I wait silently, willing him to tell me.

He shuffles closer. 'I'd been in the Middle East for two years. I was the youngest sergeant to make rank. I was surrounded by a great team who were like brothers to me. I had a shitty upbringing, as you know. My mother died in labour and my father couldn't stand the sight of me. I joined the army to serve and protect my country, to prove my life, and that my mother's death wasn't in vain.'

My heart bleeds for him. I can relate.

'We were days away from leaving the town we'd been stationed at. The locals were safe. The rebels departed. We were over the worst. Or, so we thought.' He swallows hard through the darkness.

'I sanctioned an off-the-books spin to a neighbouring town. It was my nephew, Jason's thirteenth birthday coming up and I wanted to post my St. Christopher pendant to him. The newspapers picked up the story about how the bullet had grazed my pendant and saved my life. They depicted me as some sort of national hero. I wanted Jason to have it.'

I peel my cheek from his chest, our eyes locking through the moonlight. 'That was noble.'

'It wasn't.' He shakes his head. The moonlight creeping through the cracks in the curtains casts a dim light, revealing a haunted look on his face. 'That pendant was more than just a pendant to me. It was physical proof my life mattered, even though I'd been responsible for my mother's death. I wanted him to have it because I knew he'd show my father and prove to him I was a hero, on the off chance he'd missed the media coverage.

'I was desperate to prove I'd become the man I was always meant to be. But instead, my egotistical selfish joyride put my men at risk. I'm responsible for their deaths, just as much as I'm responsible for my mother's death.'

His sorrowful eyes reach right in and grab my soul. 'What happened?'

'I drove over a landmine. The guys on the left side of the vehicle didn't stand a chance. I managed to pull out Jones, but he died in my arms shortly after.'

'Oh my God, Archie. I had no idea.' My fingers trace the names tattooed across his chest with a newfound understanding. 'It's not your fault. You didn't put that landmine there.'

He swallows hard. 'I may as well have done for all the difference it makes.'

'I wish I could crawl under your skin and take away all of your pain.' The ache in my heart is unrelenting.

'Baby, you already do. Most of it, anyway.' Firm lips seek mine in a slow, tender kiss equally full of promise and need.

Nudging me onto my back, he slips between my legs, caressing my mouth with his tongue while his palms roam across my breasts.

Pressing tiny kisses over my collarbone, he whispers, 'I wear that pendant as a reminder not to break the rules, but now look at me...' He shakes his head, but the kisses continue tracing lower and lower. 'I love you, Vic.'

'I love you, too. I've never loved a man before. In fact, I don't think I really even dated one. They were all boys in comparison. You and I... we're different. Bending the rules here is different. What harm can come to me with you in my bed?'

Even as the words slip out, I know the answer.

Because the man who protects me is the only man with any real power to hurt me. If he were to decide he couldn't do this anymore, that he didn't want me anymore, the pain would be the worst type of agony I could ever imagine.

'No one is going to harm you, baby. I promise.'

He shifts down the bed, nudging my thighs wider. Wide, smooth lips peck at my skin, dipping lower and lower below my navel until his mouth captures my sweet spot.

'I'll never get tired of doing this to you. Of teasing you and tasting you. You're mine, Vic. No one else is getting near you.' With every word, his hot breath brushes maddeningly against me.

'Archie, please.' My hips wriggle of their own accord.

'I suppose I am here to serve you.' The faint smile I hear in his tone is lost against my sex as his flat, assertive tongue runs rings around me. Thick fingers dip inside me, pumping slowly. I'm in sensory overload. It's so much more than sex. It's a union of two souls who truly see each other. It's a promise. It's a pact. It's everything.

Archie Mason has earned the title of my first love. I can only pray I'm lucky enough he'll be my last.

My thighs tremble as he quickens the pace with his swirling tongue. My fingers grasp at his cropped, mussed hair as the fireworks fizz and pop beneath my skin and the world explodes like a hot, white shooting star.

'Archie.' A moan slurs from my lips.

'For the record, I will never get tired of hearing you moan my name like that, either.' He crawls up my limp, tingling limbs and thrusts himself home in one deep long movement, stretching and filling me, drowning me in that pain/pleasure sensation that I've come to love.

My pelvis arches to take him deeper, walls clenching around him.

'You're right, you know,' he murmurs into my neck.

'I usually am, but about what specifically?' He pumps me harder, staring at me with an intensity that would melt metal. Ironic really, because that's what I had to do to him, melt that wall.

'How can something that feels so right possibly be

wrong?' Hooking my knee over his bicep, he stretches me wider, driving into my centre in a slow, deep, hypnotising rhythm. Flesh slides against flesh.

'I'm going to marry you one day, Vic. Just so you know.' His breath is ragged, his voice rough with need. It's almost more arousing than the way his swollen cock slams into me.

My body ripples around his. Every single cell inside me bursts to life. 'I'm counting on it.'

The familiar waves build and tighten. When his thumb circles my clit, I'm gone again, over the edge, into the most delicious, decadent oblivion. A climax that's so intense it's blinding. This time I'm not alone.

Archie's mouth meets mine as he spills every last drop of himself into me.

I crash on his chest again, the night terrors chased away by dreams of a future filled with love, hope and happiness.

Chapter Twenty-Two
ARCHIE

'Do we seriously have to go to Libby's?' I wait at the top of the landing, resting against the banister.

The prospect of another student party, especially a ridiculously posh one, is not my idea of a sizzling Saturday night.

Some of the medical students look down their noses at me so severely, I often do a double-take and wonder how the fuck I ended up where I did.

I didn't even sit my high school exams before I enrolled in the army.

I push away the niggle, forcing it to a box in my brain labelled 'don't go there.'

Victoria sweeps out of her bedroom in a sultry scented perfume cloud. *Our* bedroom is probably a more accurate description these days. We haven't slept apart in months. I've even moved my revolver into the bedside drawer on the left side of the bed, the bodyguard equivalent of leaving my underwear in the drawer. There's another one in the 'spare room' too, just in case.

In a black lace cocktail dress which moulds to her every curve like a pair of Spanx, Victoria is a fucking vision. Long silky hair bounces in loose waves over her shoulders and her porcelain skin shimmers with some sort of lotion that begs me to touch her.

'You look amazing.' I still can't believe the woman I've been fantasising about for years is actually mine. That it's possible we might have a future together, one that will allow us to have a relationship out in the open after she graduates.

'Thank you.' A splash of red colours her cheeks. 'You look pretty good yourself, you know.' I prefer the navy Boss suit, but I picked the black Armani because it seems to be her favourite.

'Seriously, Vic, I hate being a party pooper, but your friends are kind of a handful.' The club shooting that got me posted here in the first place appears to have been a one-off freak incident and, although there is no direct threat to Victoria's life as far as I'm aware, that's not to say there never will be.

Victoria would make an exceptional target for an opportunistic ransom kidnapping, thanks to her wealthy, famous family.

So nights like these, where there are hundreds of randoms milling round her, make me slightly nervous.

She links her arm in mine as we descend the stairs. 'That's why we're going early, before it gets rowdy. We'll show our faces and then leave. I can't just drop my friends, even if I would rather be having mind-blowing sex with my bodyguard.'

My lips brush over the scar on her clavicle. 'Mind-blowing sex sounds way more like it. You can keep the dress on. I'm gonna hitch it up around your waist and fuck you on the table in it.'

'For dessert, you can, but I made dinner reservations for us.'

'Dinner? Where?'

'It's a surprise.' Gold flecks of amusement glint in those warm eyes.

A semi-normal event like dinner out together is tempting, as long as the paps don't take over our night. 'A surprise? How am I meant to protect you if I don't know where we're going?'

'Oh Arch, I don't doubt you'd manage to protect me if you were a hundred miles away.'

It's my biggest fear. My worst nightmare, not being here if something happens. It's probably why I don't feel as guilty as I should about our relationship, because I get to be with my ward, even in her bed at night.

'I'll never be a hundred miles from you,' I promise, straightening my jacket. 'Dinner sounds nice. If you think you can control yourself in public.' I'm only half joking.

The air fizzes. Our mutual attraction is showing no sign of waning. My hand reaches beneath the dress, swiping between her legs. The scrap of lace covering her sex is flimsy enough to be ripped, which is exactly what I plan on doing the second we get back to the house.

She shamelessly grabs my cock through my suit trousers, gripping my erection. 'More like you'll need to control yourself. What would the world say if those sneaky paps got a shot of this?'

'They'd say you're fucking beautiful and I'm only human,' I shrug as I bang the front door closed behind us and open the car door for her. 'I'd probably still get the sack, though.'

.

Libby greets Victoria with a double-cheek kiss at her penthouse door. I step back before she attempts to offer the same to me. We're in public and I'm the paid protection, not her friend's boyfriend, and she'd do well to remember it.

I scan the room behind the women as they complement each other on their fashion choices.

The apartment layout might be familiar, but the crowd of faces is ever changing, although they all emit a similar aura of arrogance, snobbery and entitlement.

I have nothing in common with any of these people.

It's a miracle Victoria's so normal, given her family background. So unassuming. The opposite of self-important. She has a heart the size of the Atlantic Ocean and that's what makes her so fucking beautiful, and even more of an easy target if someone were to try to take advantage. It's not going to happen. Not on my watch.

I follow Victoria as she walks into a huge living area and a sea of bodies bumping along to a loud disco beat. The scent of excessive aftershave and alcohol hangs in the air.

A champagne fountain offers more drinks than a wedding. We pause at the table while Victoria helps herself to a gin and tonic.

My eyes land on a pair of fucking bronze sculptures. Materialistic crap. They give me the creeps.

That floppy-haired, bent-nosed neanderthal Harrison approaches us, pushing through the crowd of smiling faces until he reaches Victoria. It's not the sculptures giving me the creeps after all.

Victoria stiffens as she spots him. I step forwards, inserting myself between them before he reaches us.

'Dog.' Even though the term is derogatory, Harrison enunciates it with a certain level of begrudging respect this time. In a Ralph Lauren polo shirt and drainpipe designer jeans, he looks every bit the posh twat.

'I thought I warned you already.' My voice is dangerously low. In fairness, he's stayed well away from Victoria at the hospital.

Harrison's Adam's apple bobs up and down as he swallows

hard. 'I know. I've been working up the courage to apologise for weeks. I'm so sorry about that night.' He shuffles from one wanky over-priced loafer to the other. 'I had too much to drink. I didn't know what I was doing. I never meant to hurt you, V.'

V? Seriously? Do I need to break his legs as well as his nose?

'You shouldn't have put your hands on me. There's no excuse for that.' Victoria's head peeps from round my shoulder.

'Never put your hands on a woman again unless she asks you to, got it?' I hiss. My chest squares against him, leaving him in no doubt that I'll cheerfully crush him like a nut in a metal cracker given half the chance.

Harrison tilts his head in her direction. 'You know, perhaps we could...'

'No.' My growl is more beast than dog.

Harrison steps back. Finally. 'See you around,' he mutters, before slinking off.

My slow, controlled exhale is one of relief. 'Can we go yet?'

'Ten minutes. Let me find Mel and say hi, then we'll go for dinner.' Victoria brushes past me, her breasts grazing lingeringly against my arm. From her mischievous expression, it's no accident. I've a good mind to take her to the bathroom, but that would only delay our departure.

I catch her wrist, thumb gently stroking over it. 'I distinctly remember you promising to always finish what you start.'

She rises onto her tiptoes to lean into my ear, her hot breath teasing my earlobe. 'Oh, I will. Think of it as delayed gratification.'

Harrison's death stare stabs at me from across the room. Enlightenment dawns in his widening eyes. Fuck him. I trust his apology as far as I can throw him. And he looks like one heavy fucker.

I tail Victoria as she searches for Mel, forcing my eyes to stop straying to her perfect ass and keep watch on the crowd. Is it them I don't trust? Or myself to do my job? Either way, the quicker we escape, the better.

The second we're back in the SUV, Victoria's hungry mouth ravages mine. Fingers scour over my trousers, gripping my thigh.

'Careful, Vic, or you're about to get banged in the SUV.'

'Promises, promises.' A giggle pierces the air between us. 'I've never had car sex before.'

'We'll have to rectify that. Not here though.' I fire up the engine and switch on Victoria's seat warmer.

'Head towards East Fountainbridge. It'll be easier to park there. We can walk up.'

'The Witchery again?' I guess.

'Yes. It's only fair. The food was fabulous, although I can't say the same about the company the last time. Tonight, I'm going to have the best of both.'

'I hope you don't feel like you had to do this.' The idea that Victoria feels like she owes me or has to make up for something isn't one that I relish. She might have booked it, but no way is she paying.

'I want to go to The Witchery with my boyfriend. It should have been *our* first date that night. I'm so sorry I put you through that.'

'Don't be. If you hadn't pushed me to boiling point, I'd still be tiptoeing around your bedroom, sniffing your knickers while you slept.' It's an effort to keep a straight face as her jaw drops to her lap.

A laugh splutters from her chest as the back of her hand smacks my arm. 'Dirtbag.'

'I'm *your* dirtbag, baby.'

'Yep, just not quite a teenage one.' The same hand falls to my thigh and squeezes.

'Does my age bother you?' I might never get a better opportunity to ask, and the thought has crossed my mind a couple of times.

'With age comes experience, something which you have in spades.' Her voice takes on a husky tone, weighted with wanting.

Looks like the ten-year gap might not be a flaw after all.

At the Witchery, we're seated in the same corner as Victoria and Harrison when he brought her here and served by the same waiting staff. If they recognise her, they conceal it well.

I'm not usually into fancy tiny portions decorated with edible flowers but even I can't deny the food is fabulous. Vic orders the salt-crusted halibut and I opt for a fillet, even chancing a small glass of red wine at Victoria's insistence. What really makes it though, is the company.

'Cheers.' Vic raises her glass and clinks it against mine.

'Cheers.'

'Less than a month until graduation. Then, we'll be able to go wherever we like in public together.' She beams across the table at me.

'We kind of do anyway, but I know what you mean.' I'm still not relishing the idea of telling Ryan, but I swat the thought away for now.

The waitress clears away our plates and offers us the dessert menu. Our heads shake simultaneously. Money can't buy what I'm about to devour for pudding.

I pay the bill, practically dragging my girlfriend out of the restaurant in my desperation to get beneath that dress.

'Thank you.' The kiss she presses to my cheek is chaste, but the fevered temperature of her lips don't lie. My heart hammers in my chest. Blood pulses below. The scent of her skin inches from mine is intoxicating. It would be so easy to capture her mouth with mine.

As we step out of the restaurant into the chill night air, a camera flashes to our right. Fucking paps. 'Head down. Hang on to my arm and I'll get you back to the car asap,' I instruct, switching out of boyfriend mode and instantly into my role as her bodyguard.

'Victoria! Victoria! What are your plans for after graduation?' the pap shouts. She doesn't look up.

It takes less than a minute to hurry back to the car, across the cobblestones of the Royal Mile.

'Sneaky bastards,' I fume, conscious Victoria's kiss on my cheek may have been captured by that photographer. What if it ends up on the front pages and Ryan and Sasha see it?

'I kissed my bodyguard on the cheek,' she shrugs. 'It could have been a lot worse.'

She's right, but we're playing with fire. Knowing it and experiencing it first-hand is very different. I was a millisecond away from forgetting where we were and who we are.

I pull up close to Victoria's house in her allocated parking spot, uneasiness lingering in my gut.

'It's okay.' Her hand reaches for my thigh again.

The air hums, but this time it's not with lust. Something feels off. I scan the perimeter, every hair on my neck standing to attention.

'Did you leave the bedroom light on?'

'No. It was light when we left. I didn't put it on at all.' Her head whips up to where a dim glow radiates from behind the drawn curtains.

I grab the weapon I keep in the dash, running my thumb over the safety.

'Archie? You set the alarm, right?' Fear cracks in her voice.

Cold shame washes over me. Distracted by Victoria's

hand on my cock, I managed the unthinkable and forgot to set the fucking brand-new upgraded alarm system I personally insisted was installed.

This is the precise reason security detail should never sleep with their wards.

'No.' My admission kills me, but my mental self-loathing will have to wait until I've secured the house.

I'm caught between a rock and a hard place. I can't leave Victoria out here alone, but I can't bring her into the house either.

The front door is intact. No sign of a forced entry. Maybe she did leave the bedroom light on?

No. My gut never lies.

And it's telling me someone is here. Or at least was.

'Get your keys out of your bag and stay behind me. We're going in, okay?' She's safer with me than out here alone and unprotected.

Victoria offers a short, sharp nod.

With her sheltered behind my back, we enter the house. Tiny scratches on the pink paintwork of the front door indicate the lock has been picked.

Adrenaline pumps furiously through my chest, but the gun doesn't waver a millimetre in my hand, poised and ready, just in case.

It's silent inside. We climb the stairs and I check each floor until we get to the top. The bedroom door's ajar, which is odd as I distinctly remember Victoria closing it.

Nudging it open with my knee, I scan every inch of the room.

There's nobody here.

But there was.

Because the ivory lingerie I bought Victoria in Sublime Secrets is carefully positioned on our bed, complete with the stockings and a pair of silver stilettos. And I'm damn sure neither of us put it there.

Her eyes widen in a horror that matches my own.

Because this should never have happened.

And if I wasn't fucking my ward, it wouldn't have.

Chapter Twenty-Three
VICTORIA

My shaky fingers cling to the back of Archie's jacket.

It's bad enough someone was in my house but messing with my underwear propels this sickening scenario to a new level of appalling. My gallbladder's going to have to work overtime to break down the bile my body's rapidly producing.

Archie crosses the room, examining the lingerie without touching it. He whips out his phone, punching in three digits before holding it to his blood-red ear. Glinting topaz eyes remain focused on the bed.

'Police, please,' he barks at the operator. His jaw's set so tightly it might snap.

I watch on in shock while he explains the situation, his role, and who I am.

Within minutes, two plain-clothed police officers arrive with a forensics team and another uniformed female officer. She's not much older than me, but clearly experienced in this type of thing. While Archie remains upstairs talking to the detectives, she makes me a mug of sweet tea in the kitchen.

My whole body trembles.

Someone was in my house.

Someone was touching my things.

It's taken years, but finally I can appreciate my family's insistence on me having a bodyguard. They can never know about this, though. Sasha would insist on my immediate extraction by helicopter and lock me up in Huxley Castle forever if she got even a whiff of it.

I'm so close to graduation. I've worked so damned hard for six years. I wasn't joking when I told Archie I always finish what I start. Nothing in this world will stop me from graduating with the rest of my class.

With only one more week of placement, and a few more weeks of lectures to go, my final exams are approaching. I can't afford to miss a day.

Two hours later, everyone has gone. The house is silent once again. Archie begged me to check into a hotel, but I won't be chased out of my home by a filthy prowler. Plus, the thought of being papped again is too much.

The police have left two uniformed officers outside the house, plus the security alarms have now been set.

I'm not annoyed with Archie. Before he arrived, Jared and I never bothered setting the alarm. In some ways, it was a cheap lesson. Things could have been a lot worse.

Archie's changed into those low hanging grey sweats that I love and a plain white t-shirt. His stony expression chills me to the bone as he paces the house like a stealthy cheetah.

I pat the couch next to me. 'Sit, please.'

'I can't.' He stalks across the kitchen and back to the living area, checking each window is locked for the hundredth time. 'I fucked up tonight. Big time.'

'It happens,' I shrug.

'It shouldn't have, though. And it wouldn't have if I was doing my job properly.' Regret taints his tone. Thick fingers rake through his dirty blond hair.

'You did your job perfectly. I'm fine. Shaken, but fine. And at least there's the camera footage.' When Archie insisted on installing thirteen security cameras, it seemed excessive. Tonight, I'm grateful for them.

'It was dark. The intruder wore dark clothing and a baseball cap and never looked up once.' Archie's frustration rolls from him in palpable waves.

I gravitate towards him, halting him mid-pace. My arms slip around his waist, and he flinches, looking everywhere but at me. So we're back to this again.

'The police will get him.' Am I reassuring Archie, or myself? 'Come on. Let's go to bed. It's been a long night.' My fingers interlink with his, tugging him towards the staircase.

'I'll be up in five. Just going to check the doors again.'

In the shower, I scrub my skin with an exfoliating body wash, but I can't seem to get rid of the dirty feeling that I've been violated. Well, my privacy, at least.

I slip between the fresh sheets on Archie's bed. I didn't want to go to a hotel, but there's no way I can sleep in my own room tonight.

Feet approach up the stairs and my imagination goes to town with images of the intruder returning until the rational part of my brain reminds me it's Archie.

Still, it's a relief when his head pops round the door, followed by those burly shoulders. 'Just gonna brush my teeth. You okay?'

'Yeah,' I lie with the sound of my own heartbeat jackhammering in my ears.

I take the side of the bed farthest away from the door and burrow under the lavender-scented sheets. Archie returns, slips off his clothes and creeps in beside me, resting his back against the headboard in a sitting position. His weapon rests on the bedside locker.

'Do you think it was personal?' I ask, unsure if I really want to know.

Archie's tongue clicks against the roof of his mouth. 'He could just be some sick fuck who does this type of thing and somehow ended up in your house. Or it could be Harrison.'

'Harrison?' My hand clutches my chest. 'He literally just apologised.'

Archie cocks his head to the side. 'Seriously? We've already seen he's unhinged. I told the police to question him first.'

I don't know what's worse, the prowler being someone I know, or it being a complete stranger.

As if he can read my mind, Archie says, 'If it turns out to be a stranger, the pictures of your family they must have seen will have told him who you are. Who your family are. We ought to tell them.'

'What?' I bolt up into a sitting position, clutching the cover over my chest. 'Archie, please. If we tell them, they'll make me go home. I'm this close to graduating.' I pinch my thumb and finger in front of his face.

'We'll sleep on it. I'm not calling Ryan at this hour of the night, anyway.' Archie fluffs his pillow behind him but remains in a sitting position, poised and ready for action. Just not the kind of action we originally had in mind.

He holds me in his arms all night long, but it's the first night since we hooked up that we don't have sex.

Days pass with no sign of the police catching the intruder. Like a professional, he left no fingerprints. No DNA. Nothing. Harrison was questioned but was adamant he left Libby's house and went straight home alone afterwards. His driver confirmed it.

Archie's not convinced.

He upped the security round the house again, installing super-sensitive motion sensors on all the doors and windows.

He paces constantly, barely sitting long enough to swallow his food. With a huge amount of tears and begging, I managed to persuade him not to tell Ryan and Sasha. For all we know, it could have been a random break-in. And there's been nothing since.

Despite all this, and my best efforts at enticing him, Archie still hasn't touched me since that night. It's like he's forbidden himself until the prowler's caught or something. His rejections stings, but I understand it on some level. As if he wants to right his perceived wrong.

The only positive of his neglect is it frees up time for me to cram for my exams.

Staring into my textbook over my morning coffee, I remind myself this will be a distant memory soon enough. Once we get through the next few weeks, the summer will be our own. I'm thinking a trip around Europe might be the way to celebrate my freedom, finishing up at Huxley Castle where we can break the news we're an item.

There will be plenty of time to make up for lost time together then.

Archie strolls into the kitchen wearing a pair of bum-sculpting running shorts. 'Want to go for a gallop?' He nods at the window where the sky is so blue we could be in Spain instead of Scotland.

'Sure. I've been at this for hours. I could do with a break.' And some time with my boyfriend, even if I would prefer a different form of exercise.

It takes less than a minute to change into a sports bra and throw on my running tights. I tie my hair in a ponytail, skipping down the steps when the house alarm sounds like a siren but four times louder. My palms cup my ears trying to protect my ear drums. God only knows what the neighbours must think.

Archie's broad shoulders are tensed and ready for action.

Grabbing his gun from the kitchen table, he clicks off the safety catch and motions for me to get back upstairs. He pulls his phone from his pocket and opens up the app to view the cameras.

I hover on the bottom step, adrenaline igniting my fight or flight response in every nerve ending in my body.

'It's Ryan and Sasha.' Archie sounds as surprised as me as he punches in the code to silence the alarm.

'What?' I'm torn between excitement at seeing my sister and the worry that she might drag me away from here.

He shrugs before racing down the stairs to the front door.

'Surprise!' Ryan and Sasha shout simultaneously.

'Jesus, this place is like Fort Knox.' Ryan's low whistle resounds around the hallway and the sound of feet pad across the carpet. 'The risk of going deaf from that siren alone is enough to deter any intruders.'

Here's hoping.

Sasha is the first up the stairs. She throws herself at me, wrapping me in a huge maternal embrace. Her familiar pomegranate perfume wafts in the air around me and a tension I hadn't realised I'd been holding in my shoulders slips.

If she hadn't stepped up, taken on the role of mother, guardian, and protector, who knows where I would have ended up.

My mind goes to Lily-May again, the child whose mother died in A&E a few weeks ago.

I've thought about her every day since it happened.

Wondering where she is. If she has other family members to care for her.

'Victoria, look at you!' Sasha snaps me back to the present moment, stepping back and taking my hands as she inspects me from head to toe.

'What on earth are you doing here?' My eyes roam over

the woman who raised me, absorbing every detail of her immaculately cut summer dress and designer wedges.

'Evangeline Araceli's here meeting suppliers and she invited us to join her. It seemed like the perfect excuse to kill two birds with one stone.' Her sunny beam lights up the room. 'How have you been? Are you all set for your exams? Do you think you'll look for your postgraduate placement here or in Ireland? Tell me everything.'

'Give the girl a chance.' Ryan sweeps in behind her to hug me, flanked by his security, Pierce, and another equally buff-looking guy I don't recognise.

Archie winces, presumably at the term 'girl,' hovering awkwardly behind them.

'I can't believe you're actually here.' I didn't realise how much I missed them, and the warm fuzzy feeling their love creates, until they showed up.

Maybe a postgraduate placement in Ireland wouldn't be a bad idea after all. 'Where are you staying?'

It goes without saying they won't stay here. They never do. They need their own space, which is a polite way of saying they have wild, animated sex most nights and we have an unspoken agreement that I've heard enough of it over the years. Hearing those two at it like rabbits all night would have been enough to make me move out at eighteen, even if I hadn't planned on going to college.

Though Archie and I could give them a run for their money now. Well, we might have done before last weekend, anyway.

'At the Caledonian.' Sasha claps her hands together gleefully.

Of course. The most elite hotel in the city, situated at the bottom of Lothian Road in the heart of the West End. It boasts stunning views of Edinburgh Castle.

'Sit down, please.' I motion for them to make themselves comfortable while I put on the kettle.

Ryan, Pierce and the other security guard sit at the kitchen table while Sasha and Archie follow me to the kitchen area.

Archie busies himself firing up the Nespresso machine. 'How are the twins?'

'They're amazing. They ask about "Uncle Archie" most days.'

Sasha's words warm my soul. 'Huh! What about Aunty Vic?'

'They can't wait to have you home in the summer,' Ryan assures me.

'Little shits are robbing me blind daily,' Pierce grumbles good-naturedly.

'You should wash your mouth out with soap, and you'd be a lot richer for it,' Ryan sniggers.

'You're doing a stellar job minding my sister.' Sasha sidles up to Archie, winking at him.

Heat flames my cheeks. Is it that obvious?

'I saw the picture of you two on the Royal Mile.' Ah, the shot taken outside the Witchery, where my lips were pressed to Archie's cheek.

Eagle eyes volley between us, seeking answers to a question she didn't have to ask.

'Don't be so ridiculous,' Ryan calls from across the room. 'Archie's a professional. Leave them alone, Sasha. Stop your meddling. You know the first rule of security is never get involved with the ward. Isn't that right, Arch?'

'Absolutely.'

Thank you, Ryan.

Not.

Whatever distance has been between Archie and me this week, it's just doubled.

Chapter Twenty-Four
ARCHIE

'I've been asked to speak at the hospital's annual summer fundraiser at the Usher Hall next week,' Victoria announces as we walk through the hospital corridors to her final shift on A&E. This place has become so familiar over the past few months, the smell of disinfectant and doom barely registers in my nostrils.

My arm brushes hers, sending shocks jolting through me. Even though Ryan and Sasha's visit last week resurrected a lot of internal conflict, I can't fight the feelings I have for my ward.

'Probably not a good idea, given the police are no further forwards with catching the prowler. He could be out there still, waiting for an opportunity.'

'To do what? Sniff my underwear in public?' She rolls her eyes, extracting a hairband from her scrub pocket and tying those loose, bouncing curls into a secure knot on top of her head.

I arch my eyebrows. 'The only reason I agreed not to tell Ryan and Sasha is because you agreed to keep a low profile and do as I recommend. Is your FOMO getting to you?'

'No! Don't be daft. It's a work function to raise badly needed funds for the hospital. There's no way I can turn it down. And I don't want to. The hospital has given me so much over the last six years, I want to give something back before I go.'

I sidestep a couple of nurses speed walking past. 'Can't you buy a few raffle tickets instead?'

'Come on, Archie. You know how important this is to me. The dean himself called me personally. I'm not going to turn it down. It'll be full of doctors and surgeons. I'm pretty sure there'll be no creepers there.' She pauses, one hand hovering on the door to A&E.

Using my shoulder, I open the door for her and motion her to go ahead. 'They're the worst creeps from what I've seen.'

'Huh. Thank you very much. I thought you liked my fetishes.'

'Present company excluded, of course.' I shoot her a wink. 'Look, say a few words if you must, but I'll need to be on that stage with you.' The closer we get to the ward, the louder the noise buzzes around us.

'Is that really necessary?' Slim, neatly trimmed fingernails roam over her NHS ID badge pinned to the front of her scrub top.

'Are you embarrassed to be seen with me in front of your doctor friends?' It's meant to be a joke, but somehow it comes out sounding serious. That deep-rooted sense of inadequacy rears its ugly head.

Her head whips up, pupils narrowing in on me. 'Don't be so ridiculous, Archie. You know me better than that.'

She's right. I do.

She's nothing like the rest of these toffs. She's educated *and* kind. She'd never dream of looking down her nose at anyone. I won't miss them when we go back to Ireland. 'Sorry.'

We haven't been intimate in a few days and it's affecting me. Something I'll rectify tonight.

'Look, I have to attend the fundraiser, anyway. Does it really make much difference if I'm in the crowd or on the stage?'

She has a point, I suppose.

'Email me the details and I'll scope out the venue.' If it's mostly hospital staff and their families and friends, it probably isn't much more risky than her coming here most days, anyway.

'Doctor Sexton,' Doctor Dickson barks from a nearby cubicle. 'Your shift started five minutes ago.'

Victoria snaps on a pair of gloves from a wall-mounted box and struts towards the patient he's attending to. I take a seat in the waiting area to watch.

A fire in a city bakery creates a challenging shift treating burn victims.

I could watch Victoria work all day long and never tire of it. She has such a knack with people. A compassion most never accomplish.

Harrison struts by, glaring like he wants to kill me. Mind you, I'd want to kill him too if Victoria shared her bed with him every night. The police might have ruled him out of their investigation, but I haven't. He has an edge to him. An attitude. Like he's above everyone and everything, including the law.

When Victoria eventually gets a fifteen-minute break, she heads to the reception area instead of the hospital canteen. 'What are you doing?'

She sweeps a few stray strands of hair behind her ear. 'I just need to check something. I can't get that kid out of my mind.'

I don't need to ask which kid, even though fifteen passed through here today already. Lily-May has been on my mind too.

A harassed-looking receptionist glances up with a sigh as we approach. 'Doctor Sexton.' She nods a greeting.

'Hi...' Victoria's eyes dart to the woman's NHS ID card, '...Violet. I wonder if you can help me. Can you check on a previous patient for me? Her name is Lily-May Fitzpatrick. You might remember her? She was treated here a couple of weeks ago for shock. Her mother collapsed in the waiting area and sadly died.'

Violet's grey tight curls bounce as she nods her head. 'I remember. The poor girl.' Weathered fingers tap away at a keyboard on the desk.

'I can't stop thinking about her, wondering what happened to her,' Victoria says.

Violet squints at her computer screen. 'It says she was discharged into the care of social services.'

Victoria's teeth worry at her lower lip. 'That's what I feared.'

'It's not a bad system.' Violet's tone convinces neither of us.

'Would you want your daughter to end up there?' Victoria blows out a huge puff of frustration. 'Can you get the case worker assigned to Lily-May on the phone, please?'

Violet taps a biro thoughtfully on the desk. 'Forgive me, Doctor Sexton. I know I'm only the receptionist, but Lily-May was discharged. It was terrible what happened to her, but she's no longer a concern of ours. Contacting her is against protocol.'

Victoria straightens her spine and clears her throat with an air of authority. 'I think we can both agree this was an exceptional case. I'd simply like to speak to her before I leave this hospital, or I'll spend the rest of my life wondering if she's okay.'

Violet shrugs. 'I'm not making that call, but I won't stop you. It's your registration you're risking.' She turns her screen around, flashing Victoria the contact details. Victoria takes a screenshot on her phone.

'I didn't see that,' Violet says. 'Storing patient contact details for personal use is a breach of patient confidentiality.' What a jobsworth.

'It's for a good cause, I promise.' Victoria whirls on her toes, thanks Violet and struts towards the vending machine. The coffee's crap, but it's hot.

'I have a job for you,' she whispers in my ear as she taps something on the screen of her phone.

'Another one?' My phone vibrates in my pocket. The child's contact details.

'Ryan knows someone that can find out things. The guy who does the background checks on all the staff. I've heard Sasha and Chloe talking about him. Apparently, there's nothing he can't find out. Can you please enquire into who is caring for this child? I know if I ring the social worker, they won't tell me a thing.'

My heart quadruples in my chest. Victoria Sexton has the biggest heart I've ever known. She has the world at her fingertips, and yet she gives and gives and gives.

'I'll do what I can.' We reach the vending machine and I punch the button for an Americano, holding a plastic cup under the nub. 'But I can't promise you'll like what I find.'

The harsh truth is, if the child hasn't been taken in by a relative, she's either in a foster home or with a foster family.

'Let me worry about that.' Victoria takes the cup I offer, adding two sweeteners and stirring with the wooden stick.

I grab a second cup for myself. 'Are you sad this is your last day?'

Victoria gazes at me from under those huge black lashes. 'It won't be my last day on A&E. I think I've found my spiritual home.'

'Here?' It's a battle to keep the surprise from my voice. I knew there was a chance we might be here for another couple of years, but she'd mentioned applying in Ireland, too.

'Not necessarily this hospital. I might apply to Belfast. But A&E is definitely where I see myself long term.'

Belfast? Where did that come from? I sort of assumed if we weren't here, we'd be heading back to Huxley Castle. Back to my cabin. Back to the twins. Back to her family, the family I've chosen as my own over the years.

Jen, one of the nurses I've come to recognise from the ward, approaches the coffee machine and we step back, allowing her to get her caffeine fix.

She shoots me a curious smile before turning her attention to Victoria. 'Are you coming for the leaving drinks tonight? We can't send you off without a cocktail or two for the road.'

Victoria downs the remaining coffee from her cup before dumping it into the recycling bin. 'Absolutely. I wouldn't miss it for the world.'

'Brilliant.' A smile light's Jen's face all the way to the corners of her eyes. 'I'm going to miss you so much.'

Victoria links her arm through Jen's as they turn in the direction of the ward. I follow with the realisation it could be a long night.

And another one without any intimacy.

The drinks take place in a bustling old pub called Doctor's, not far from campus. It's one of the bars the medical students regularly frequent. Do they go there because of its name? Or did they name it Doctor's because it's always been popular among the medical students?

Several dusty-looking chandeliers hang from the red painted ceiling and cast a low light on the otherwise dingy room. In contrast to the sunny summer evening outside, the place is dull. Mahogany wood lines the walls and bar top like so many of these Gothic-themed establishments in Edinburgh.

Victoria's changed into a pair of wet-look leather leggings and a black off-the-shoulder top revealing the lace strap of her bra. She may as well get a megaphone and invite every creep in the place to cop an eyeful of her lingerie. At least tonight the house alarm is on.

From my position in the corner, I pull up my phone and check the cameras at home. It's all quiet. This time of year, though, the nights are bright until after eleven. Someone would have to be off their head to think they could get away with creeping around Victoria's house without being spotted. Mind you, they'd have to be off their head to want to.

But Victoria does have a way of enticing men to do things they wouldn't normally do. Myself included. I've never fucked a ward in my life, let alone fallen in love with one.

Ryan's comments the other day hit hard. *'Don't be ridiculous, Archie's a professional.'*

What will he say when we come out as a couple in a few weeks?

Will he be disappointed in me? Or will he finally stop seeing Victoria as a girl when she graduates?

With her talk of Belfast earlier, will we have anything left to announce?

Clearly, her plans are different from mine. Things were supposed to get easier after graduation. I'm beginning to realise I might have been wrong.

Libby and Mel arrive, both having finished their respective placements. The number of patrons double, bodies squashing everywhere. I move in closer to Victoria, who's deep in conversation with another student doctor, Ally, a quiet girl from Inverness.

Jen arrives with Doctor Dickhead in tow. He looks equally smarmy out of his white coat, wearing an ill-fitting suit and striped tie. Black bags linger beneath his eyes, and he looks as though he's lost about half a stone in a week. Brushing his body against Victoria, he makes a beeline for the bar.

'Sorry, I didn't mean to knock into you.' His hand drops to her waist and his eyes drop to her bra strap. 'Can I buy you a drink?'

'No, thank you. I just got one.' With a quick, polite flash of teeth, Victoria resumes her conversation with Ally.

A flicker of annoyance flips over Doctor Dickhead's face, but I don't have time to analyse it because Harrison stalks over. From his bloodshot eyes, I gather he's already well lubricated.

'Victoria,' Harrison slurs, clumsily shoving Ally to one side.

I step in front of the women, shielding them with my body.

'Get out of my way, dog. We both know you're not going to assault me in front of all these witnesses.' His breath reeks of whiskey.

'Don't push me or you'll find out.' My heel presses over his tan leather loafer, pinning him in position.

'You're fucking him, Victoria, aren't you?' Wild accusatory eyes peer past me, round me and over my shoulder as he tries to read my girlfriend.

Is there any need to completely deny it now she's finished her hospital placement? These people are no longer her colleagues and mentors as of today. There's no reason to care what they think. She could give him enough, without actually spelling it out.

'I saw the picture *The Sun* printed of you both on the Royal Mile. Your lips were all over his face.' Harrison's features screw into an ugly ball.

Don't deny us entirely.

Show him you're mine without actually spelling it out for him.

'What? No, Harrison. Don't be ridiculous.' Disgust rings in her cold tone. As if the idea of being with someone like me is so repulsive.

Victoria's words rip through my insides.

I know we can't openly admit our relationship yet, so why do I feel like she just did a Judas on me?

Chapter Twenty-Five
VICTORIA

Tonight is the hospital fundraiser at the Usher Hall. With lectures done, assignments completed and final exams behind me, I feel like I'm waiting in no man's land.

The official graduation is weeks away. I'm sure I've passed. Not to be egotistical or big-headed, but I put too much work in not to have succeeded.

Sure, there were a lot of parties before Archie arrived, but work was always my priority. I studied day and night, absorbing every detailed fact my greedy eyes could devour.

I should be ecstatic. Finally, I can read romance novels instead of textbooks again, and party all night without fearing being called into work. Though I haven't been out partying in ages, truth be told. These days, I prefer to scroll through pictures of other people's nights out, admiring the fashion from the comfort of my boyfriend's arms.

Change is coming. It makes me uneasy.

The graduation I once looked forward to is now a terrifying reality. In my bubble of placements, lectures, exams and assignments, there was stability, routine and structure.

Now, it's out into the unknown.

My night terrors are at an all-time high, where I dream of falling into oblivion. I see the faces of the patients I couldn't save. And Lily-May, who I eventually discovered is now living in a care home in Oban, in the West Highlands of Scotland.

I'm still contemplating what I can do about that.

Archie's not been himself since Sasha and Ryan's visit. There's a distance between us. Well, as much distance as there can be when he's paid to remain within five feet of me at all times. It's more like a mental distance. Like the shield's been half resurrected, and I don't know why.

He comes to my bed every night. Holds me while I scream in my sleep. The sex has been less frequent. Less frantic. More meaningful, in some respects. Slow and deep and loving. But when it's over, it's like he withdraws his feelings along with his man parts.

Fastening tiny pearl studs to my ears, I glance at him in the bathroom mirror where he's dry shaving next to me. His sculpted skin glistens with residual droplets from his shower. Broad shoulders beg to be touched. The urge to dig my fingernails into his back is primal. Where once I wouldn't have hesitated, a fear of rejection lingers.

I stand in my lingerie, make-up applied, and hair done. Once he would have leapt on me. 'Is everything okay between us, Arch?'

I hate that I need his reassurance. I hate that everything is up in the air.

'Everything is fine.' Deep topaz lakes shimmer back at me, eyes so blue I could dive straight into them.

'I was thinking we could do a few weeks around Europe after graduation. Before we return to Ireland. What do you think?' I ask.

His fingers halt, holding his electric razor an inch from his jaw. 'It's entirely up to you. I go where you go.' He doesn't exactly sound overjoyed about it.

'What's that supposed to mean? I thought we were a team?' Like an uncontrollable child in a sweet shop, my hands reach for his bare torso, tracing the perfect planes of his six-pack.

'So did I, Vic, then you started talking about Belfast and I don't know...' He places the razor on the gleaming white bathroom countertop, turning to face me.

My eyes search his expression for words he's not actually saying, but come up blank. Confusion hangs like steam in the air between us. 'We talked about going back to Ireland, Arch.'

'Yeah. I thought you meant the Republic of Ireland. Our home. I didn't realise you meant Belfast.' A strong hand cups my chin with affection. 'I didn't want to bring it up while you were in the middle of your exams, but now they're over, this is a conversation we need to have.'

'You know I can't move back to Huxley castle, not yet. I love my family more than words, but no matter how many children Sasha and Ryan have of their own, I'll always be treated like one of them. I could study for ten medical degrees and I'll always be a baby to them. I can't live like that. Not after everything I've achieved at university and living independently. I'd like to be close enough to visit regularly, but not actually living under their roof.'

'What about my roof?' Archie's fingers rake through his dirty blond hair.

The cabin Archie bought on the Huxley estate is stunning, as are they all. It's as big as the house we live in now, but bordering the edge of a small forest on my family's estate. But can I really picture myself living there?

'Maybe one day, but first I have two-year medical post qualification training program. I didn't get this degree for fun.

I'm going to be a doctor. Belfast would be a great compromise for both of us.'

Archie's lips purse together thoughtfully. 'Where do I fit into this scenario? You know I can't remain as your security once we tell your family about us.'

'I know,' I sigh. 'But I'm hoping they won't insist on another bodyguard. After all, no one has more incentive to protect me than you.'

The intensity of his stare penetrates my soul. 'So, you *do* want me to go to Belfast with you?'

'Yes! As my boyfriend, though. Not my bodyguard.'

My heart hammers in my chest, waiting for confirmation of what I'd wrongly assumed was a given.

'You're not ashamed that we're worlds apart, socially? I'm never going to fit in with your doctor friends.'

'Don't be ridiculous.' My fingers continue to caress his taut stomach.

He stiffens beneath my touch. 'That's what you said to Harrison when he asked if we were together. Only I'm pretty sure that night your tone was filled with way more disgust.'

'My disgust was aimed at him. Not the suggestion of you and me. Fuck, Archie, you know how I feel about you. I'm crazy with lust anytime you're near. I think about you every second of every day. I had no idea this is what love felt like. You might be my first love, but even I can tell what we have is something phenomenal. Something that some people never experience in their entire life. How did I get lucky enough to find it so young?'

'You are so young. It's one of the things that worries me.' His Adam's apple bobs up and down. 'Your ambitions are very different from mine. One day, I'd like to move back to Huxley Castle. To go home. Is that something you see in *your* future? After you finish your training?'

Torrid flames in his irises indicate this is a deal breaker for him.

His fingers travel over my spine, darting over the back of my lace bra. 'You know, I consider your family as my own. They welcomed me as so much more than an employee. They saved my life. Offered me friendship. My own home. I'm closer to them than my own blood. Your nephew and niece are already like my own. I don't want to lose that connection. I might never have another one like it.'

'You won't. And one day, that connection will be made official. I remember you promising you were going to marry me.' My hips press against his suggestively. Damn that towel.

'Careful, Vic, that almost sounds like a proposal.' Devilment dances over his full, plump lips. I glimpse a flash of *my* Archie. Thank God. We're okay. Everything is going to be okay.

'You wish.' My palm bounces off his chest as I shove it playfully.

'So, a few years in Belfast. Then maybe home?' he checks.

'It's not hard to picture us together at Huxley, with a family of our own, raising children alongside my sisters. But not yet. Not now.' To be honest, I don't know if I'll ever be able to settle at Huxley as an adult, but if it means that much to him, I'd try.

'You want children?' His tone is tainted with hope.

'I want *your* children.' I tug at the white fluffy towel round his waist. It drops to the floor silently. 'So, we'd better get practising, so we know what to do when the time is right.'

His hard length presses against the thin fabric of my panties, another stunning set from Sublime Secrets.

'I know exactly what to do, baby.' His fingers whip the lace aside and swipe across my sex. A carnal glint lights his eyes as he sweeps over my secret slickness. Nudging my bum up to rest on the bathroom countertop, he parts my thighs wide.

His mouth fastens against mine as he continues his relentless assault on my sweet spot. 'You. Are. Soaking.'

'You have that effect on me.'

'Ditto.' He nudges his erection against my entrance while his thumb moves to circle my clit.

'If you keep that up much longer, I'm going to come all over the tip of your cock.' My lips murmur against the pulse throbbing in his neck.

'Quite the dirty mouth you have, young lady.' His voice is husky as he nudges into my centre, inch by glorious inch. 'No one in their right mind would treat you like a child if they heard the filth that rolled from that pretty little tongue. I hope your speech tonight is a lot cleaner.'

'Archie, I...' Words escape me as he pumps me long and hard. My fingers grip the marble, hanging on as his every thrust pushes me closer to the edge.

His tongue plunders my mouth, teeth nip at my lower lip and that thumb increases the pressure on my clit. The world evaporates around us. All I can see and feel is him as my orgasm rips so powerfully through me it's debilitating.

Seconds later, his release follows mine as he moans my name into my mouth like I'm some sort of goddess.

He places a tender kiss on my lips, tugging my underwear back into place as if it's still wearable. It's ruined. And so am I for anyone else other than him.

Already, I'm lusting after my next hit.

The Usher Hall is on Lothian Road, not far from the Caledonian Hotel, where Sasha and Ryan stayed a few weeks ago.

The annual fundraiser is partly a review of the hospital's

achievements over the previous year, a chance for everyone to hear how last year's funds have been spent, and to find out the difference the money has made in securing the future of the Royal Infirmary, one of the best NHS hospitals in Scotland.

There are formal awards for staff who have surpassed themselves in the line of duty and informal tongue-in-cheek awards for categories like 'Best Dressed Doctor,' which is kind of hilarious considering we all wear the same hospital-issued scrubs. Last year, the title went to my friend, Mel, who changes her hair and glasses as often as I change my underwear.

Four rows of traffic block the road outside. The street is wedged with elegantly dressed women in cocktail dresses and men sporting suits and dickie bows.

'We're going to be late.' I gaze at the unmoving traffic surrounding us. 'It would be so much easier if I could hop out while you parked,' I suggest to Archie.

'Not going to happen, baby.' His hand falls to my thigh where my Isabel Marant chiffon dress has risen four inches above my knee. 'And who's fault is it that we're late?' Amorous eyes dart sideways with a smile.

'It was worth it.' We needed it. The talk and the intimacy.

'You're not on until the second half, don't panic.' He offers my leg a reassuring squeeze.

Eventually, the traffic crawls along and we find a spot to abandon the car. The grey paving outside the Usher Hall is absolutely thronged with reporters, what looks like a television crew, and a tonne of paparazzi.

Jesus, who are they expecting? The King?

Hanging onto Archie's arm, I negotiate the pavement in my high heels, almost at the entrance now. My phone vibrates in my tiny silver clutch, but I ignore it. It vibrates again at the exact moment Archie's phone rings. He pulls it out of his pocket as I locate mine amongst my lipliner and mascara.

'Libby.' My head cocks to the side as I notice seventeen other missed calls from Mel, Sasha, and even Chloe.

Archie holds up his phone for me to see. It's Ryan.

Our eyebrows arch in unison.

Archie swipes to answer. 'Hello?'

'I don't know what the fuck is going on over there with Victoria, but the two of you are all over the papers. Find somewhere to lock down. Now!' Ryan barks.

A sense of sick dread sweeps over me as the crowd turns to face us. What feels like a thousand voices vie for my attention. Our attention.

'Victoria, is it true you're having an affair with your bodyguard?' One particularly aggressive reporter shoves his microphone in my face.

'Mr Mason, do you have anything to say about Doctor Hughes' allegation that you assaulted him?' someone else shouts.

'Victoria, isn't he old enough to be your father?'

'You won't get away with assaulting a doctor,' someone else shrieks.

Archie's arm is around my shoulder in an instant, swatting the crowd out of our path like they're overgrown wasps. Parasites. That's exactly what they are.

Fucking Harrison. What was he thinking of, going to the press?

Archie takes the initiative and guides me back to the car, away from the glaring spotlight of the press mob. He bundles me into the passenger seat of the SUV while cameras flash all around us. I haven't had this much attention since Ryan and Sasha's movie came out four years ago. I haven't missed it a bit. I'm not cut out for this life.

I don't speak until the car merges into a row of slow, but thankfully moving traffic. 'What actually just happened?'

'Looks like Harrison went to the press and spun his own story about that night.'

'Why would he do that? And why now? Why not at the time?' My curls swing as my head shakes in disgust.

'He's got nothing else to lose. And nothing better to do.' Archie slams the gear stick into fourth and presses his foot to the gas.

Chapter Twenty-Six
ARCHIE

Fucking Harrison. He was always going to be trouble. But no one could have anticipated how much of a circus he'd create. Although every cloud has a silver lining, as now I don't have to spend the night in a room full of people all far more educated than me.

The quicker I get Victoria home, the better.

The street outside Victoria's house is now also swarmed with as many paparazzi and reporters as the Usher Hall.

And from the way they're camped out, it looks as though they have no intention of going anywhere tonight.

'This is a disaster.' Victoria clutches her phone. Sasha's name flashes relentlessly across the front of it. 'If I answer this, she'll insist we return to Huxley Castle and I'm not ready to face them yet.'

Neither am I.

Ryan's tone was positively lethal on the phone. On the plus side, I no longer need to wonder how he'll take the news that I'm sleeping with his sister-in-law because I know. He's taken it about as well as a bullet in his back.

I abused a position of trust and remained on his payroll

while I kept Victoria's bed warm, breaking the first rule of my contract.

I should have refused to take the job. Or the money. But then he would have known something was up. Especially when I didn't return to Huxley.

But now he knows anyway, and it's a million times worse than I feared.

If only I'd admitted my feelings for Victoria to him when he asked me to take the position.

What a fucking idiot. I should have insisted someone else step in the second I fucked up. I'll never forgive myself, so why should I expect him to?

The idea he thinks badly of me is worse than the entire world believing I beat Harrison to a pulp. Ryan's friendship and respect mean everything to me. Not because he's a rock star, but because he's a man of honour. A family man. And I've violated his trust in the worst possible way.

'Where will we go?' Victoria voices my exact thoughts. 'Everyone will be looking for us. A hotel is too risky. Someone's bound to spot us and sell us down the river to the paps.'

Victoria isn't like her sisters, both of whom have taken naturally to the limelight. She wears her heart on her sleeve and there's no way she can spin this into something it's not, like a well-planned PR stunt. If she's confronted by the press, she's more likely than not to admit everything.

Would that be such a bad thing, though?

Would anyone believe me when I protest I've been fighting this attraction for years until Victoria was old enough to make an educated decision? Ten years isn't a huge gap, it's just, I suppose, she's so young.

No. They'd make me out to be some sort of paedophile because that's what sells papers. No one cares about true love.

And I doubt they'll believe that when I attacked that

slimebag Harrison Hughes, it was only because I was protecting Victoria.

No.

'Do you have any friends we could try?' I ask. It's a long shot. I've met most of Victoria's friends over the past few months, and none of them have seemed particularly discreet.

Her porcelain skin is positively drained of any colour it did possess. 'Libby?'

Libby's penthouse is pretty secure, but it's too obvious. Victoria's been photographed with her too many times, at too many high-profile parties over the years.

'We wouldn't make it as far as the elevator.' My index finger thrums furiously over the steering wheel as I cruise round the city aimlessly, wracking my brain for any solution other than the one that keeps coming to the forefront of my brain.

My phone rings again. It's my sister, Andrea. I cancel it instinctively, but it gives me an idea.

My mouth runs away with itself before I can stop it. 'There is a place where no one would look for us.'

'Where?' Hope sparks in Victoria's voice for the first time since we left the house.

'It's a long drive.' The warning in my voice is clear, even if the reason isn't.

Tired honey-coloured eyes dart to mine. 'It has to be better than aimlessly driving around the city.'

I'm not sure I agree, but it's safe. I'm long overdue a visit. And no one will ever find us there.

I drive through the night for five hours straight until the Scottish mountains are nothing more than a blurry memory.

Victoria's temple presses against the side of the car, but from the way she's breathing, I guess she's awake. After hours of brightly lit motorway, the sleepy English town of Somerton looks like a ghost town.

It feels like one too.

I have no memories of my mother, obviously. She died in labour. But every time I returned, I feel her presence. I imagine her in the overgrown lawn picking flowers. By all accounts, she loved to be outdoors.

Dad couldn't stick the place after she died. He went to work on the oil rigs, out of choice rather than necessity, and left Andrea to take care of me, while a young local farmer, Roger Hamley, was left to manage the farm.

Did Dad regret moving away when Roger took a shine to my sister and moved in with us? Or was it a relief that there was another man to take care of us in his absence?

Andrea and Roger must have been married for almost twenty years now. Their son, my nephew, Jason, is twenty this year.

My sister, Andrea, raised me as though I was her son, in the same way Sasha raised Victoria. We have uncannily similar stories, although my mother died so I could live.

And although my father might not have died, he couldn't bear the sight of me, blaming me for my mother's death.

I negotiate the SUV through miles of winding countryside and up a long winding dirt track towards the old house. Cattle occupy the fields on our left, sheep to the right.

'Where are we? Is this a farm?' Victoria's arms lift above her head in a cramped stretch.

'Yep. It's Hope Farm.' It would be funny if it wasn't so depressing. The only thing I hoped for was to leave and never return. Because the two weeks' leave Dad got off from the rigs each month, he ensured I had no hope of having any self-confidence left.

'What is this place?' Victoria gazes through the darkness. It's so remote. There's not another house for miles.

'It's where I was born.'

The farmhouse appears in the bright gaze of the headlights. Its beige stonework is more weathered than I remember and the windowsills could do with a good sanding and a thorough lick of fresh paint. Plant pots, overflowing with purple pansy swaying in the warm breeze, bracket the weathered-looking front door.

Huge stables flank the main house. They used to be home to two horses, Penelope and Peter, two thoroughbreds, which I used to groom daily as a teenager. I have no idea if they're still alive.

The car slows to a stop next to an old Massey Ferguson tractor which I learnt to drive when I was just a boy.

Nostalgia sweeps through my blood. Tiny hairs prick on my forearms and neck. 'Ready?' Am I asking Victoria? Or myself?

'You grew up here?' She squints through the darkness.

'Tending to the land was one of my favourite pastimes as a kid.' My fingers are poised on the door handle, still not fully committed to getting out. Even if Andrea does welcome us with open arms, it won't erase years of torment.

'Wow, it must have been idyllic.' Victoria exhales slowly.

'Not really. My father was abusive. He blamed me for the death of my mother. The two weeks each month he was away on the oil rig were heaven. The other two weeks were hell.' It's the first time I've said it out loud.

Warm hands reach out to me. 'Oh, Arch, I'm so sorry. I had no idea.'

'It's fine. Well, it's not fine, but if he's still breathing, he'll be an old man at this stage. He can't hurt me now.'

Not physically, anyway.

FALLING FOR MY BODYGUARD 227

'Does he still live here?' Victoria rakes her fingers through my hair, cradling my head. It feels like heaven.

'My sister Andrea and her husband, Roger, live here. I'm not sure about Dad. He'd be over eighty now, if he's still alive.'

'Why don't you speak to your sister?' Victoria asks.

'It's not as though I'm *not* talking to her, but every time I answer her calls, she wants me to come home. Wants to talk about Dad.' My throat bobs with emotion. 'I can't do it, you know? He did what he did, and I did what I did. We all have our crosses to bear. Talking about it won't fix it. It just forces you to relive it, over and over.'

Before Victoria can answer, the lantern lights on either side of the front door flick on.

Andrea appears in the doorway dressed in a floral nightdress that reaches her knees, her blonde tousled hair matted on one side. Roger appears at her side wearing an expression of worry, a shotgun resting against his shoulder.

I hurriedly step out of the car before he feels the need to use it. 'Andie, it's me, Archie.' I raise my hand to wave, like it's normal for me to land on her doorstep in the early hours of the morning.

'Archie? Oh, my God! I saw the news earlier. Thank God you've finally come home.'

She leaps out of the doorway, over two cement steps and straight into my arms, burying her nose in my neck.

Did the past sixteen years even happen? Because it feels like I've never been away. I pat her hair awkwardly as she cries into my chest. 'I'm sorry. I should have come sooner.' Until this moment, it never occurred to me how much my absence hurt her. All I cared about was getting away from *him*.

'You're damn right you should have done,' she scolds,

stepping back. 'Now, this must be Victoria Sexton, Ireland's answer to the Kardashians, although way classier.'

'Oh, God, I'm nothing like them! You shouldn't believe everything you read in the press.' Victoria steps forwards, extending a hand. Andie ignores it and sweeps her into one of her maternal hugs.

'And what about the part where you're having an illicit relationship with my brother, who is shock, horror, more than ten years older than you?' Andie's eyes widen mockingly.

Victoria looks at me and I shrug. 'That part's true.' Even with all the shit, knowing Ryan is probably sending Pierce over with instructions to assassinate me, introducing my sister to the woman I want to marry still manages to bring a smile to my lips.

'You do know there's a warrant out for your arrest?' Roger steps forwards, the gun now hanging by his side. He grabs my hand and shakes it firmly.

'I'll take care of it. I just didn't fancy doing it from a dingy Scottish cell. There was a scuffle, but...'

'A scuffle where you broke that guy's nose in his own kitchen?' Roger arches a thick, bushy eyebrow.

'He put his hands on Victoria. He won't press charges, because if he does, she will press charges of her own. He's just causing trouble,' I say.

'It will all blow over,' Victoria assures us. 'I'm no stranger to a scandal in the press. In a few days, they'll be talking about someone else. But for now...' She bites her lower lip.

I finish the sentence for her. 'We need to lie low.'

'Well, come on in. What are you waiting for?' Andie's arms open wide in a welcoming gesture, ushering Victoria up the steps and into the hallway.

Roger hangs back, resting a palm on top of mine. 'You should probably know *he's* here.'

I should have guessed the old bastard's too stubborn to die. 'Where?'

'In Jason's old room.' He nods towards an upstairs. 'He's not very mobile these days, and his medication seems to knock him out most of the time. A nurse comes twice a day and Andie takes his meals up to him, so you don't have to see him until you're ready. Or if you're ready.'

Will I ever be ready?

'And Jason?'

'He signed up to the army.' Roger's chest puffs with pride. 'He wanted to be a hero, like his uncle Archie.'

'I'm no hero.'

'Of course, because everyone carries an injured comrade seven kilometres across the desert with a broken leg.'

'And then led him to his death a year later.' My fingers instinctively go to the St. Christopher round my neck.

Roger grabs my shoulder, twisting me to face him. Crickets chirp all around us. Victoria and Andie are probably wondering where we are.

'Look at me now, boy.' Roger's only twenty years older than me, but I'll always be a boy to him, just like Victoria will always be a girl to Ryan. 'It wasn't your fault. You didn't plant that landmine.'

'So people keep telling me, but it doesn't change the fact those men are dead because of me.'

Roger shakes his head. 'I hope you stay long enough for me to knock some sense into you.'

'Good luck with that.' I slap his back and usher him into the house, trying not to picture the old man upstairs or the way a shred of hope sparked to discover he's still alive.

Stupidly, somewhere deep down, the young boy still lurks.

The one that's determined to make him proud, even though he can't stand the sight of me.

Chapter Twenty-Seven

VICTORIA

The farm is a stunning, quaint lakeside retreat in the middle of the Cotswolds countryside. Surrounded by animals and nature, it's beyond therapeutic, a place to unplug from city life and the rest of humanity. Even the wi-fi is delightfully shocking.

Of all the places Archie could take me to hide out, this has to be the best.

It's our third day here and the way I feel right now, I could stay forever.

The bedroom we've been allocated is at the back of the house overlooking a crystal blue lake and the finest chartreuse-coloured land. There's not another house as far as the eye can see. No one in their right mind would ever think to look for us here.

Sasha's frantic phone calls have eventually subsided now I've reassured her we're safe, though it took an age to convince her not to send a helicopter.

I haven't got a stitch of my own clothing, but Andie has kindly lent me some of hers, and with Archie by my side, I have everything I could possibly need.

After the intensity of the last few months, this is better than any European holiday I could have planned. Even the weather has been amazing. Twenty-six degrees of pure sunshine and powder blue skies that extend as far as the eye can see.

Andie and Roger are the perfect hosts, cooking delicious homemade meals grown in their garden, serving fine wine, and regaling me with tales of Archie's boyish antics. Ones where his father was clearly not around.

Andie mentioned her father is in the house, but he rarely makes it out of his bedroom these days. Old age has taken a grip of him, weathering him down by the day. Archie hasn't seen him, as far as I know. Nor has he mentioned him.

I wish he'd open up to me. Talk to me. But it's not my place to pry. Families are complicated. I know from experience.

I thought city life in the UK offered freedom, but the city has nothing on this place. Each day, I roam the fields with Archie by my side, pointing out landmarks and amusing me with memories of his childhood, the happier ones at least.

Sprawled across a chequered blanket a few feet from the edge of a lake, we laze under the midday sun, picking from a wicker picnic basket Andie packed for us. She's really pulling out all the stops. The basket is overflowing with local cheeses, fresh juicy apples, home-grown strawberries and even a bottle of chilled champagne.

Archie watches with a smirk as I sink my teeth into an apple with a satisfying crunch. 'If your bark is worse than your bite, I'm not sure I ever want to hear it.'

'Smart ass. Take your t-shirt off and you won't have to.'

That perfect Cupid's bow flattens into a broad, wide smile. His arms snake out to capture me, tugging me tightly against his chest. 'Fancy a bit of alfresco fun, huh?'

'I'll take whatever I can get.' The original wooden flooring in the farmhouse squeaks almost as much as the bed. Though I don't know if that's what stops Archie reaching out for me or knowing the man who made his childhood an utter misery could be listening.

Out here, in the open, neither is an issue. When we're outside, the cloud that hovers over him lifts. When we're inside the house, his gaze permanently returns to the wooden beams along the ceiling, though it's not them he's seeing. It's the man who lies above them. His father is the proverbial elephant in the room above.

In one swift jerk, Archie removes his t-shirt. My fingers automatically roam over his scars, with a fresh insight that the deepest ones he wears are on the inside.

Perhaps it's not only the people who present at A&E who need help to heal.

Our lips fasten, deepening into a kiss loaded with tenderness. Archie nudges me onto my back with one huge broad shoulder while his hand bunches up the yellow summer dress I'm wearing around my waist. Deft hands slip off my underwear. Powerful hips wriggle between my thighs.

With the sun beating down on my face and the man I love pressing down on top of me, I think I may actually have died and gone to heaven. We needed this. Needed the break. Needed some time together away from the spotlight.

Archie takes his time, pressing slow, languorous kisses all over my body. Goosebumps tear across my sensitive skin with every loving stroke, every gentle caress. He's behaving like I'm fragile this time. Truly, I think he's the fragile one and he's projecting. Either way, I'm revelling in his touch. Basking in his undivided attention.

When he slips inside me, it's slow. Sensual. We've joined like this so many times before, but this is different. On another level. Bringing me here has forced him to face up to his past. Reveal his vulnerabilities to me. And for that, I only love him more.

His pelvis rocks against mine, driving us into a mutual oblivion until we're shaking and shuddering, moaning each other's names.

'I love you.' His voice is thick with emotion.

'And I love you.'

His cheek presses against my chest, my haywire heart out of control.

'I wish we could stay here forever,' I tell him.

'Really?' Surprise taints his tone.

'Yeah. I mean, look at this place. It's so peaceful. So tranquil.'

He slides out of me and flops onto his back, taking my hand and pressing his lips against the back of it. 'Isn't Huxley Castle equally tranquil?'

'It might be if it wasn't filled with glamorous visitors clawing over each other to meet the rock star who lives there.' My head turns and I raise the hand that Archie isn't holding to shield the sun from my eyes. 'And don't get me started on the four-year-old divas who run wild on the grounds.'

He sniggers. 'Ha. You love them really.'

'You know I do.' It occurs to me that Andie and Roger's son, Jason, would have been about the same age as Bella and Blake are when Archie enrolled in the army. No wonder he's so attached to the twins.

'Come on.' He pulls me into a seated position.

'Come on what? I'll have you know, I'm in post-coital bliss and I'm thinking about a nap.' Sublimely satiated and more relaxed than I've been in years, perhaps even my entire life, I'm seconds away from drifting off.

'Let's go for a dip in the lake.' Archie effortlessly scoops me up into his arms, pretending to throw me in.

'Don't even think about it.' My palm strikes his back with a slapping sound. 'Besides, I don't have a swimsuit.'

'Oh, baby.' He places me down and pulls Andie's dress over my head. 'You don't need one.'

The sun does feel amazing on my bare skin. 'Skinny dipping? What if someone sees?'

A lascivious grin lights his face. 'You weren't too concerned about anyone "seeing" a minute ago.'

'That's because the only thing they'd have seen is your pert ass bobbing up and down on top of me.'

He snorts, all other troubles temporarily forgotten.

Scanning the scenery, there's not a sinner or saint on the horizon. I dip a tentative toe in the water and squeal. 'It's absolutely freezing.'

'It's beautiful once you're in, I promise.' He drops his shorts and tosses them onto the blanket.

My greedy eyes devour him, desperate to commit this moment to memory forever. He shoots me a wink before diving gracefully underneath the cool blue lake, resurfacing a few metres in, rubbing the water from his eyes. 'Get in. It's glorious.'

I dive in, the cold shock stealing the breath from my lungs. I'd follow Archie Mason anywhere.

Resurfacing next to him, I sweep the water from my lashes with a grin. The cold shock subsides, and the water feels amazing. I bob next to Archie until his hands find my hips and settle there.

'Will you go to see him?' The question leaves my lips before I have time to stop it. Maybe there's no better time given the way we just reconnected.

The lake has nothing on the colour of those deep blue pools staring back at me. 'I don't know.'

'I'm not going to presume to understand, but from what

Andie said, it might be your last chance.' I'm treading deep water, in and out of the lake.

'I feel as though if I go to him, it's admitting he still has some sort of power over me. Does that make sense?' He pulls my chest flush with his. 'And if I don't go to him, I feel like it's my way of saying I've risen above what he's done to me. Made my peace with it.'

'But have you, though?'

Archie's shoulders shrug beneath the water.

'Maybe you should truly make peace, instead of pretending to.'

'Maybe.' Fair eyebrows burrow into a doubtful frown.

'You don't have to decide today.' For the first time in my life, I hope the media scandal goes on and on and on because I'd happily spend the rest of the summer here in this idyllic bliss.

'Nice time at the lake earlier?' My cheeks flush scarlet as Roger wiggles his eyebrows suggestively over the dinner table.

Thankfully, Andie's upstairs seeing to her father. One less person to witness my embarrassment.

'Fabulous, thank you.' Archie is unfazed. 'Nothing like the simple pleasures in life.' He winks at his brother-in-law.

Ground swallow me whole, please.

A hacking noise from upstairs prevents Roger from commenting further. I'd put money on Archie's father having a forty-a-day habit in his time. His cough is relentless, but this bout sounds dangerously alarming.

'Help! Someone help! He's choking!' Andie cries from the landing.

I leap to my feet, banging my hip on the table in my rush.

Taking the stairs two at a time, I feel Archie behind me rather than see him.

In the room across the landing to ours, an elderly man is propped up in a double bed, his neck supported on a mound of pillows. Navy pyjamas do nothing to hide his frail, thinning frame. Andie's next to him, attempting to force him forwards in the bed, as she slaps the space between his shoulder blades.

'A piece of chicken!' she shouts without stopping.

'I'm a doctor. Let me at him.' I push her aside, watching as his face turns increasingly purple with each passing second.

Before I can do anything, Archie yanks his father from his bed into a standing position, holding him from the front as crumpled sheets scatter to the floor. Archie's hands lock into position on his father's abdomen, and he begins abdominal thrusts.

On the fifth squeeze, the piece of chicken flies up and bursts out of his mouth.

'Welcome fucking home, son,' Archie pants sarcastically, but the relief in his tone is obvious.

He might pretend not to care for his father, but we all just saw the truth of the matter.

His father straightens himself as much as he physically can to look at Archie in the face.

His leathery skin is whiter than the bedsheets. 'Thank you,' he says, his gravelly voice ragged with exertion.

Archie places him back onto the bed like he weighs nothing before grabbing my waist with trembling fingers. His pulse thumps furiously in his temple. I squeeze his hand, hoping to silently convey how proud of him I am.

Leaving his demons at the door to save the man who unleashed them on him.

If that doesn't make him a hero, nothing will.

Chapter Twenty-Eight
ARCHIE

My heart beats at what feels like a million miles an hour as I take in every detail of the frail old man before me. The man who knocked out every ounce of confidence I ever had. Who relentlessly reminded me my mother died to bring me into this world and I'd better make something of myself.

He's about half the size of his former self. Weathered skin hangs from his slack jaws. His shoulders are lost in those cotton pyjamas.

Andie fusses over him, tucking him back in. 'Jesus, Dad, you scared the life out of us. What an introduction, hey?' Andie turns to Victoria. 'Victoria, this is our father, Wesley.'

'Dad, this is Victoria, Archie's erm…'

'Girlfriend,' Victoria announces, grasping his clenched fist and unravelling it with her slim fingers until his hand is slack in hers. She emits a natural radiance. An authenticity that not even Dad could miss. A kindness, a wholesomeness. Her smile is positively dazzling.

Dad's thin pursed lips lift into a half smile/half grimace. 'Pleased to meet you.' His voice is hoarse. I suppose he did just almost choke to death.

'Victoria's a doctor.' Andie repeats what Victoria already told him, doing her best to fill the awkward silence. 'Although we didn't need a doctor in the end, did we?'

Andie's hand brushes over mine. 'Thank God you were here.'

My father's eyes rise to meet mine. The whites are yellow and gunky. Narrow, dark pupils stare expressionlessly at me. Awkwardness hangs in the air between us. Years of unspoken resentment loom like a black, thunderous cloud overhead.

I don't speak.

Where would I even start?

Dad bristles and breaks the silence. 'Thank you.' His words sound thick, strained, unnatural.

My head nods, but my lips refuse to budge.

Something about being in front of him makes me feel like an inadequate child again. The weight of his eternal disappointment returns to my shoulders.

When Andie's satisfied Dad's tucked in tight enough he can barely move, she turns to me. 'Would you like a minute?'

My father's eyes lock with mine in a hard stare. Like he's waiting.

The ball's in my court.

Victoria sidesteps towards the door and squeezes my arm in encouragement as she passes. Her words from earlier at the lake flash through my mind.

'Maybe you should truly make peace, instead of pretending to.'

We're never going to be close. I'll always be a disappointment to him. But if there's a way to let go of some of the animosity between us, perhaps it's time to find out?

My head nods again and something that looks suspiciously like a fleeting flicker of hope flashes across my father's face.

Andie smooths her hand over her dress, beaming in approval. 'I'll put the kettle on.'

She follows Victoria out of the room, leaving me with the man I've spent most of my life avoiding.

My back rests against the wall as I try to find something appropriate to say. "How've you been?" isn't quite going to cut it.

'Thank you. Really.' Dad swallows hard, wincing as he readjusts himself in the bed. 'I'm sure it was tempting to watch with a bag of popcorn while your old man got his comeuppance in front of your eyes.'

'Don't be ridiculous, Dad. I never wished you any harm.'

All I ever wanted was your approval.

'I suppose I wouldn't blame you if you did.' He shifts uncomfortably beneath the covers. 'Wasn't exactly the most loving father, was I?'

'You could say that.' My arms fold across my chest. 'But I guess you had your reasons.'

He swallows hard. 'I loved your mother more than anything on this earth. She was my absolute everything. Each time she walked into a room, she lit it up brighter than a shooting star. When she died...' He shakes his head sadly.

'You blamed me. I know.' My jaw locks.

'I did. And I'm sorry for that, son. Really, I am.' He gulps in a large breath before exhaling slowly. 'It was easier to blame you than to blame myself.'

'It was a tragedy.' Her death. His treatment of me.

Our lack of relationship.

Shame it took him reaching death's door to realise it.

'Why blame anyone?' I don't get it. His cruelty was unnecessary. We'd all lost enough without losing each other in the process.

'It was me who pushed so hard for a second baby.' Glassy eyes stare out of the open sash window, gazing over the driveway, seeing something that's no longer there. 'Andie was a surprise. Your mother was only nineteen. We tried so hard for a second child, but we weren't blessed with another.'

It's the most he's ever said to me that didn't involve telling me I was a worthless little shit.

'Your mother knew how much I wanted another child. A boy to work the farm with me. To carry my name. So she went to some fancy doctor in London and got some sort of treatment. I don't know what.' His hand swats away something imaginary in front of him. 'But it worked. Within three months, she was pregnant again, aged thirty-nine.'

I swallow hard, every picture of my mother I've ever seen racing to the forefront of my mind. Her long blonde hair. Big blue eyes. Andie always says I'm the image of her.

No wonder he found it hard to look at me.

'Then that night, everything changed. I got what I always wanted, but it cost me more than I was prepared to pay. Each time I looked at you, all I could see was what I lost.'

My eyes seek out his sombre ones. Something like understanding passes between us.

I can't forgive him, but I do sort of understand.

If anything happened to Victoria, I don't think I could live with myself. Especially if I had some sort of role in it. Which I'm always going to have, given it's my job to watch over her.

'It was me I blamed, really. Not you. You just bore the brunt of it. For that, I'm sorry.' His voice cracks with emotion.

His head falls to his hands.

Shoulders shake in a silent sob.

To see a hard man like my father cry is akin to witnessing the ocean dry up. It's unfathomable.

The bed dips under my weight as my backside perches tentatively on the edge of the mattress. A cautious hand extends to grab mine. It's almost lost in my huge palm.

'She'd be so goddamn proud of you, son.'

The words I've waited to hear for my entire life.

Every mistake I've ever made flashes through my mind. The landmine. Almost throttling Harrison. Abusing Ryan's trust.

As if he can read my mind, he says, 'We're only human.'

'Isn't that the truth?' I agree.

His head flops back on to the pillow. Tired eyes flutter closed. 'Will you visit me tomorrow or do I have to choke on another piece of chicken to get your backside up those stairs?'

'I'll be up in the morning. I'm sure the real doctor would like to check on you, too.' I pat his hand before standing.

'She's a beauty. Take care of her.'

Tiptoeing out of the room, I leave the door half-open in case there's any more drama tonight.

The swirling blades of a helicopter overhead rouse me from a deep slumber. The back of Victoria's naked body moulds perfectly against the front of mine. It takes a second to work out where we are. Mad dreams have plagued my subconscious for the past few nights. Dreams where we decide to stay here and build a house overlooking the lake.

In my dreams I'm working the farm again, raising a family here. Teaching my children to swim in the lake. Giving them the childhood I almost had, with a mother and father who adore them and the space to run free. Catching up on lost time with my sister and Roger. Spending whatever time my father has left on this earth with him. Being here to greet my nephew when he returns from his first tour.

But dreams are all they'll ever be.

Some tiny part of me deep down always knew I'd have to come home at some point and confront my demons. The ones that didn't originate in the Middle East. But I didn't expect to feel such a sense of relief, acceptance and contentment.

The weight on my shoulders has miraculously lightened after last night.

This morning, it's a pleasure to wake up in my childhood home. To have breakfast with my woman and my family without tiptoeing around, avoiding one room in particular.

Rome wasn't built in a day, but last night provided a pretty good foundation to work with.

'Good morning.' Victoria stirs as my teeth nip at her earlobe. The summer sun beats through the open window, straight onto the light cotton blankets strewn across us. It's another glorious day.

'For a second there, when the helicopter passed overhead, I thought we were in Huxley Castle.' Helicopters coming and going are a daily occurrence there.

'Oh God, don't,' she moans into her pillow. 'We'd never get away with alfresco fun over there.'

'Doctor Sexton, am I to believe you're looking for a repeat of yesterday?'

'You'd better believe it.' She rolls round to face me, devilment dancing in those gigantic eyes. The highlights streaking her thick chestnut hair are brighter from the few days soaking in the sunshine. Dad was right. She's a beauty.

'I'm so glad Harrison outed us to the world and started his own personal witch-hunt because otherwise we'd never have come here. I never thought I'd see the day, but I actually might shake his hand if I ever see him again.' My fingers trace the perfect outline of her lips.

'You'll see him at my graduation. If Sasha and Ryan's PR team sort everything out before then,' she groans.

'Any word from them?' I don't recall the house phone ringing last night. Even a dodgy network can't keep Sasha from checking in on her baby sister.

An engine thrums in the distance, purring closer and closer with each second.

The bedroom door bursts open. Roger appears wearing only a pair of once white Y-fronts, clutching the shotgun over his protruding belly. 'Are you two expecting company?'

'No.' Victoria pulls the covers higher over herself.

'Well, we've got some.' Roger tosses me the gun and makes a quick exit. Presumably to get another one.

'Wait.' Victoria leaps out of bed, scratching around for yesterday's discarded clothing. 'The helicopter. Do you think it could be Sasha and Ryan?'

Sounds like something they'd do - just arrive without announcing it. Knowing Sasha, she probably can't rest until she's seen Victoria with her own eyes.

And as sure as God, the helicopter lands on the flattest field at Hope Farm.

Two minutes later, I'm forced to face another demon. A raven-haired rock star who's ready to pummel me to death.

'Archie Mason, get your fucking ass down here right now. You've got some explaining to do.' Ryan's voice reverberates through the open window, followed by the unmistakable sound of Sasha Sexton's tinkling laugh.

Victoria arches her eyebrows at me and shakes her head. 'There was me thinking my father died years ago.'

Victoria and I tear down the stairs in time to see Andie almost faint at the front door. I suppose it's not every day the world's hottest rock star lands on your doorstep.

Ryan's black eyes glare at me. 'We've just about cleaned up your mess.' He folds his arms across his broad chest, his jaw clenched so tightly it might break.

My eyes avert to the ground. 'Sorry, boss.'

Sasha pushes past her husband into the hallway, searching eyes seeking out her sister. 'Vic! Are you okay?'

Satisfied she's in one piece, she yanks her into a huge

embrace before turning to me. 'Archie Mason, you'd better look after my baby sister like she's the most precious thing in this entire world.' Her voice is stern as her index finger points at my chest, but a smile plays on her pink lips.

'She is the most precious thing in *MY* entire world. I promise I'll take care of her. We were going to tell you, I promise. We wanted to get home first.'

Home. Do I still even have one?

'You're coming home?' Sasha squeals in excitement.

'For the summer, anyway.' Victoria sets her straight before she starts planning our wedding. Though I wouldn't be averse to it.

I step outside to face Ryan, man to man. 'I'm sorry, Ry. I broke your trust. It'll never happen again.'

'You're damn right it won't.' His stance is rigid. Unforgiving.

'I had no intention of falling for her, but it was a foregone conclusion before I even got to Edinburgh.' I swallow the lump forming in my throat. The past twenty-four hours have been a rollercoaster of emotions. Who am I kidding? It's been a rollercoaster for the past six months, and longer.

'I avoided her for years because of the way she makes me feel. I love her, man.'

Ryan's expression softens. If anyone understands what it's like to be in love with a woman, it's him.

'You fucking lied to me, Archie.'

'It was more of an omission.' My defence is feeble. My apology isn't. 'Ryan, I'm so fucking sorry, man. I swear. We were going to tell you at the graduation. This isn't some casual hook-up. It's the real deal for us. I swear it.'

'You should have told me.' His hands fall to his side. 'Just take care of her, okay?' His tone is as reluctant as his acceptance.

'I didn't touch the salary you wired me.'

'I know you didn't. But why? Why do you continue to lay your life on the line for my family without taking any payment?'

My eyes meet his. 'Because you and Jayden dragged me out of my own personal hell by giving me a job, a purpose, when all I wanted to do was die, like I should have done along with my men on that final tour of duty. Because your family has become *my* family over the years. Because it's a fucking honour.'

'Then you'd better pay up.' He extends an upturned palm.

'I'll wire every cent back to you.' I pull out my phone, intending to do it there and then.

But Ryan shakes his head. 'Not the salary, Arch. I need good men like you on my payroll. But you owe the twins a fiver for the swear jar. They made me promise if I heard you swear, you'd pay up.' A small smile lifts his lips before he slaps my back in an awkward man hug.

'Guard her with your fucking life,' Ryan mutters into my ear. 'Or it won't be me coming after your balls with a carving knife.' He nods at his wife, who is smothering Victoria with hugs and kisses.

'Of course. You have my word.' Not because Sasha scares me, but because a life without Victoria does.

Chapter Twenty-Nine
VICTORIA

As the saying goes, all good things must come to an end. The scandal has died down. Angela, Sasha and Ryan's PR manager released an official statement to the press announcing that Archie and I are in a loving, committed relationship and that we wish to have our privacy respected as we enjoy this special time in our lives.

The Harrison situation was defused by the testimony of several other medical students. Apparently, I'm not the first woman he's laid his grubby hands on uninvited. Hopefully, I'll be the last. None of them have pressed charges against him, though. I can only assume mummy and daddy had to dig deep into their pockets to make the threat of court cases disappear.

The past couple of weeks at Hope Farm have easily been the best two weeks of my life. I've been all over the world with Ryan and Sasha, on tours and movie premieres and a million other red-carpet events. New York. Vegas. The Maldives. But nowhere has called to me like the picturesque Cotswolds countryside.

Archie's home is so beautifully remote. We only ventured

into the small nearby town a few times, but nobody batted an eyelid. It's the first chance I've had to be truly anonymous since Ryan Cooper came back into my sister's life all those years ago.

Huxley Castle looks remote from the outside but growing up, it was always filled with guests, strangers, and staff. Even before my family became famous, there were always eyes on me. I was 'poor Victoria' the girl who survived the car crash that killed her parents.

Here, I'm no one and I've loved every minute of it.

I haven't put on a flick of make-up since I arrived. Haven't seen a designer dress, let alone put one on. We've walked the land, been shooting, swum in the lake, sipped champagne... and other delicacies, you could say.

But the best part has been watching Archie build a bond with his father he never thought possible.

The smile gracing Archie's lips is no longer a false one to mask the hurt he's hiding. It's genuine. Warm. Overflowing with happiness.

I doubt I'll ever use my Instagram account again. Being unplugged from the pressure of social media platforms has been utterly empowering. I've missed chatting to Libby and Mel, but the past couple of weeks have taught me I don't need to be in constant contact to feel part of a friendship group. I don't need to check everyone's social media updates the second they post them.

While suffering from FOMO, I was actually missing out on so much more - the minute details of the real world.

The tiny details are really the big things. Like the subtle way Archie gravitates to me, like I'm the sun and he's the earth.

If he did that when we were in Edinburgh, I missed it. Maybe because my nose was permanently buried in my phone. Or maybe because he was so busy watching everything around us. Scanning for danger.

It's been a real eye-opener. I feel as if I've matured into the woman I've always meant to be. I've been searching for something my entire life, but I never imagined it was solitude. Simplicity. Love and laughter.

I don't want to give up medicine, or the madness of A&E, but imagine finishing a busy shift and coming home to this. It's a prospect I can't get out of my head.

I don't know if I'll ever be able to move home to Huxley Castle with Archie, but maybe there's an alternative solution…

As we bid Andie and Roger farewell, a lump forms in my throat.

Wesley said his goodbyes earlier and is currently taking an afternoon nap, although I think it might be his way of avoiding having to say goodbye. Andie throws her arms around me, pressing her tiny frame against mine. 'Come back as soon as you can, and as often as you can.'

'We will,' I promise. She might not be quite so enthusiastic if she knew how quickly I'm imagining us returning. Or for how long.

Archie's Adam's apple bobs up and down and his eyes look suspiciously glassy as he gazes at the upstairs window where his father is supposed to be sleeping. The curtain twitches and Archie raises a hand. 'We'll definitely be back in a couple of months.'

'Take care of each other,' Andie urges, with Roger at her side. A sombre expression etches on his sullen face as he wraps an arm around his wife's shoulder.

Archie opens the passenger door of the car and I slip in.

I've been off the radar for the last couple of weeks, but in the best possible way. The prospect of going back to the real world seems colourless in comparison to the violet flower baskets overflowing with pansies. The ice-blue lake. The rolling emerald countryside.

The engine starts and I raise a hand, wondering why tears are threatening at the corners of my eyes. This is not my home. They're not my family.

But if you get married, they will be.

The second we reach civilisation again, my phone beeps with a million notifications. I can't bring myself to look at any of them.

Archie's phone pings with a voicemail. He lets the message from Declan, the guy Ryan uses to find out things, play over the car's handsfree system. 'Archie, I have an update on Lily-May, the girl you asked me to look into. No blood relation has come forward to take her in. They're interviewing families for a more long-term solution right now. I'll keep an eye on the situation and keep you posted on the outcome. Cheers.'

Archie casts his eyes towards me.

Is he thinking what I'm thinking? Or has the sunshine and family time gone straight to my head?

My mind churns faster than the wheels of the car, silently swirling with possibilities and weighing the risk.

The drive back to Edinburgh takes an age. The traffic is horrendous. The air seems thicker. Polluted. My lungs feel jammed with smoke and smog.

'You're quiet.' Archie's gaze flicks sideways to me.

I nod, unsure whether to voice the mad ideas floating around my head on autopilot. 'Is it mad that I miss your sister already?'

'I know the feeling. How did I let all those years pass? All that time I'll never get back.' His hand falls to my thigh, his thumb brushing tiny light strokes over my skin. It's not just sensual. It's loving.

I've never felt more loved by anyone.

The sky is streaked with pink and orange by the time we pull up outside the house. It's only been a few weeks, but it feels so much longer.

Marissa and Kristina are outside their own house. Kristina locks the door then Marissa double-checks it, testing the brass handle with a twist.

They are both immaculately dressed as usual. Flawlessly applied make-up accentuates Kristina's already stunning cheekbones and lips. Before I might have asked where they were going with the hope of being invited along too.

Now, I can't get into the house quickly enough.

I wave and watch as they hop into a taxi that waits for them, grateful for once that there's no time for small talk.

The alarm isn't set. Miriam, the cleaner, must have been in. Archie tuts but doesn't say a word.

Inside, everything looks exactly as it was when we left. The "country style" kitchen looks laughable in comparison to the true, authentic country kitchen in the Cotswolds. It's about as authentic as a fifty-year-old's tight, flawless forehead.

I open the fridge. Miriam has at least emptied and restocked it. The thought of mouldy food turns my stomach. Blood, bodily fluids and bullet wounds, no problem. But maggots are in a league of their own.

I light a candle, hoping to create some sort of cosy ambience, but I just don't feel any ounce of joy at being home. Because it's dawning like the brightest sunrise that whatever shade I paint the front door, the walls or any other room, this house has never felt like home.

It's missing love and laughter and purpose.

It's the most stunning cage a bird could be homed in, but the beauty doesn't take away the desire to fly free.

I am that bird.

Archie pours us both a whiskey from the crystal decanter. We have nothing else to do. Given we left without a single item of clothing, there's nothing to unpack.

'Can I say something crazy?' We both say, simultaneously.

Archie's bright blue eyes lock with mine, swirling with compassion and a depth I could drown in. I'm still scratching the surface with this amazingly layered man, and I can't wait to get all the way to the bottom and back again.

He pulls my hips to settle against his as he rests on the kitchen counter. 'You first.'

'It's going to sound really far out there, but I've had this mad idea that's been plaguing me the entire way home.'

'Go on.' Earnest pupils gaze into mine.

'I think we should consider moving to the countryside.' I swallow the feeling of silliness rising inside. 'Specifically, the Cotswolds countryside.'

Archie's head tilts to the side as if he's deliberately putting his ear lower to my lips to check he heard me right. 'It's like you plucked the words straight from my mind.'

Swirling his whiskey around the crystal tumbler, he stares at me thoughtfully. 'Why though? How could you think it's the right thing for you? You have your career to consider. You're so young. It's so quiet there. What could the countryside offer you? I'm not trying to dissuade you. The opposite, in fact, but I want to understand why.'

Taking a sip of whiskey, I search for the right words. 'It might be quiet, but I've never had as much freedom. Never felt less pressure to conform to what I'm "supposed to be." The youngest "Sexton Sister", following in the footsteps of my two super-successful, high-profile sisters.

'I didn't realise it before, but I prefer the quiet life. The lack of pressure. I love the busy ward and the pressure in the hospital, but that's where it stops. I don't want that pace in my personal life. I want to build a home that feels like a home. One that I can truly unplug in.' My hand sweeps around the kitchen to reinforce my point. 'A sanctuary that actually is a sanctuary and not just fashionably designed to look like one.'

'Really?' Archie's pupils search mine, brimming with hope and possibility.

'Yes. I want to settle somewhere outside of the limelight. Somewhere we can raise a family without being hounded by the paparazzi. Somewhere we're not looking over our shoulders. I've always craved a normal life. During these past couple of weeks, it's the first time I've felt anything close to normal in years.'

Archie exhales slowly, drawing me closer into his chest. He's my home. His chest. His arms. Enveloped by his love.

'Baby, I want that too. All of it and more. I'm tired of looking for reasons to worry, instead of reasons to live.'

'Exactly.' We are on the same page. 'I can apply to do my postgraduate placement in a hospital in Oxford or Gloucester. I don't need to be in a city to do the work I love.'

'And I can help Andie and Roger look after Dad and run the farm. It's a lot of work for them. We can build a house nearby, but not too close.' His hand roams to my ass and squeezes. 'I want to be able to ravage you in the meadows anytime I feel like it.'

My hips buck against his at the suggestion. 'Oh my God, it sounds like absolute heaven.'

'What about *your* family?' His voice drops.

'I love them so much, but being apart from them has allowed me to find myself. I don't need to be babysat anymore.'

'Don't I know it.' His pelvis nudges deeper against mine.

'Also, I know this sounds even crazier, but do you think they'd consider us as foster parents for Lily-May? I can't get her out of my head, Archie.'

His teeth catch his lower lip. 'I've been waiting for you to say that. When you asked me to look into her background, I knew this day would come. Is it crazy? Absolutely. Am I up for the challenge? Also, absolutely.'

The squeal that erupts from my throat is one of excitement, hope, and wonder. 'Are we really doing this?'

'Fuck it, why not? If we don't try, we'll never know.' Archie raises his glass in a toast.

'Everyone's going to think we're utterly bananas.'

'*Everyone* doesn't matter.' Warm lips seek mine, cementing our newfound plans.

A feeling of purpose I'd been missing since my placement ended settles in my stomach. 'You know this calls for champagne, right?'

Archie sets down his whiskey on the counter before lifting me into his arms and positioning my backside on the granite while he searches the fridge.

'This is a travesty! We're out of champagne. You're definitely not following the usual path of the Sexton sisters. If Chloe heard about this, she'd set up a counselling hotline or something.'

'First world problems.' My eyes rise to the ceiling. 'Will you pop out to the off-licence on the corner?'

Archie's head jerks in my direction. 'I can't leave you.'

'Oh, come on, Arch. It's not like someone's going to steal me. Lock the door. I'll grab a quick shower. I feel revolting after that drive. Then we can really start the celebrations, okay?'

A doubtful look forms on his handsome face.

'Seriously? I'll barely have turned the water on, and you'll be back. Go. Please. Or I will call Chloe and get that champagne hotline set up.'

Archie reluctantly grabs his keys from the kitchen table. 'I see you'll compromise on the countryside, but not on your drink of choice. You're more like your sisters than you think,' he teases.

'Only because we're celebrating.'

He darts over to me, pressing a kiss on my lips. 'I'll be two minutes. Not even. Will you be okay?'

'For two minutes?' I roll my eyes. 'I think I'll manage. Come on, Arch. You've never babied me before. Don't start now.'

'Two minutes,' he reiterates, intensely.

I hop off the worktop, opening the overhead cupboard in search of champagne flutes.

The front door bangs closed. The handle rattles as Archie checks it's locked.

The exasperated sigh about to leave my lips is trapped and smothered by the cold, clammy hand that clamps over my mouth.

I'm dragged backwards, panic raging in my chest, as a familiar voice hisses in my ear. 'Welcome home, Doctor Sexton.'

Chapter Thirty
ARCHIE

There's a queue in the off-licence. A white-haired woman tuts impatiently behind the glass-walled counter, pursing her deeply lined lips as the customer she's serving counts out pennies from a small, worn purse.

Two teenagers giggle in front of me, nudging each other's ribs. If their nervous laughter doesn't give them away, their overly made-up faces definitely reveal they're underage. The white-haired woman doesn't seem to care. The teenagers take their time ordering what seems like every flavour of alcopop in the shop. I check my watch for the tenth time in two minutes.

I should be back by now. I shouldn't have left her.

She's a grown woman. In a locked house.

I pull up the security cameras on my phone to double-check. The front door is closed. The motion sensor lights haven't been activated since I left.

She's okay.

Eventually the teenagers hand over their money, practically running out of the store as if worried the shop assistant might change her mind.

'Can I get a bottle of Bollinger, please?' The good stuff is on the floor-to-ceiling shelving behind the counter.

I dig into my pocket for my wallet. 'Actually, better make it two.'

'Someone's celebrating...' The assistant's pursed lips crinkle tighter as if celebrating's frowned upon.

'Yep.' My eyes flick to my wristwatch again.

The assistant rings my purchases through the till, nowhere near quickly enough for my liking, and I hand over my card, punching in the pin so fast my fingers skim the wrong digits. It takes three attempts to get it right.

'Do you want a bag?' she calls, but I'm already jogging through aisle upon aisle of Pinot Noir and Pinot Grigio.

My gut is on fire.

Every hair on my body prickles to attention.

Something's wrong.

My instincts are screaming at me.

Like a sixth sense, I just know. I feel it with every single fibre of my being.

I sprint the two hundred metres to Victoria's house, my breath burning the lining of my lungs. The front door's still locked. There's no sign of forced entry. So why is every electrified nerve ending screaming she's in trouble?

I insert the key in the lock with shaky fingers and force the door open.

My boots pound the stairs up to the first floor. The kitchen's empty. I drop the bottles onto the counter. 'Vic?' Panic weighs my tone. 'Victoria?'

I scan the living room with eagle eyes. There's not so much as a cushion out of place.

I run for the stairs up to the third floor. The bedroom door's closed, but even with the Saturday night traffic passing outside the sash windows, Victoria's muffled cries are audible.

It takes two seconds to grab a gun from my bedside

locker. Two seconds which I can't undo. Two seconds that may as well be ten minutes.

My boot connects with Victoria's bedroom door hard enough to shatter the wood into splinters.

Victoria's wrists are bound with a pinstripe tie above her head, her pretty mouth gagged with masking tape. She's on the bed, surrounded by an array of her own exquisite lingerie.

Doctor Dickhead leers over her. A long sharp knife glints in his hand.

'Ahh, Victoria's resident dog. And lover, I believe.' The strap of the summer dress Andie insisted she have this morning has slipped down, revealing Victoria's creamy collarbone. He runs a hand across her bare skin. I hate that he can see her like this, let alone touch her. Rage courses through my arteries, priming every muscle for action.

I point my pistol at his head. 'Get your hands off her.' My tone's lethal, yet somehow it invokes a smile from the sick, twisted fuck.

My ward.

My everything.

Outwardly, my hand doesn't shake even a millimetre. Internally, I'm quivering with enough rage and adrenaline to fuel a world war.

He presses the knife against her throat. 'I wouldn't do that if I were you.' A pinched smile curls his thin lips upwards. His voice is playful. Unhinged. He's enjoying himself. 'We've been waiting for you, haven't we, Victoria?' She flinches as unwelcome fingers stroke her glossy hair fanned out across the pillow.

I could probably put a bullet in his head before he had time to press that knife into her neck, and if it was any other of my wards lying on that bed I wouldn't hesitate, but what if he hurts her?

What if that knife pierces her throat?

What if I can't save her?

Stone-cold eyes mock me from across the room. 'You always did like to watch us together, didn't you? Well, you're in for a treat. We're going to give you quite the show tonight, aren't we, Victoria?' The knife slides lower over her heart and she whimpers behind the tape covering her mouth.

Mad, beady eyes dart to the lingerie he's put out on display. 'Quite an impressive collection.'

The dirty bastard. I should have known Harrison didn't have the cunning to execute this type of horror show.

Victoria's eyes meet with mine, pleading silently. Her body is rigid on the bed where we've made love so many times.

'This has to be my personal favourite.' He lifts a scarlet thong and presses it against his face with a long, slow appreciative inhale.

It plays out in slow motion before me.

But there's nothing slow about my reaction.

My finger pulls the trigger. The bullet exits the chamber with a crack, flies across the room, and penetrates Doctor Dickhead's shoulder. He crashes backwards against Victoria's vanity station. A mirror resting on top of it wobbles and smashes onto his head. A million fragments of glass flicker against the thick crimson liquid pooling round him.

I'm on him before he can understand what's happened.

He's no match for me. Nor ever would be. It's an abomination that he got close enough to find out, but I can't allow myself to think about that right now.

'It's okay, Vic. Everything's okay.' With my knee on his chest, I pry the knife from his hand. Blood continues to pool around him. Not enough to be fatal, but enough to ensure he won't be getting up anytime soon.

I pull my phone from my pocket and dial 999 for the

second time in this bedroom. The operator assures me a patrol will be with us in under three minutes.

My eyes return to Victoria. Silent tears stream down her pale cheeks as she wriggles across the bed. I rip the tape from her mouth without lifting my knee from Doctor Dickhead's chest. 'You're safe, sweetheart. You're safe.'

She rocks upwards into a sitting position, teeth tearing at the tie around her wrists. 'You seriously thought you'd get away with this?' Her high-pitched yells are wild, like an animal caught in a trap.

A low, disturbing chuckle slips from Doctor Dickhead's lips.

Dangerous creep. I use his own knife to cut Victoria's hands free.

'It was worth a try,' he hisses from beneath me.

'You'd throw your life away, all your years studying, just to hurt me?' She gingerly rubs the chaffed skin on her wrists.

'Not to hurt you. To have you.' His eyes roam over her lasciviously even as the blood drains out of him. His attention returns to me. 'Shoot me in the head. End this for good.'

It's tempting. Oh, so tempting. But I've killed enough men in my time. And he's no longer a threat. There's no way he'll be released. No chance on God's green earth. And I narrowly missed charges for assaulting one doctor. I'm not prepared to go down for killing another.

Victoria stands on shaky legs, backing away from the bed towards the doorway. 'You're like a man who's got nothing to lose.'

His eyes flutter closed. 'You always were my brightest student.'

Their exchange means nothing to me.

Sirens wail in the distance. They get louder with each passing second. 'Go and let them in. I'll stay here.' If they break down the door, I'll have to find a replacement. Impossible at this hour of the night.

Victoria nods, glassy-eyed and trembling. I hate that he's done this to her. I hate that I gave him the opportunity.

I might not have been two hundred miles away, but when it came to it, two hundred metres was too far.

I fucked up.

I'm ruined.

We're both ruined.

There's a reason why you're not supposed to fuck the ward, let alone fall in love with them.

I can't watch her back if I'm on my own. I did the unforgivable. I overestimated my own abilities. I'm fucking worse than Jared.

Victoria needs a man who can protect her.

That man clearly isn't me.

She could have died because I bent the rules. Again.

The St. Christopher pendant scalds the skin around my neck. So much for serving as a reminder.

Two uniformed police officers burst into the room, flanked by two plainclothes detectives. Doctor Dickhead is taken away in an ambulance to the hospital where he used to work.

He'll never work anywhere again. Not unless you count scrubbing prison toilets.

The police take statements. I email them CCTV footage from the previous few days. If I wasn't so busy shagging my ward, I might have kept a better eye on it myself.

It looks as if our intruder slipped in behind the cleaner and hid in the house for four hours before we arrived home. He had no way of knowing we were coming. Sheer bad luck on our part. Or rather sheer neglect on mine.

I almost had it all.

'Is it too soon to go back to the Cotswolds?' Victoria asks.

We watch from the kitchen as the forensics team traipses up the stairs, covered head to toe in white suits.

I pull her into me, inhaling the scent of her skin. Memorising the shape of her curves as they mould against me for the final time.

'We're not going back to the Cotswolds, sweetheart.' No point delaying the inevitable.

'What are you talking about?' Her eyes flash up to mine.

A huge sigh whooshes from my lungs. 'I can't protect you, even with security cameras, a top-of-the-range alarm and police swarming within a mile radius. There's no way I can bring you to the countryside where you'd only have me. It's not enough. I'm not enough. Your safety is way more important than my happiness.'

'Our happiness,' she corrects me.

'You call this happiness?' My index finger points to the floor above, the image of her bound and gagged on the bed permanently etched into my brain.

'Arch.' Panic taints her tone. 'What are you saying?'

'I'm saying we're over. I've been selfish for too long. I'm not what you need.' Every sliver of skin aches in a silent protest as I take a step back from her.

She follows. Angry fists pound my chest as if she's trying to shock my heart back into the familiar rhythm we've slipped into. 'You're what I *want*! Doesn't that count for something?'

'It's not enough. I'm sorry.' My feet shuffle backwards, dragging me away from her.

'You mean, *I'm* not enough,' she yells. 'You're sick of babysitting me. Sick of suffering these creeps who won't leave us alone. Admit it, I'm not enough to outweigh the hassle of being with a Sexton.'

I can't admit it. Because it's not true. But if I deny it, I'm giving her false hope.

'Pierce is on his way. He's going to step in until they can find a permanent replacement for me.'

'Don't do this, Archie.' She runs at me, desperate fingers clinging to my shirt.

It takes every bit of self-control I have to peel her from me and push her into the arms of a female police officer.

Chapter Thirty-One

VICTORIA

I hadn't planned on spending the remainder of my summer at Huxley Castle, but with the gaping hole Archie left in my chest when he ripped my heart straight from it, I couldn't survive anywhere else.

A part of me thought he might show up here at some point. If not to see me, then to return to his cabin. But then again, why would he? It might have been his home once but, now he's been reunited with his own family, he no longer needs mine to plug that void in his life.

The nights are endless without him. The terrors back in full force. I'm falling into oblivion. Not because of what happened with David Dickson, but because a future without Archie is like staring into the biggest, blackest hole of my life.

Sasha and I sit on the outdoor furniture, positioned near the edge of the dolphin-shaped water feature. We watch on as the twins run ragged, squealing and chasing each other on the pristinely manicured lawns of the garden, not a care in the world between them.

My mind strays to Lily-May. Is she okay? Did a family foster her?

I'm in no position to care for her right now. I can't even care for myself.

The rhythmic trickling of water is supposed to be therapeutic. So far, it's doing nothing to ease my troubled mind.

'How are you holding up?' Sasha's perfectly blow-dried curls bounce in the soft summer breeze.

She's asked me the same question every day for the past twenty-eight days.

My answer never changes. 'Hanging in there.'

It's the truth. I'm suspended in mid-air, waiting for something. What, I don't know.

With each day that passes, it's becoming increasingly clear Archie isn't coming back. Maybe I'm simply waiting to feel something other than crushing agony every time my delinquent brain summons the image of his huge oceanic eyes. The way his lips curl in a reluctant smile. The feel of his firm, rippled torso beneath my fingertips.

The fear I had that night, tied up and gagged, has nothing on the fear that plagues me now.

I can't fathom a life without Archie. And I don't want to, either. His lost presence has consumed every minute of my day and night for a month. It's been like losing a limb. A part of me is missing, and the pain is more excruciating than anything I've ever experienced.

Sasha shoots me a sympathetic smile. 'I have a surprise for you.'

Unless it's Archie himself, I'm not interested. Forcing a half-smile, I do a poor job of feigning interest.

'They'll be here in...' Sasha squints at her phone through the sunlight, 'two minutes.'

'Who?' A twinge of hope flickers inside me.

The only person I'm remotely interested in seeing, other than Archie, is Chloe. Where Sasha took on the role of my mother when she passed, Chloe has always remained my cool, older sister.

Chloe's married to Ryan's older brother, Jayden. They live in Santa Monica with their five-year-old daughter, Pippa, and their two-year-old son, Jayden Junior.

I used to wonder what might have happened if Ryan and Jayden had had another brother. Though Archie kind of was an adopted brother to them, which is one of the reasons Ryan is taking this entire situation almost as badly as I am.

Right on cue, a granite grey Audi Q7 crunches over the long gravel driveway, pulling to a stop at the front of the castle, where James, one of the castle's long-standing porters, waits between huge white pillars.

The passenger door flies open before James can open it, and my sun-kissed sister leaps out and throws her arms around him.

'James. You haven't aged a day. Seriously, I need to know your skin care regime,' Chloe teases him affectionately.

'Soap and a face cloth, and that's only if I've got time.' James grins, awkwardly returning Chloe's hug. 'Welcome home, Miss Sexton.'

'It's Mrs Cooper, now, James, I'll have you know.' Chloe pushes oversized Chanel sunglasses on top of her head and scans the castle grounds, her eyes falling to me and Sasha as we cross the garden to reach her.

'Ladies!' she squeals, running towards us in six-inch stilettos. It seems motherhood hasn't made her any more practical, not when it comes to fashion, at least.

Jayden slips out from the driver's side, raising a hand in a silent salute. Like Ryan, his hair's so dark it's almost black. They share a lot of the same physical attributes apparently, something I know way more about than I'd care to. My sisters have absolutely no filter when it comes to discussing their husbands' anatomy. Yuck.

We meet somewhere on the gravel to form a Sexton sister group hug. Tears roll across my cheekbones. Tears of relief to be surrounded by the two women who raised me. Tears of loss. Tears of heartache. Tears, tears and more tears.

'Oh, sweetie.' Chloe steps back, lifting my chin with her finger, forcing me to meet her azure eyes. 'This too shall pass.'

I swipe my tears with the back of my hand. 'Well, right now, it's passing like a fucking elephant-sized kidney stone.'

'You owe us a fiver,' Bella and Blake screech excitedly from my waist. They high five each other before offering their upturned palms.

'It's going to have to be an I owe you, I'm afraid.' My palm ruffles Blake's hair, dark like his daddy's. 'Unless you take cards?'

'Where's Pippa and Jay?' Blake asks Chloe, too excited to even acknowledge her properly.

'Uncle Jayden is unbuckling their seatbelts right now.' Chloe ruffles Blake's hair.

Bella tugs her mammy's hand. 'Why is Aunty Vic crying again?'

'Because she's so happy to see her favourite sister.' Chloe winks at Bella and hands her a fiver for my debt. 'Go see your cousins.'

'Grown-ups are so weird.' Bella takes the note and stuffs it in the pocket of her shorts, hugs Chloe and runs over to the Jeep where Jayden is unloading the kids.

'It's so good to have you home,' Sasha gushes, linking Chloe's arm on one side and mine on the other, steering us back towards the fountain.

'It's so good to be home.' Chloe inhales a lungful of air. She winks at her husband across the lawn as he puts a baseball cap on Jayden Junior. 'Is it too early for champagne?'

'It's never too early for champagne,' Sasha assures her, encouraging us to sit on the white intricately weaved wicker benches, laden with plump, plush pastel cushions. 'I'll go rustle up some and leave you two to catch up.'

Code for, '*Leave Chloe to talk some sense into you.*'

Sasha heads back towards the castle entrance and kisses her brother-in-law on the cheek before disappearing inside, leaving Jayden to haul Chloe's enormous suitcase from the boot, assisted by a red-faced puffing James.

'Come over here and give your Aunty Vic a kiss!' Chloe shouts at her offspring, but they're too busy playing with their cousins.

Chloe sidles closer, eyes raking over me.

I've lost about half a stone since I got here. Accidentally, that is. My stomach just can't tolerate food.

'Oh honey, want to talk about it?'

A sigh leaves my lips as I shrug. 'What's there to say?'

'I know Archie was your first love, and that is something that will stay with you forever, but trust me when I say this, no one marries their first love.'

'Sasha did.' Even if Ryan did disappear off the face of the earth during that time.

Chloe arches a single eyebrow. 'True, but that's a rare exception to the rule. And they were both with other people in between, even if it was only for a night.' She crosses one long, slim denim-clad leg over the other. 'I had to kiss a load of frogs before I found my prince.'

'I can't imagine ever feeling for anyone else the way I feel about Archie.' I gave him every single part of me. There's nothing left to give to anyone else. Not now, not ever.

Chloe stares at me hard. 'I know, honey, I know. There's nothing like that first love feeling. It's all consuming. It's obsessive, addictive.'

'I love him so fucking much it hurts.' I glance round to check where the twins are. Looks like I got away with that F-bomb. 'But in the end, it wasn't enough. I wasn't enough.'

'Oh, sweetie, it's not you. Can't you see that? It's not you at all. Archie fucked up big time. He was supposed to be guarding you and he left you alone. It doesn't take a psychiatrist to work out he broke up with you because he's trying to do the right thing by you.'

'So, why does it feel so fucking wrong, then?'

'Have you heard from him?' Chloe's eyes stray towards the far side of the estate, to where Archie's cabin is situated.

'Not a single word.' That's the worst of it. I lost my boyfriend. And my best friend too. Along with all my hopes and plans for the future. I neglect to mention I've tried to call Archie's mobile every day only to reach his voicemail.

'The worst thing about it is I finally found myself with him. Like, really found what I wanted. Where I wanted to be. And he ripped it all away from me, along with my heart. I don't know where I'm going. What I'm doing. I don't want to do anything other than what we planned.'

'You're so young, Vic. I know it hurts like hell, but the pain will ease. You will meet somebody else. Someone who deserves you.' Her thumb brushes away a single tear, but the next one replaces it just as quickly.

'It was me who sent him out for that stupid champagne. He was only gone for five minutes, and he shot the man who tried to hurt me. He did his damn job in the end. I'm fine, physically anyway. The culprit is behind bars, for now, at least.'

'What do you mean for now?' Concern colours Chloe's tone.

'He's dying, Chloe. Stage four cancer. He said it himself. He had nothing to lose. He'll be six-foot under before the year's out.'

'Good riddance. Hopefully, the devil's got room for him in hell.' Chloe shudders despite the summer sun.

Chapter Thirty-Two
ARCHIE

The countryside seems less quaint and more barren without Victoria to share it with.

The lake is nowhere near as enticing when I'm sitting by it alone.

And my family is nowhere near as endearing when they have an opinion they can't stop pressing upon a person.

For twenty-eight days straight, I've worked the land. Sanded the windows and door. Repainted every inch of the place, including the stables, which are currently empty. I've worked my fingers to the bone, hoping enough manual labour will serve to knock me out at night, or at least serve as a punishment for my utter stupidity.

Stupidity which almost cost me everything. The only saving grace is that Victoria is alive and healthy. No thanks to me.

Pierce will protect her. She's in good hands.

Whose hands will she be in next, though?

The thought tortures me. Which lucky bastard will get to keep her? I was a fool to believe it could ever have been me.

'Archie, there's a phone call for you,' Andie yells across the field from the farmhouse.

Hope and dread spark and duel in my sternum. Nobody knows I'm here.

Dusting the dirt from my hands, I push myself up from the grass and trudge across the field, in through the open back door.

My own phone is dead in my bedroom. It seemed pointless charging it when there's no network here, anyway. The only person I actually want to hear from is better off not being able to reach me.

I take the receiver from Andie's outstretched hand with a raised eyebrow. She shrugs.

'Hello?'

'There you are.' It's Declan, Ryan's fixer and finder. The guy who ran Harrison's background check. Shame I didn't think to get him to do one on Doctor Dickhead too.

'Declan, how can I help?' He must have heard I no longer work for Ryan.

Declan clears his throat. 'I'm following up on that case you asked me to keep an eye on. The girl.'

'Lily-May?' I've thought of her every day, but I'm in no position to do anything for her right now. A single man, with no references or experience with kids, other than babysitting the Cooper twins. No social worker in their right mind would consider me a suitable foster parent for Lily-May, no matter how hard I fought. A female doctor and her partner, however, would have been an entirely different story.

'She's in trouble. She ran away from the foster home twice before ending up back in A&E with some questionable bruises. I thought you'd want to know.'

Damn right I want to know.

But what can I do about it?

'Do you know of any *relatives* who might be willing to take her on?' His meaning is clear.

Could *I* do it?

Step up and actually do something meaningful with my life?

Silence rings in my ears.

'Does Victoria know about this?' I'm sure she'd want to know. We might not be able to foster Lily-May like we'd originally hoped, but surely we could do something for the child we can both relate to on so many levels.

'She's not taking any calls,' Declan says, revealing nothing about her whereabouts. Did she stay in Edinburgh? Go to Belfast to prepare for her next placement? Go to Europe like she mentioned?

It's none of my business. I have no right to know.

But one thing I do know with absolute certainty is she'd want me to help Lily-May.

I couldn't protect Victoria, but there's no reason I can't protect a little girl. Especially here, with the help of my sister.

Would Lily-May want that? Something in my soul stirs. I was born to serve and protect, even if I haven't always been the best at it.

'I'd love to do it, but I can't imagine for one minute they'd think I was suitable. However, my sister and her husband have a fabulous home for a child.' My gaze meets Andie's. She's leaning against the kitchen doorway, not even bothering to pretend she's not eavesdropping.

I shoot her a silent plea with my eyes.

She mouths, 'What the fuck?' At least it's not a straight no.

'I might be able to fabricate some sort of distant relative claim to Lily-May if you send me on enough paperwork,' Declan says. 'Passports, birth certificates. Give me everything you've got, and I'll do the rest.'

What am I doing? Taking on a child I've met only a handful of times. One who wants to be with Victoria as much as I do.

At least we have that in common.

I know nothing about raising kids.

Am I trying to impress Victoria? Or is it because I want a second chance at protecting someone I care about, even if it is a four-and-a-half-foot hellraiser?

I honestly don't know.

But I do know I can't abandon her. She's clearly not happy where she is.

'Give me an hour to reach civilisation and a fax machine,' I say.

'You'll want to get some sort of wi-fi network booster if you're planning on staying down there in the sticks,' Declan advises.

'I like being off grid,' I admit.

'Isn't it lonely?'

'It might not be for much longer.' Oh God, what am I doing?

The sound of his chuckle drifts through the receiver before he hangs up.

Andie stalks across the room. 'You can't seriously be thinking about adopting a child?'

'Deadly serious. Well, foster at first.'

'What the actual fuck, Archie?' Her hands rise in an exasperated gesture.

'Victoria and I had decided we wanted to try to help Lily-May before... before *that* night.'

When I arrived here, pale-faced and broken-hearted, Andie coaxed the whole sorry story out of me, minus the part where Victoria and I had discussed trying to foster Lily-May together.

'So you want to honour your word to Victoria?' Andie asks.

Do I? Is that what this is?

'In some ways, yes, but it's so much more than that. Lily-May's mother died in the hospital on Victoria's shift. We forged a bond with her. Both of us saw ourselves in her. When Mum died, I had you. When Victoria's parents died, she had her sisters. But Lily-May has no one. I had hoped she'd find a nice family, given Victoria and I obviously couldn't take her on anymore, but she hasn't, Andie. I can't leave her there, knowing she's miserable.'

'Archie, we're talking about adopting a child. Or fostering, at least.' She blows out a long, slow breath. 'A child who's going to need stability, security and love. If you do this, there's no going back. It's a bigger commitment than marriage. You can't divorce a child.'

'I know. But I can give her what she needs. Security. Stability. A family, if you don't mind being part of this.'

I made a lot of mistakes in my life which I can't fix, but I can do as much good for others as possible to make up for it.

Andie flips a tea towel over her shoulder and stretches her hands out towards me. 'You spoke about building a house here. Is this why? Are you really going to settle here? Or are you going to swan off for another fifteen years and leave me to raise this kid?'

'When we came last month, I didn't expect to feel the way I did about all of you, and about this place.' I lean on the freshly painted hall wall for support. 'I missed you all so much. Missed this house. Missed having a home. I thought I found one at Huxley Castle with Victoria's family, but I was only playing happy families there. Trying to fill the void of my own.'

Andie's features knit into a sympathetic expression. Her

mouth opens, but I silence her with a raised finger, needing her to hear what I have to say.

'Coming home after all these years was more terrifying than going into battle. War is filled with nameless faces. Enemies you don't know. Coming home, I thought I was my father's enemy. And facing the scorn on his face, his disappointment in me, was one of the most daunting confrontations in my life.'

'You were never my enemy, son,' a croaky voice calls from up the stairs. 'I was my own enemy and you bore the brunt of it. I'm sorry, lad.'

Of course, he's been listening to every word. This old house holds no secrets.

'We've been over this. No need to keep apologising,' I shout up the stairs.

I place a hand on my sister's shoulder. 'I know it's asking a lot, not only having me here but a child you don't even know, but she's a great kid and I'll take full responsibility for her.'

Andie sighs. 'I think you've completely and utterly lost the plot.'

'Did you ever get a gut feeling about something? A feeling so powerful you can't override it, no matter how crazy it sounds?' My hand grips her shoulder gently.

Andie's mouth opens and closes again. 'I... er... I suppose I got that when I held you for the first time. I was only a teenager. I had no idea what to do with a newborn. I'd never even changed a nappy before. But I knew we'd be okay. That we'd work it out. And we did.'

'So, you understand then?' I release her shoulder with a smile.

She moistens her lips. 'You were my brother. My blood. There was no way I was going to let anyone else raise you.'

'Well, Lily-May doesn't have that luxury.' My hands grip the banister as I turn for the stairs, taking them two at a time. I need to find my passport and other identification papers for Declan. 'I'm going to give her a chance.'

A croaky cough emanates from behind Dad's half-open bedroom door. 'Speaking of chances, I think it's time you gave yourself one, son.'

When I pop my head round the door, my father lifts his head from his pillow, beckoning me in with a crooked finger.

'In here now, Archie,' he wheezes, straightening himself in the bed. 'It's about time I gave you some fatherly advice, to prepare you for the role you're volunteering for.'

Fatherly advice? Huh, what does he know about it?

But maybe it's finally time to let bygones be bygones. I perch on the edge of the mattress.

Roger was more of a father to me than my own father ever was. I may have forgiven him for that, but I'll never forget.

Narrow eyes hone in on me. 'Look at you, rushing in to save a life again. You can't help yourself, can you?'

'It's not about me, Dad.' Heat flashes up my neck. We're wasting time.

'It *is* about you, son. You're forever trying to make up for things that were out of your control. Your mother's death. The death of your men in the Middle East. The crazed behaviour of Victoria's tutor. It's not down to you to save the world. You owe it nothing.'

For a man who I felt I barely knew my entire life, he certainly seems to know me.

'I blame myself.' He raps his chest with his palm. 'I put a lot of nonsense in your head when you were a kid because I was hurting. You matter, Archie. You don't need to save the world to prove it. Taking on someone else's kid is a huge responsibility. There's a chance it won't work out. You'll fuck up. Make bad decisions because that's what people do. We're only human. Are you going to walk away from Lily-May as quickly as you walked away from Victoria, and say she's better off without you, too? Because if the answer is yes, then you should stay away and let someone else step up.'

My head shakes in disbelief. 'You think I just walked away from Victoria? I had to tear my soul away from hers, inch by painful inch. It's for her own benefit. I fucked up. Unforgivably so.'

'Don't you think it should be up to Victoria to decide if what happened is forgivable or not? Did you give her a say in it? Or did you decide to punish yourself for your mistakes and punish her in the process?' A hacking cough interrupts him. He points at a glass of water sitting on the locker next to the bed.

While I watch him take three long, slow sips, his words wash over me.

There's a grain of truth to his words.

I am punishing myself for my mistakes. But I deserve to be punished. I bent the rules again. I never learn.

Which is why I'm thinking of bending them again by claiming to be some sort of distant relative of Lily-May's. It's the only way I can save her.

Dad clears his throat and sets the glass down with a shaky hand. 'The woman I met was head over heels in love with you. Victoria worshipped every bone in your body. Love can be hard work, son. But when you find it, it's worth fighting for. What your mother and I had, it was a once in a lifetime kind of love.' Yellow eyes cloud wistfully.

'That's why I behaved so badly when it was ripped away from me. My behaviour towards you was inexcusable. If I could turn back the clock on how I treated you, I would. But I can't. Should I continue to punish myself? Rehashing all the things I could have done differently?'

'Jeez, Dad, no. Life is short. Let's move past it and enjoy what's left.' I rest my hand over the back of his.

A small smile lifts his lips. 'Exactly. Move past it and enjoy what's left. Tomorrow is promised to none of us.' He's nailed Victoria's sentiment exactly.

'Take it from me, you and Victoria have that once in a lifetime kind of love. Maybe you should take a good look in the mirror and understand it's not just Lily-May who deserves a fighting chance at happiness, stability and love. You do, too.'

Maybe he's right. We were so unbelievably good together. Maybe I didn't fit into her world. I'm nowhere near as educated as her, or sophisticated. But we share the same goals. The same ideals.

Could I really be her first and last love?

One thing's for sure, I won't find out hiding here.

Chapter Thirty-Three
VICTORIA

A stack of application forms fill my childhood bedroom at Huxley Castle. It feels wrong making decisions about a future without Archie, but he's left me no choice. I flip my phone over, trying to muster enough willpower not to call him for the millionth time.

He made his decision. It doesn't matter how wrong I think it is, I can't change his mind. Primarily, because I can't get hold of him, though that hasn't stopped me trying.

I tap his name on the screen, but the call doesn't even ring. It goes straight to voicemail again. Either he's blocked my number, or he's gone back to Andie's without me. I'm not sure which is worse.

With graduation only two weeks away, I can't stop thinking about him. He should be there. With me. He was *supposed* to be there. It's the day we were going to come out to my family and finally tell them about our relationship.

The past few mornings, I've dragged myself out of bed to run the trails on the estate, staring at his cabin, wondering if he'll ever return.

It looks bleak and empty, which is precisely how I feel right now.

I can't go on like this, mourning a man who's not dead, but simply doesn't want me and the endless drama that's associated with being part of this family. I can't even blame him. The second I got a taste of the quiet life, it's all I wanted too.

Life isn't a romance novel.

He's not coming back for me.

It's time to move on.

Watching Sasha with the twins constantly reminds me of Lily-May. Would the state let me adopt her as a single woman? Or do they only consider nuclear families? I have no idea.

It's something I need to find out just as soon as I've filled in these postgraduate placement application forms. Perhaps if I start looking forwards, I'll stop dwelling on what's behind me.

How is it possible I can have two men following me everywhere and still feel so lonely?

Sasha booked us all into the Caledonian Hotel as a 'graduation treat', but we both know the truth is, I can't bear to go back to my own house.

Not because of the bad memories but because of the good ones.

My hotel suite is large enough to house an entire family, which only serves to reinforce how alone I am.

Not so long ago, I was desperate for solitude, peace, and sanctuary. Careful what you wish for, right?

A buzz sounds from the vanity table. My phone vibrating against the glass top. Where once it used to buzz constantly with social media notifications, it's been quiet for weeks now.

It has to be Libby, or Mel, calling to try to coax me out for a few drinks when the official grad business is over.

I can't face it. It'll be hard enough sitting through dinner with my family. I catch a glimpse of my reflection in the enormous gilded mirror. The ever-present circles under my eyes are concealed with layers of make-up, but there's a hollowness around them that radiates from my soul.

'Blocked number' punctuates the screen. My heart leaps in my chest. Archie?

'Hello?' I press it against my ear and hold my breath.

'Doctor Sexton?' It's a woman's voice I don't recognise.

I exhale heavily. 'Yes, that's me.'

'My name is Lucinda Wright. I'm a social worker. I'm looking after Lily-May's case.'

It might not be Archie, but this could just be the second-best thing.

'You got my messages?' I'd left one every day for the past two weeks, urging her to call me back.

'I did.' Her stern voice echoes down the line. 'You know I'm not supposed to discuss the child with you. I know you were there with Lily-May when her mother died, and I admire the interest you've expressed in wanting to foster her, but I can't help you, I'm afraid.'

Can't or won't?

I never pull the family card. The thought of it usually turns my stomach, but in this case, I'll pull any string I can if it means helping Lily-May.

'Lucinda, I'm not sure if you know who I am, but I'm offering to change Lily-May's life forever. Give her a home. Provide for her. Shower her with love and affection. I know there's a huge amount of red tape to get through but, I can assure you, the child will not be better cared for by anyone else.'

'That may be the case, Doctor Sexton. I'm well aware of

your family's fame and fortune, but that doesn't change the fact you're not a blood relative.' Her clipped tone rings through my ear.

I push my glasses higher up onto my nose. My eyes have been too dry for contact lenses the past month due to all the tears. 'But in the absence of one—'

Lucinda cuts off my protests mid-sentence. 'Someone came forward.'

'What? Who?' My spine stiffens.

'I'm afraid that's confidential. But she's no longer in the care of the state.'

I don't know if I'm horrified or relieved.

Both, probably.

'Good day, Doctor Sexton. Please don't call me again.' She disconnects the call with a definitive click.

Am I destined to lose everyone I care about?

Three raps sound from outside my door. It can only be my sisters.

'Come in.' The thick plush carpet dips beneath my feet as I cross the enormous room to greet them.

My sisters look equally stunning in their graduation frock glory. A simple but stunning topaz Alexander McQueen dress clings to Sasha's slim frame. Chloe, never one to blend in, wears a flared hem Valentino in a shade of fire engine red.

Their glamorous attire entirely complies with the image the media paints of them.

'Oh, honey.' Sasha's worried eyes take in my puffy ones.

Chloe clicks her tongue against the roof of her mouth. 'Come now, sweetie, let's get you fixed up. We can't have you crying at your own graduation. Sasha will be bawling enough for all of us,' she jokes.

'I could cheerfully throttle Archie, you know.' Sasha holds up a bottle of champagne. 'Ryan almost did. He gave him hell for leaving you that night.'

A jolt of something powerful surges through my sternum. 'Ryan spoke to Archie?'

'Of course. Archie called to tell him he was resigning.' Sasha smooths the hair back from my face while Chloe fetches some champagne flutes from the minibar.

'Did he say where he was going?' I'm only torturing myself, but I can't help it.

'To stay with his family. Ryan said he sounded devastated. Archie isn't a bad guy, you know. Okay, he messed up, but haven't we all, at some point?' Sasha's slim fingers dust imaginary fluff off her dress. 'I thought he'd have come back for you, you know.'

So did I. Clearly, we were both wrong.

Tears prick at the back of my eyelids again. 'I'm not enough for him.'

'Oh, sweetheart, it's not that at all. Archie needs to get his head straight. It's not you, it's him.' Sasha's gentle hand tilts my face up to look at hers.

'I'm banning that man's name from being mentioned again today, girls, okay?' Chloe pops the champagne cork, sending it whizzing through the air. It hits the wall with a bang.

Dave, my newly assigned bodyguard, flies through the door. 'Everything okay, ladies?'

'It is now.' Chloe raises the bottle of champagne to him in a toast.

He doesn't smile. His surliness must come with the job.

An hour later, my sisters have given me a full make over.

'You look beautiful.' Sasha eyes my Bottega Veneta silk dress, dyed a gorgeous shade of jade green. Even with a slashed neckline, it's a million times more conservative than the ones I used to wear for a night out in the city.

'Thank you.' I examine my reflection in the gilded full-length mirror. Not bad for a woman who's spent the last six weeks crying.

'I can't believe it's your graduation! Six years seemed like a long time, but it flew by.' Sasha twists her wrists, a wistful expression creasing her face. 'I wish Mam and Dad could see you now. They'd be so proud of you! Who'd have thought we'd have a doctor in the family?'

'You know I still have a long way to go...' The postgraduate placement looms at the forefront of my mind.

'Did you decide where you're going to apply?' Chloe asks. 'You know, you could always come to the States for a couple of years. We'd love to have you, and their health care system is out of this world.'

If I hadn't fallen head over heels in love with Archie, I probably would have jumped at the chance. 'Thanks, but my applications went off last week.'

'Last week?' Sasha squeals. 'Why didn't you tell me? Don't keep us in suspense. Where did you apply to? Please tell me you're coming home.'

Home. It isn't a place, it's a person.

Don't go there Victoria. You'll ruin your make-up. Again.

'I applied for three.' My finger zips over my lips. 'I'm not saying another word until I get an offer.'

'You'll get offered all of them, trust me.' Chloe pats my arm loyally.

I hope so. But if I only got one, at least the decision would be taken out of my hands.

'Could you do your placement in Dublin?' Sasha is like a dog with a bone.

'It's easier if it's UK based.' Which is a saving grace because it's easier than admitting out loud that it's not I *can't* come home, it's that I don't want to.

My sisters still baby me.

They probably always will, to some extent. I am ten years

younger than them, I suppose. But that doesn't stop me hating it. Archie was the only person I didn't mind calling me baby, purely because he never treated me like one. He treated me like a woman. His woman. His queen.

My throat thickens.

The suite door flies open again. This time it's Ryan, followed by his brother, Jayden. They both look every bit like Hollywood stars, in similar tailored Tom Ford suits which showcase their gym-toned bodies.

My heart flips. Not because of the men, but because of the way they look at their women, my sisters. The adoration is inescapable.

My four nieces and nephews traipse in behind them. Graduation is an affair the whole family insisted on attending.

'Aunty Vic, you look so beautiful,' Pippa squeals, running a small hand over the jade fabric falling from my waist.

'You look beautiful too, honey.' Her long dark hair falls in soft waves, exactly like her mother's. She's even wearing a similar red dress.

'Twinning.' I eye Chloe and shake my head.

'Can't even buy anything without her wanting one in her size.' Chloe rolls her eyes exasperatedly, but the smirk on her scarlet lips says she loves it really.

Bella, Blake and Jayden Junior run around the suite wreaking havoc. 'Careful.' Visions of my glass Byredo perfume bottle smashing into a trillion pieces spring to mind.

Ryan turns his attention to me. 'Looking good, pipsqueak. Hard to believe you're all grown up.' He presses a kiss to my temple before wolf-whistling at his wife.

Yuck.

'I grew up six years ago. It's just none of you got the memo.' I down the remainder of my champagne and force a smile onto my face.

Jayden greets Chloe like they've been separated for a

month, not an hour. We'll be lucky if he lets her out of this room the way he's sucking her face off.

I clear my throat loudly. 'Right, let's get this show on the road then, shall we?'

It might not be the graduation I hoped for, but it's still a rite of passage. I worked damn hard for this. I wouldn't miss it for the world.

Paparazzi swarm the street outside the entrance of the Caledonian. Ryan's increased the security detail. Fourteen guards flank us as we get into the waiting limo to make the short journey to the Royal College of Surgeons.

Cameras flash from every direction. My sisters continue their conversation, holding their children by the hand, not one of them fazed by the circus surrounding us. Uneasiness eats me alive.

My mind strays to Lily-May. How is it possible to miss her when I only knew her so briefly?

I take a deep breath, gazing through the tinted windows at the sea of faces on the street outside.

Twin pools of bright blue pop from amidst the screaming crowd. I jolt forwards, craning my neck to get a better look, every fibre in my body fizzing to life.

The car moves forwards and I lose my line of sight.

Either the glass of champagne is hitting me hard, or Archie Mason was in the crowd outside the Caledonian, waiting to catch a glimpse of me.

Chapter Thirty-Four
ARCHIE

I was too late. The street was too busy. I'm so accustomed to being in the inner circle, I underestimated the crowds that had gathered to see the Sextons and how long it takes to navigate through them.

My assertive elbows part the crowd like Moses parting the Red Sea. 'Quick, let's get up to the Royal College, although it's probably mobbed up there too,' I yell.

'Would you not just phone her?' Roger suggests, readjusting the tie Andie insisted he wear.

'It doesn't quite deliver the same gesture, does it? Me coming all the way here to beg her to take me back, only to call her on the phone? It's going to take more than a quick, "I'm sorry", to undo all the hurt I caused.'

I shoot Lily-May a wink as we half-walk, half-jog up Lothian Road with Roger puffing every step of the way. A taxi pulls to a stop alongside us to let out a couple of Japanese tourists, and I grab the door before it closes.

'You free?' I pant.

The driver scoffs. 'No. It'll cost ya.'

'I'll pay double. Just take us to the Royal College of

Surgeons ASAP, please.' I usher my family into the back of the taxi before hopping into the front next to the driver. 'I'll need you to let me out first and keep this lot with you for a few minutes, if that's okay?'

'Nae bother once the metre is running.' The driver chomps on a piece of gum hard. 'Double, you say?'

'Yep.'

'Nicolson Street, aye?' he confirms.

'That's the one.' I toss a hundred quid onto his lap, and he grins.

Traffic moves ridiculously slowly. My biggest fear is they'll close the doors and I won't get to see Victoria graduate. Celebrating her success is something I'm determined to do, not just today, but every day. If she'll have me.

The grand grey building of the Royal College looms in the distance. People swarm the streets like ants, shrieking and whooping. I'm pretty sure they're not here to see Victoria, but her rock star brother-in-law and his super stylish wife.

'Pull in.' I turn to Andie. 'Let me find a way in first and I'll come and get you, okay?'

My eyes drift to the little girl with the strawberry blonde hair and earnest olive eyes sitting by her side. The one who's been discharged into my care.

On paper, we're cousins. In reality, we're still figuring this thing out.

All I know is that when I showed up for her at that foster home, she ran so freely into my arms, I knew nobody would question my lies, especially when Declan had done a terrifyingly good job creating a paper trail.

'You okay?' I mouth.

Lily-May nods and sticks a thumb up. 'Go get her, Archie.'

'Be careful,' Andie urges as I slip out of the car.

'Always.'

I take off up the street, bobbing and weaving through the crowds, bypassing the media circus outside the college building and darting into the grounds behind it.

If I could just get to Victoria, reach her before she gets up on that stage...

I glimpse the Sextons' limo pulling away. The cargo must already be inside. Using the side entrance, I strut in like I own the place. Or at least like I have the same level of education as every other guy in a suit here today.

Imposter syndrome creeps in.

You'll never fit into her life. You're not part of this world.

I give myself a mental kick in the butt.

We're going to start our own world. Far away from all this bullshit, if she'll still have me, that is.

I weave through two elderly gentlemen heartily slapping each other's backs. Their accents would make the Prince of Wales himself question if he needed elocution lessons.

I don't fit in here. I shouldn't be here.

Fuck it. Apart from being a brainiac, and from a ridiculously wealthy family, Victoria doesn't exactly fit in either.

Two suited, bulky figures flank the corridor branching off to the right. I'd know they were private security from a mile off, even before I saw their tiny, discreet earpieces.

They eye each other warily as I approach. 'I'm here to see Victoria.'

The taller of the two snorts. 'Yeah, so are the other million outside.'

'Just tell her I'm here.' I nod towards the door they're blocking. 'Tell them it's Archie. I really need to see her.'

'Yeah, sure. Will I stick the kettle on while I'm at it? Maybe shove a broom up my ass and sweep the floor too?' His smart mouth goads me.

His companion laughs, and without thinking, I grab his wrist and twist it behind his back.

He holds his other hand up in surrender without even attempting to put up a fight.

Fucking hell, where did Ryan find these guys? On the door of a nightclub? They might look the part, but they sure don't act it.

The other guy lunges for me, taking a swing at my head, but I dodge his fist, extending a foot, so he trips, landing on the floor with a thud.

These guys are no fun.

I open the door without releasing the first guy's wrist. 'She's not there,' he cries out in pain. 'They've gone up already. This is a private passage leading to the great hall, but they'll come out this way later.'

'Here's what's going to happen, okay?' I tighten my grip on his arm, inching it a fraction higher. 'I'm going to call my family and tell them to come in this way and you're going to let us all pass.'

'Who the hell are you?' Wild eyes dart back over his shoulder.

'I'm her bodyguard.'

His eyes widen.

I fire off a text to Andie, instructing her to come in the side entrance.

The security guy on the floor groans and glances around the floor as if he's looking for a weapon. 'Don't even think about it,' I caution.

'Ryan warned us you might arrive.'

'Did he now?' I'm not in Ryan's good books, understandably, but neither are these two meatheads going to be when he hears how effortlessly I breached Victoria's security.

'Know one thing. I'm not here for trouble. I'm here to make peace.' I slacken the grip on his wrist, easing it slightly lower down his spine.

'You're going an unusual way about it, mate,' the guy on the floor sneers.

Footsteps approach. I glance round, expecting to see my sister and Roger with Lily-May. Instead, I come face to face with Pierce.

'What the fuck, Archie?' His hands fly into the air. 'Could you not have just called her?'

'That's what I said,' Roger pipes up from behind, still fiddling with his tie.

'You guys don't have a romantic bone in your body,' I tut.

'I'll talk to you two later.' Pierce glances between the two security guards. He motions for us to follow him down the corridor. 'Come on then. Seeing as you've come this far. Sasha said you'd show up.' His shoulders shrug as his lips purse in a grim line. 'Ryan's going to take a little more convincing.'

I fall in line next to Pierce. 'How is Victoria?'

'As you'd expect. You broke her heart. Left her on the worst night of her life.' He shoots me a sidewards glare.

'I fucked up.' I swallow hard. 'Then I didn't know what to do, so I fucked up some more.'

'Are you done fucking up now?' Pierce asks.

I nod.

'In there.' Pierce motions to a closed arched doorway. Applause thunders from behind it.

'It's already started?' Sweat beads on my back beneath my suit.

He nods. 'Find a seat at the back and stand when her name gets called, if you want her to see you.'

I pause in the doorway, my hand hovering over the brass handle.

'You've got this, Archie.' Lily-May whispers up at me.

'Who's this?' Pierce's eyes volley between us.

'He's my new dad,' Lily-May announces proudly. 'And now we need to find me a mum.' She slips her little hand over mine and pushes until the handle drops. Another burst of applause creates the perfect distraction as we enter the magnificent room.

A high dome-like ceiling arches overhead. The walls are lined with row upon row of bookshelves overflowing with encyclopaedia-like spines. Gold backed chairs form line after line of seating and a makeshift stage is assembled at the front of the room.

Victoria and her family stand out a mile, assigned their own row, most of which is filled by suited security detail on either side of the Sexton sisters.

Even the children are present, sitting quietly for once. They must have been well-warned. Or bribed. Not one of them looks around as we slip into the only free seats left, right on the back row. Lily-May slips onto my knee while Andie and Roger take the seats on either side of me.

We watch as the university dean calls out each graduate's name one by one and they take to the stage to shake his hand, pose for a photo, and collect their scroll while their families watch on.

'Harrison Hughes.' A frown flickers across the dean's weather-worn face.

Harrison stands and an insignificant flutter of applause follows. He might not have been charged with assaulting any of the women who came forward, but he's clearly not as popular as he was.

Wanker.

It takes an eternity for the dean to work through all the graduates alphabetically.

I itch to make eye contact with Victoria. Ache to talk to her. Burn to touch her.

'Victoria Sexton,' the dean announces, and the audience goes wild. Victoria's sisters' shameless whoops and cheers ring out obtrusively in the hall crammed with conservative, stuffy old money. The kids stand on their chairs and jump like performing monkeys.

But none of them cheer louder than the little girl on my lap.

My legs force my chair backwards so I can stand, clutching Lily-May to my chest like a human shield. Like she might safeguard my heart if Victoria breaks it by not taking me back.

Victoria struts across the stage in a rich navy graduation gown and cap. Four-inch glittering heels click across the flooring.

Staring directly ahead at the scroll, she takes the dean's hand and shakes it. I silently will her to look up. To look at me. To feel me. Feel the weight of the words I'm not proficient enough to articulate.

Her head lifts a fraction, curious gold-flecked eyes dart to her sisters.

Look at me, woman.

Let me tell you I love you.

Her head whips up and her gaze eventually locks with mine, before darting to Lily-May and back again

'I'm so sorry,' I mouth.

Her jaw drops. The scroll falls from her hand, the sound of it hitting the stage lost to the continuous thundering applause.

She shimmies to the edge of the stage and hops off, leaving everyone in the room flabbergasted.

'Where is she going?' Chloe shouts. The applause dies down while people watch and wait to see if Victoria has truly lost the plot.

'Follow her,' Ryan's distinctive gravelly voice barks at the security.

Heads and necks crane as Victoria runs the length of the

red-carpeted walkway. With Lily-May still in my arms, I jog towards her until we meet in the middle of the room.

'I'm so sorry, baby.' My palm cradles the back of her neck, tugging her towards me. 'If you'll have me, I swear I'll never leave your side again. I fucked up. I'm so sorry.'

Victoria bites her lower lip, tears welling in her gigantic hazel eyes. Before she can say for sure either way, we're set upon by two screeching four-year-olds, Bella and Blake.

'You owe us a fiver, Uncle Archie.'

Chapter Thirty-Five
VICTORIA

He's here. He's actually here. And so is Lily-May.

But what does it mean?

'Archie?' My arms automatically go to Lily-May, but I don't take her from him. Apart from the fact she's too heavy for me, she clings to Archie like a koala clings to a tree.

'Victoria, I'm so sorry, baby. I should never have left you.' Archie's palm cups my chin with a familiar tenderness I've been craving.

'It was the worst night of my life,' I confess in a hushed whisper. 'Not what happened, but you leaving me.'

'I know, baby. I'm so sorry.' Archie's thumb brushes away the solitary tear that streaks down my cheek.

'I didn't think you'd ever come back to me. I didn't know if I'd ever see you again.' I swallow the surge of emotion rising in my throat. 'I don't know if I'll ever get over it. I've lost so much in my life already, I couldn't bear to lose anyone else.'

'I promise, I'll never go anywhere again, if you'll have me,' Archie says, his earnest eyes searching mine, reaching right into my soul and squeezing my very core.

'Doctor Sexton, take your seat please,' the dean demands from the front.

My lips chew my lower lip. 'I have to go.'

But my feet lock to the floor, hands fixed on Lily-May's cherub-like cheeks.

'Doctor Sexton.' The dean's tone is decidedly less patient this time.

'Victoria, if you'll have me, I'll never go anywhere again.' Bright blue eyes search mine.

I can't answer him. Because if I do, I'm letting him back in and leaving myself wide open to be hurt all over again. I need a commitment. I need to know he's serious. That he's not going to run at the first sign of trouble because he's taken it upon himself to decide what's right for me.

It's a battle to drag my body away from him and back to my seat. Like trying to tear the sun from the sky. Every inch of me wants to cling to him like Lily-May, but I'm an adult woman and it's my graduation.

I'm only present physically as the remaining few members of my class collect their scrolls. Thoughts whirl around my head like a tornado.

How can I trust him not to run out on me again when I need him the most?

How can I build my life around someone who leaves at the first sign of trouble?

How can I give him another chance when he's so unwilling to pay himself the same respect?

And what the hell is he doing with Lily-May?

Shit! He's the 'relation!'

He did that for her. For me. For us.

A hot swell of emotion surges within, along with a million questions.

Finally, the last person accepts their scroll and we're ushered outside to the high-walled gardens for the official photos. Chloe steps into line on my right, leaving Jayden and Ryan leading the kids by their hands.

People stare as we pass, flanked by enough bodyguards to set up our own security firm. My classmates gawp in awe at the spectacle my family brings. Their presence here overshadows everything else.

That's why we need to leave as soon as possible.

And so I can get Archie alone to ask him what he's doing here and what it really means, and whether he's planning on staying.

'I knew he'd come back!' Sasha drapes an arm over my shoulder, jade eyes boring into mine. 'I thought you'd be happier.'

'I am happy. I'm simply in shock.' My hand clasps my chest, fingering the slash neckline of my dress.

'You need to set some ground rules if you're taking him back,' Chloe hisses in my ear. 'He put you through hell and back. Make sure he knows you won't tolerate that again. Be strong.'

She's right. It's so tempting to run back into Archie's arms, but how can I trust him not to hurt me again? Not to decide what's best for me without even consulting me?

Waiting staff pass around flutes filled with fizzing champagne. I don't need any. My stomach is bubbling enough as it is. Bubbling with hope, excitement, and trepidation.

I feel Archie's presence. He gravitates around me, never letting me out of his sight. When he was first assigned to me, it used to irritate the life out of me. Now, I love being the focus of his attention. It's all I've ever wanted.

Archie weaves closer with Lily-May at his side and Andie and Roger at his back. My stomach soars with a trillion butterflies.

If I knew he wouldn't leave me again, if he could offer me some sort of security, I'd leap into his arms in a heartbeat.

But does anyone really have that kind of security?

Sometimes people don't choose to leave, they're taken.

In which case, does that mean to protect myself I'll never let anyone in again? It's a pretty miserable prospect.

More miserable than I've been the past six weeks, though?

'Congratulations, Doctor Sexton.' Andie weaves through my security, swathing me in a warm embrace. Roger pats my back awkwardly.

'Thank you so much for coming. I can't believe you're all here.' I turn to my favourite seven-year-old. 'Lily-May, we have so much to catch up on.'

'We have the rest of our lives for that, if you'll have us.' Archie steps forward, taking my hands in his. Something cold and hard presses from his palm into mine and before I know what's happening, he's on two knees on the grass, looking up at me.

'Victoria Sexton...'

'*Doctor* Victoria Sexton!' someone shouts from behind me, and giggles ensue.

'Doctor Victoria Sexton,' Archie begins again, his tone fraught with nerves. 'I have loved you since long before I ever should have done. And I will love you for as many years as we have left on this planet, and even longer after that. I don't want to just be your first love. I want to be your last love. Will you do me the enormous honour of becoming my wife?'

I open my palm to find the most beautiful diamond solitaire nestled into a plain gold band. 'It was my mother's. If you don't like it, we can buy something else.' Liquid topaz eyes gaze up at me.

'I... it's beautiful.' How much more security can one person offer?

Tomorrow is promised to none. I've always said we should live for today. Tears stream down my cheeks. 'Yes, Archie. I will marry you.'

He slips the ring onto my finger. 'I swear to you, Vic, I'll never leave you again.'

'I know.' And somehow, I just do.

I trust him.

Trust his sincerity.

Trust what we have.

My sisters whoop and cheer behind me, with Libby and Mel screeching alongside them. Archie leaps to his feet. His hot lips crash against mine in an urgent, frenzied kiss. He tastes like mint and mojitos, but mostly he tastes like home.

His fingers stretch over my spine, pulling my body against his. I groan into his mouth. Cameras flash and families cheer, but they all fade into the background.

When we eventually break apart, Lily-May runs to our side, her strawberry blonde hair bouncing behind her back.

My lips press against her temple, and she wraps her small arms around both of us, burying into my side. 'How did you get them to agree to let you foster her?'

'She's my cousin, don't you know?' Archie winks and pulls her between us again.

A blood relative. Of course. 'I'll ask no more questions.'

His fingers brush over the ring on my fourth finger. 'Enough questions have been asked today already.'

'Not quite enough. I do have one more.' Ryan steps forwards, a grim expression carved onto his face.

'Ryan,' I warn.

He squares up to Archie. 'Are you planning on sticking around this time?'

'I am. I promise. I'll take care of her, Ryan. Not because it's my job, but because it's my life's purpose.' Archie's flat palm rests across his heart.

Ryan's frown melts into a smile and he slaps Archie's back. 'Thank God for that. It wasn't just Vic you walked out on, it was all of us. You know you've been like a brother to Jayden and me since you saved our asses in that bar in LA.'

'I'm sorry. It won't happen again.' Archie's voice rings with conviction.

'I know.' Ryan nods.

Archie's family joins us at the Caledonian for my graduation/engagement dinner in a private dining room overlooking Edinburgh Castle.

'Do you think I'm too young to get married?' I ask Chloe across the table. Archie flanks my right, while Lily-May sits to my left, pushing steamed broccoli around her plate with a screwed-up face.

Chloe swallows what she's chewing before answering. 'No. You're a grown woman. A strong, confident, beautiful woman.'

'Can I have that in writing?' I raise my champagne glass in salute.

'The strong, confident, beautiful part?' Chloe's head tilts in question.

'No, the grown woman part. You and Sasha have babied me since forever,' I say. Archie squeezes my thigh beneath the table.

'Only because you didn't have parents to baby you,' Sasha interrupts from next to Chloe. 'You want to be treated like a sister and not a child, that's fine. But we want details you might not be prepared to share.'

'Ha.' I know exactly the type of details those two are hankering after. 'Deal. You'll get your details, although you'll be lucky if you don't hear them through the walls.'

'Oh God, who will mind the child?' Chloe asks. 'You'll have to think of these things now!'

'I will,' Andie offers from further up the table.

'Cheers to having another sister.' I raise my glass again. 'To family.'

'To family,' everyone choruses, clinking crystal.

We retire to Sasha and Ryan's penthouse suite after dinner to enjoy several more bottles of champagne in a place the children can relax, too.

Lily-May nestles between Bella and Blake on the couch, watching the Lion King with her shoes kicked off and a bowl of popcorn on her lap. She's already fitting in like she's been here forever.

When the party eventually wraps up, Andie makes good on her promise to keep Lily-May for the night, leaving Archie and me free to make up properly.

Electricity buzzes in the air, carrying the weight of my excited anticipation. Soon, we'll be exploring each other's bodies once again. After kissing our foster daughter goodnight and bidding our less than subtle cat-calling family goodbye, we practically run down the corridor.

Two security guards stand poised outside our suite. Archie nods before closing the door on them.

'I half-thought you might dismiss them.' The lock twists shut with a satisfying click.

Alone at last.

'No, they can stay. That way, I can focus every bit of attention on you.' His finger curls upwards as he motions for me to come closer.

'I can't believe you're mine.' His breathy whisper tickles my ear as he inhales the scent of my hair deep into his lungs.

'You better believe it. It's probably plastered over every news site in the world right now.' I wouldn't know. My phone is switched off. Everyone I want to hear from is under the one roof.

'I've missed you so fucking much, Vic.' Warm hands roam the length of my spine before cupping my ass.

His impressive erection throbs between us as his lips capture mine again. I can't wait. It's been too long. A yelp of disappointment emerges from my throat as he breaks our kiss, tugging me towards the huge four-poster bed.

'You look so fucking beautiful today, but that dress needs to come off now.' Hungry eyes roam over my body.

My fingers reach round and unzip the back of the silk. It falls to the floor to reveal his favourite ivory lingerie.

A low whistle of appreciation pierces the air.

'Leave the shoes on. I'm going to do what I should have done to you the first day you wore this lingerie for me.' He drops to his knees, parting my legs wide enough for his shoulders to slip between them. His mouth presses over the ivory silk, a hum of satisfaction vibrating through both of us. When his tongue dips beneath the material, a jolt of electricity sparks right the way to my soul.

My legs quake and tremble as his expert tongue swipes the length of me. I'm blinded by a dizzying desire for him to fill me up.

'Archie, please.'

Watching him down there, doing that to me, is enough to get me off alone, but I need him inside me.

'Tell me what you want and it's yours,' he murmurs against my clit.

'You. You're all I've ever wanted.' Heaving him upwards, I undo his belt, freeing his glistening length.

He pushes me onto the bed, not bothering to remove his clothes or the soaked scrap of silk covering my sex. Instead, he yanks it to the side and slides himself into me, driving us both to an inevitably quick, simultaneous finish.

'Just making up for lost time,' he jokes, as his heart hammers against mine.

My orgasm has barely subsided, and I'm already greedy for the next one. 'In that case, I'll need you to do that again in about three minutes.'

'I won't even need two.' His hips thrust against mine as he thickens inside me again.

'I'm counting on it.' The diamond glittering on my left hand reminds me we don't only have all night to make up that lost time, but forever.

The next morning, I wake naturally in Archie's arms, his heart thudding against mine in our own unique beat. For the first time in weeks, the night terrors didn't come.

'Morning, baby,' he whispers, instinctively knowing I'm awake even though my back is pressed to his front.

'Good morning.' If there's a heaven, I think I've found it. 'What are we doing?'

His lips nuzzle into the sensitive skin below my earlobe. 'Today? Or for the rest of our lives?'

'Both,' I smile, knowing the two are one and the same.

EPILOGUE
Two Years Later

Victoria

Chloe was right. I was offered all three placements for my postgraduate position. Obviously, I accepted the one in Oxford, at a small A&E department forty minutes from the farmhouse Archie built for us.

The bare soles of my feet pad across the marbled tiled flooring of the authentic country kitchen towards an enormous corner window. The expansive, picturesque view from our new home is like something from a glossy home-style magazine.

My heart skips a beat as my gaze roams the rural landscape. The setting sun renders it a warm shade of coral above the rustic horizon. Cattle and sheep graze in the neighbouring fields and we even have three horses in our brand-new stables.

There's no traffic. No pollution. And what's more, no paparazzi.

I never take the peace or freedom for granted. It's all I've ever wanted, and I'll never tire of it.

Our new house is nothing like the castle I was raised in,

but it is complete with an indoor swimming pool and jacuzzi. Archie still loves getting wet with me, but the lake's too cold for skinny-dipping this time of year.

Mind you, there's nothing skinny about me at the minute.

My swollen stomach stretches the cream woollen dress that clings to my skin as I stir a pan of sumptuous-smelling gravy. While heat radiates from the Aga, the life growing within me warms my insides.

Lily-May bends over a huge cherry wood table working on her homework. She's thrived over the past two years, slipping into a life with us more effortlessly than we could have hoped. She even says she wants to be a doctor when she grows up.

Her nostrils flare as the scent of rosemary wafts through the air. A leg of lamb roasts in the oven alongside some of our homegrown potatoes and carrots.

Tonight we're celebrating the end of my postgraduate placement and the official start of my maternity leave. Andie and Roger are on their way over for dinner. Chloe and Jayden are currently somewhere over the Atlantic on a private jet, and Sasha and Ryan's helicopter should be landing on our purpose-built helipad any minute now.

Sasha continues to baby me. But in my current condition, I kind of like being fussed over.

Libby's still living the party life in Edinburgh, while Mel swapped her nights out for nights in with an Italian stallion called Riccardo, who rents a room from her in the house she bought. My old house, to be precise. There was no point in keeping it. Not when we have no intention of going back.

Archie kept his cabin. It serves as the perfect holiday home each time we return to Huxley Castle. This way, we have the best of both worlds.

The back door opens and closes with a bang. 'Honey, I'm home,' Archie calls from the utility room. It's an ongoing joke because he's never not here. Neither of us wanders too far from the house, but when we do, I know I'm safe with him by my side. We don't need a throng of security surrounding us. Not here.

Archie strips down to his black boxer briefs, shoving his filthy farming clothes straight into the washing machine.

The intricate tattoo inked across his chest has another name scrawled in italics, weaving around the cross. His father, Wesley, sadly died last year, but not before we got to spend some quality time with him. If our baby is a boy, we'll name him after his grandfather.

'How are my girls?' Archie stalks across the room, capturing my mouth with his, before approaching Lily-May and pressing his lips against her temple.

'Ah, Dad! Put some clothes on! Aunty Sasha will be here in a minute!' Lily-May squeals.

'Worried, I'll embarrass you?' Archie motions to his bare torso and laughs.

'Yep. Can you see why?' Lily-May shakes her head at me. 'What will she think of us if you're strutting round here with no clothes on?'

'Will you explain to our daughter that apart from the fact Ryan probably struts around half-naked in his house, it doesn't matter what other people think?' Archie nuzzles my neck from behind as I continue to stir the gravy.

My head rolls back to rest against my husband's huge chest. The St. Christopher he used to wear around his neck as a reminder to play it safe has been melted and reshaped into a signet ring he wears on the fourth finger of his left hand. 'Other people are always going to have an opinion. Their views are their own responsibility.'

'Semi-nakedness is not an opinion,' Lily-May mutters, and we snigger.

The back door opens again. Andie makes a huge show of

pretending to shield her eyes. 'Holy moly, put some clothes on, brother, will you?'

'Thank you!' Lily-May slaps the table.

Archie pulls on a white, torso-hugging top and a pair of grey sweats from the top of the laundry basket. My eyes are drawn to the perfect V lines disappearing beneath the fabric. The pregnancy hormones have rendered me insatiable. On the plus side, at least I have 'details' to report to my sisters when they arrive.

The door opens and closes again. This time it's Roger. 'Something smells good.' His tubby tummy isn't a patch on mine these days.

An elbow nudges my ribs from the inside, and my lips curl up into an excited smile.

The low thrum of a chopper hums in the distance.

'They're here,' Lily-May shrieks, pointing up to the sky.

I gaze upwards with a smile.

I might have lost my parents in the beginning.

But I gained an entire family in the end.

THE END

Not quite had enough of Archie & Victoria's romance? Click here for a bonus epilogue... https://dl.bookfunnel.com/v7n7gakmy8

Other Books in the series:
FALLING FOR MY FORBIDDEN FLING click to learn more My Book
FALLING FOR THE ROCK STAR AT CHRISTMAS click to learn more My Book
Turn over for a sneak peak...

ALSO BY LYNDSEY GALLAGHER

FALLING FOR MY FORBIDDEN FLING
Click here to download... My Book
A RED HOT enemies-to-lovers romance with ALL the FIERY feels.

CHLOE

Even the name **Jayden Cooper** sends a hot flush of irritation through my veins.

His rockstar brother might be about to marry my darling sister, but that does **not** make us family.

That arrogant tongue and those smouldering eyes push buttons I had no idea I owned.

Going on tour with Jayden is almost as inconvenient as the hate-fuelled lust that steals the air straight from my lungs every time he's near.

Eight cities.

Eight concerts.

Eight chances to fall in love with a man I'm supposed to hate.

JAYDEN

I've been through hell to get to where I am today.

I'm *the* best agent in Hollywood's cut-throat industry because I clawed and dragged myself there inch by excruciating inch.

Which is why I refuse to be bossed around by a pushy, Prada-wearing princess when it comes to organising my Rockstar brother's farewell tour. I've got bigger fish to fry, starting with upholding a promise I made a lifetime ago...

The fact I want to bend the aforementioned Prada-wearing princess over my desk is utterly irrelevant, as well as highly inconvenient.

But Chloe is about to find out the hard way, what goes on tour stays on tour.

Click here to learn more.... Or keep turning the pages for the first two chapters...

FALLING FOR THE ROCK STAR AT CHRISTMAS

Sexton Sisters Series

A steamy second chance rockstar romance with ALL the festive feels.

SASHA

Ten years ago, I inherited our family castle and sole care of my youngest sister. More Cinderella, than Sleeping Beauty, at the mere age of twenty-eight I have a teenager to raise and a hotel to run. If the hotel is to survive past Christmas, I need a lottery win, a miracle, or Prince Charming himself to sweep in with a humongous... wad of cash.

When my super successful middle sister announces she's coming home for the holiday season, I'm determined to put my problems aside and make this the most fabulous Christmas ever. Especially as it might just be the last one in our family home.

I didn't factor in the return of my first love, **Ryan Cooper**. Back then he was the boy next door. Now, he's a world famous singer/song writer. We were supposed to go the States together. He left without me. Now he's back. Rumour is he has writers block. Apparently this is a last-ditch attempt to find inspiration before his record label pulls the plug permanently.

And guess where he wants to stay? You have it in one- the most inspiring castle hotel in Dublin's fair city.

Every woman in the city wants to pull this Hollywood Christmas cracker. Except me. I'm going to avoid him at all costs.

Easier said than done when he's parading around under my roof, with enough heat exuding from his molten eyes to melt every square inch of snow from the peaks of the Dublin mountains...

***FALLING FOR THE ROCK STAR AT CHRISTMAS* is an *OPEN DOOR* steamy, love conquers all, stand alone romance, with no cliffhanger- and a guaranteed happy ever after.**

Click to learn more...

My Book

PROFESSIONAL PLAYERS SERIES

Five Steamy Contemporary Stand Alone Sports Romance Novels. HEA guaranteed. Perfect for fans of Amy Daws, Meghan Quinn and Lucy Score.

My Book

LOVE & OTHER MUSHY STUFF

A STEAMY, FAKE-DATING, SPORTS ROMANCE WITH ALL THE FEELS!

ABBY

I need a man.

Not in my bed, but for my radio show.

I'm an eternally single agony aunt responsible for dishing out romantic advice to the nation.

It would be funny if it weren't so tragic. I desperately need to up my ratings.

What better way than to employ one of the country's hottest rugby players to offer his take on love and other mushy stuff to the frenzied females of the nation?

Callum Connolly is the classic example of male perfection.

He's everything I need for my show and everything I don't need in my life...

CALLUM

I'm not looking for *the one*, merely for *the next one*.

That is, until my teammates bet I can't keep the same woman long enough to bring to my best friend's wedding.

How hard can it be to date the same woman for three months?

When I bump into a beautiful DJ in a hotel spa, we strike an unlikely but alluring deal. I'll feature on her show and help up her ratings, if she fake dates me until after the wedding.

I don't bank on falling for her.

Especially when nailing her proves harder than nailing the most elusive touchdown ever...

A FULL-LENGTH STANDALONE ROMANCE FULL OF HEAT, HEART & A GUARANTEED HAPPY EVER AFTER.

NO CLIFF-HANGER. NO CHEATING. BOOK 1 OF A WIDER SERIES WITH OVERLAPPING CHARACTERS.

https://mybook.to/Love_OtherMushyStuff

What reviewers are saying:

★★★★★ *Sassy, sexy, funny and poignant- what a rollercoaster read!*

★★★★★ *A gorgeous must read with an 'ugly truth' vibe.*

★★★★★ *Another belter from Lyndsey Gallagher. Pure steam. Gave me all the Valentine's feels. Her books just keep getting better!*

★★★★★ *Steamy, sweet and funny!*

★★★★★ *Laughed out loud at this new steamy contemporary romance. Written in the first person, you feel like you're pulled directly into their world, the two alternating viewpoints between him and her were a real treat. The chemistry betweem Abby & Callum bounced off each page, and the banter between the lads was hilarious. Roll on July- can't wait for the next book in the series.*

★★★★★ *If you like your romances sassy, sexy, funny and poignant, this ones for you. It has it all- the playboy rugby player who's never made it past the first date; the radio presenter who's emotionally battered and bruise by the man who broke her heart, and the 'will they, won't they' rollercoaster ride they embark on after they first set eyes on each other and the sparks fly. A definite page-turner.*

LOVE & OTHER GAMES

AN OPEN DOOR, STEAMY, ENEMIES-TO-LOVERS, FORCED PROXIMITY SPORTS ROMANCE.

EMMA

I spent one mind-blowing night with the country's hottest rugby hooker.

It was the best night of my life.

Transcendent, in fact.

And foolishly, I believed **Eddie Harrington** when he swore the feeling was mutual.

But it turns out, the man is a notorious player off the pitch, as well as on it.

They don't call him "Hooker Harrington" for nothing.

One year later, I board a flight to my best friends beach wedding, dreaming of sun, sea and sangria. The last person I expect to find in the seat next to mine is Eddie "love-them-and-leave-them" Harrington.

His best friend is about to marry mine.

I *hate* the ground he walks on, but to keep the peace, I'll play nicely.

Even when a mad twist of fate forces us to share a romantic, idyllic honeymoon suite, complete with only one ginormous, rose petal-covered bed.

Eddie is certain his practiced tactics will earn him a replay, but this time around, I'm sticking firmly to my game plan.

Even if the chemistry between us is hotter than the Croatian sun...

https://mybook.to/Love_

AMAZON REVIEWS:

★★★★★ *Lyndsey Gallagher has done it again. This book is absolutely AMAZING! You are instantly pulled into the pages and won't want to put it down.*

★★★★★ *Another brilliant read by the talented Lyndsey Gallgher. A really fun follow on from Love & Other Mushy Stuff. A real page-turner. The twists and turns in this book make it another exceptional read.*

★★★★★ *What's not to love about this book? Gorgeous idyllic setting, a bit of forced proximity (oh no we have to share a room) and the blossoming relationship between Eddie & Emma. I loved this story and could not put it down.*

LOVE & OTHER LIES

A SINGLE DAD/ NANNY STEAMY SPORTS ROMANCE WITH ALL THE FEELS!

KERRY

Who's unlucky enough to get sacked and evicted in the same week?

Me. That's who.

But a chance phone call with a witty, velvet-voiced stranger provides a stunning solution to both my problems.

Nathan's looking for a live-in nanny for his sunny five-year-old daughter and as fate has it, I have a degree in childcare, even though I swore I'd never use it.

Taking this job will force me to face demons I've been hiding from for a long time, but I have no choice but to accept.

It's only when I reach the magnificent Georgian house, my new home for the summer, I realise Nathan "the velvet-voiced stranger" is actually Nathan Kennedy, Ireland's most successful rugby player, and the only man I ever kissed when my boyfriend and I were on a break.

I can only pray one tiny (hot as hell) blip in my past doesn't ruin my future.

I need this job more than I've ever needed anything.

And worryingly, now I'm here, I want it more than I ever wanted anything too.

As the summer heats up, so does the escalating chemistry with my new boss.

Nathan's advances are becoming harder to resist.

And this time round, he swears he's playing for keeps...

A FULL-LENGTH STANDALONE, FORCED PROXIMITY ROMANCE WITH NO CHEATING , COMPLETE WITH A HUGE, HEARTFELT HAPPY EVER AFTER.

https://mybook.to/ProfessionalPlayers

What reviewers are saying:

★★★★★ *AN ABSOLUTE PAGE TURNER - GALLAGHER HAS DONE IT AGAIN!*

★★★★★ *SEXY, SWEET & LAUGH OUT LOUD FUNNY*

★★★★★ *THE PERFECT ROMANTIC ESCAPE TO IRELAND*

LOVE & OTHER FORBIDDEN THINGS

A STEAMY, OPEN DOOR, BROTHERS-BEST-FRIEND, SPORTS ROMANCE WITH A GUARANTEED HEA!

AMY

I've always been a good girl, but for the first time in my life, I'm ready to do something bad...

Hot, half-naked men lurk everywhere I turn.

But the one whose soul screams to mine wears the number six jersey, along with a look of sheer uninhibited desire.

Six has always been my lucky number, but it's hard to see how this will end auspiciously for either of us.

Ollie Quinn is my brother's teammate.

And thanks to my recent appointment as the team's physiotherapist, he's now my patient too.

He might be newly single and ready to mingle, but he is utterly off-limits.

Does that stop me?

Of course not.

Chemistry crackles like an invisible circuit between us and it's too much for either of us to compete with.

OLLIE

Injuries sustained on the pitch seem minimal compared to what Eddie Harrington might do if he finds out I'm sleeping with his little sister.

But Amy is everything I never knew I needed and I couldn't give her up if I tried.

Is it simply the temptation of tasting the forbidden fruit?

Or will forbidden turn into forever?

https://mybook.to/OQPw

What reviewers are saying:

★★★★★ *SEXY, SASSY, COMPLETELY UNPUTDOWNABLE!*

★★★★★ *WITH EXPLOSIVE CHEMISTRY AND TRULY IRRESISTIBLE CHARACTERS, THIS BOOK WAS IMPOSSIBLE TO LEAVE DOWN.*

★★★★★ *SIZZLINGLY ADDICTIVE!*

LOVE & OTHER VOWS

THE ULTIMATE STEAMY, OPEN DOOR, CELEBRITY, SECOND CHANCE ROMANCE GUARANTEED TO GIVE YOU ALL THE FEELS!

MARCUS

Once upon a time, I was the captain of the national rugby team, surrounded by the loyalty and laughter of my teammates, basking in the glory each winning match brought our country.

Now, I'm a stay-at-home-dad to my two beautiful, bubbly, busy girls while my stunning wife, Shelly, slides, shakes and shimmies her pert little ass all over national television as part of the newest, sexiest, celebrity dance show.

I don't resent her.

She's my world.

But if I tell you I'm struggling to adjust, it's an understatement.

SHELLY

After years of flying solo with the kids while my husband travelled the world with his teammates, the light has finally emerged at the end of a long and lonely tunnel.

Living in Marcus's shadow has been hard but now, I'm finally getting my chance to shine.

I never dreamed I'd be offered a place on the hottest new dance show around.

Nor did I dream I'd be paired up with Marcus's oldest rival either, though.

And they weren't just rivals on the pitch.

We have a whole lot of history. And history has an awful habit of repeating itself.

Marcus and I vowed to stay together through sickness and health, but can we survive the pressure brought by fame and wealth?

https://mybook.to/love_and_other_vows

WHAT REVIEWERS ARE SAYING:

Sarah Foster

★★★★★ Fabulous romance and an epic finale to an incredible series!

Lyndsey Gallagher is a phenomenal writer and storyteller. Every book of hers is an unputdownable steamy page-turner and I fall in love with every character she creates.

If you love steamy contemporary romance then you need this book in your life!

Emily H

★★★★★ Another cracking book!

Well she's done it again! Honestly Lyndsey keeps writing absolute page turners. I loved this book - it was weird that the main characters were together already and there wouldn't be a meet cute or a chase but that did not matter at all. Marcus and Shelley are brilliant characters and once again some of my favourites (hello Callum!) make an appearance. This is a brilliant, fast paced story. I devoured it. Thanks Lyndsey!

TRINA G

★★★★★ Great read that starts with a bang!!!!!

This book did not disappoint. Another great steamy read that, once I started, I couldn't put down!!!!!

AFTERWORD

Dear Reader,

Thank you so much for reading Falling For My Bodyguard. I really hope you enjoyed Archie and Victoria's story. It was so much fun to write!

If you're not already part of my reader group, Lyndsey's Book Lushes, come hang out with us here...

https://www.facebook.com/groups/530398645913222

We'd love to have you! Plus you get first peeks at everything!

Or alternatively join. Me on my brand new Patreon account. https://patreon.com/Lyndsey_Gallagher_Spicy_Romance_Writer?utm_medium=clipboard_copy&utm_source=copyLink&utm_campaign=creatorshare_creator&utm_content=join_link

I'm going to miss those Sexton sisters and their gorgeous men, but fear not... I am almost halfway into writing a new book, the first of a brand new series and it's heating up nicely!

A movie star, an art teacher, and one incredibly embarrassing viral video...

I can't wait to share it with you!

Lots of love,
Lyndsey xxx

Turn over for a sneak peak...

THE CHRISTMAS CRUSH
A STEAMY CELEBRITY ROMANCE STORY WITH ALL THE FESTIVE FEELS!

Ground, please swallow me whole.

One drunken night out and suddenly I'm the face (and boobs) of every viral holiday meme going.

If I want to keep my teaching job at the Catholic girls' school, or have my pearl-clutching family look me in the eye ever again, I need a time machine. Or a Christmas miracle.

To escape this mortifying circus, I flee to my BFF's gorgeous holiday villa on Ireland's west coast.

Foolproof plan: spend the rest of the holiday season licking my wounds. Somewhere peaceful. Tranquil. Totally off the radar.

Minor flaw: half of Hollywood is here to film a Hallmark Christmas movie.

Major flaw: Nate Jackson, Hollywood's hottest actor and my all-time celebrity crush is starring in it. And somehow, after the surrealist night of my life, I'm cast as an utterly unlikely extra.

My quiet Christmas just got crazy. But the craziest part of this entire scenario?

Turns out Nate Jackson is crazy about me.

Is it a Christmas miracle, or a fleeting festive crush?

He's the brightest star on the Christmas tree and I'm like the joke from the Christmas cracker.

We're a match made in Hallmark hell, so why does it feel like heaven?

Click here to preorder.... https://mybook.to/The_Christmas_Crush

You may even recognise the film Nate is filming! ;)

ACKNOWLEDGMENTS

First of all, thanks to YOU, dear reader, for choosing my book. Because of romance lovers like you, I get to do my dream job, conjuring up hot rock stars/bodyguards/ rugby players all in the name of "work!"

Thanks for taking a chance on my books when there are so many amazing romance stories out there!

Secondly, thank you so much to my beautiful bookish bestie Sara Madderson. Not only is she an amazing author, but she's also an incredible human being!

Last but not least, thank you to my fabulous husband, the most amazing man I know, and a total ride! ;) He's going to kill me for writing this- if he ever reads it!

It's one sure way to find out! XXX

ABOUT THE AUTHOR

Lyndsey Gallagher writes spicy romance stories featuring swoon-worthy heroes, sassy heroines and copious amounts of champagne. Her books are dripping with heat, heart and guaranteed happy ever afters.

She lives in the west of Ireland with her two children, two fur babies, and her endlessly patient husband. Lyndsey loves long walks, deep talks and more chocolate than is healthy. But let's be honest, no good story ever started with a salad...

For more info, bonus epilogues and freebies sign up to www.lyndseygallagherauthor.com